TEDDY

A. PHILL BABCOCK

Order this book online at www.trafford.com
or email orders@trafford.com

Most Trafford titles are also available at major online book retailers.

Print information available on the last page.

ISBN: 978-1-4669-9558-1 (sc)
ISBN: 978-1-4669-9557-4 (e)

Trafford rev. 06/02/2016

www.trafford.com

North America & international
toll-free: 1 888 232 4444 (USA & Canada)
fax: 812 355 4082

CHAPTER 1

THAT MORNING WAS JUST another rotten, windy, freezing, early wintry one as I started to pedal my bicycle from home to my folk's Confectionary Store, a distance of six miles. It was fall 1951, and we lived in Daisy Junction. I certainly knew how to get to my folks store even if I bicycled backward, if I dared, but it wasn't advisable with our winters because Daisy Junction was only one-hundred miles from the Canadian border and about two-hundred miles from New Hampshire.

Leaving at a dark five in the morning, I'd arrive before six. I remember swearing to myself, This morning is the worst I have experience in the two years since my morning job at Mom and Dad's place of business started.

Our Confectionary Store sold various candies, ice cream, breakfast and lunch. We also had a soda fountain with booths and tables. Everything in our store was home made, and Dad never let a request or sale pass him by.

That morning my bike light screwed up and I could see only a short distance, and I had just put new batteries in last night.

To add to the misery, the damn streets were full of chuck holes, and where water once stood it was now ice. Turn the bicycle wrong, and you're down.

Then add the hellish, cold head wind that seemed to slam me from every direction. There's no way to get away from that damnable Arctic wind blasting from the North Pole straight down at this miserable town.

My head and face were numb, even with my wool watch cap pulled low over my eyes. I had a bandana around my nose and mouth, nearly frozen from my breath.

I decided then and there, When I grow up, I'm gonna leave this country so fast people will forget I once lived here. I just don't want to live here any longer than I have to, fighting this weather. Right now, living in a California or Arizona desert sounded great, but for then, six mornings a week, I bicycled to our All American Cafe. Sundays were off days because in Daisy Junction no business could be open, movies and gas stations included because of the Blue Laws.

I pumped my bike on streets that could shake the fillings out of anyone riding in a car, and it's worse on my bicycle.

Halfway into my miserable ride, I thought, Why can't our elected, so called, public conscious, Aldermen, fix our streets, instead of stuffing their 'certain' money in their pockets.

This money came from 'certain' business houses we had in Daisy Junction like gambling and prostitution, just three blocks from our police station.

I was an eighteen-year old student at Daisy Junction High School and that was the morning I was hoping I will get the chance to 'feel up', that's right, 'feel up' our morning waitress Dee Dee, right in Mom and Dad's cafe kitchen. I was not kidding because it was something to help me forget the miserable bike ride. So I'm dreaming, I'll soon have her tits in my hands, and find out what French Kissing is. This thing had been building for quite some time and, yes sir, those were two mysteries I longed to know about from listening to the Senior boys in gym class when they discuss some of our well exposed and well used high school girls.

And then I blew my front tire four blocks from our store because of those darn overlooked chuck holes and had to push the bike the rest of the way, but the fantasies were still clear.

Six days a week, I swept and mopped the store, then fixed my breakfast and before eight o-clock, on the school days, I walked to Daisy Junction High School just three blocks away.

That's six mornings I'm alone in our store, until seven o'clock, when that damn Dee Dee, our morning waitress, arrived.

* * *

That morning, while I'm in the kitchen reading the sports page of our local paper and just finishing my breakfast, our back door banged wide open, and a sudden a blast of our frigid, winter wind blew in. The newspaper I'm reading, sailed all over the kitchen. Shit, I knew immediately who the cause was. It's that damn Katerina, 'Dee Dee' Kisonovich, our morning waitress.

Almost every morning, Dee Dee tried to tease me in some way or other. She's in her late twenties and had been my baby sitter when I was younger.

This dark haired teaser still thought she could order me around and at times she acted as if she really owned me.

Dee Dee was about five-feet-one or two, thin, and kinda well stacked, like Lisa Roberts, a girl the big boys in our gym class talked about. Lisa was really something; like Dee Dee, always showing off her tits while her rear end flipped from side to side.

That morning Dee Dee had a red face from the freezing wind as she dashed into our kitchen and loudly exclaimed, "Everything I have is frozen, I mean everything."

We would be the only two in the store until eight in the morning when our morning cook, Cookie, arrived.

So this dark-haired, blue-eyed, tit-bouncing, Slovenian sex-pot, stood in middle of our kitchen that cold morning with her legs apart and her hands on her hips.

She narrowed her blue eyes and stared at me. I used to hate her when she stared at me like that because I knew she was a teaser.

Her face had a shining-crimson-red-hue from the brutal, cold wind outside because she always walked to work. Her house was about half mile from our store, if you cut the corners. She was breathing very rapidly, smiling. I figured the teaser was thinking of something that involved me and I was suddenly uncomfortable.

Dee Dee quickly shook off her thick, black wool coat and hooked it on a hanger with her purse. Then she turned and walked right to where I'm sitting and stared right at me with those dark blue eyes.

Oh God! I'm thinking, How I wish I could be in front of the store next to one of the big windows because Dee Dee had something on her mind, and in some way it would concern me.

It was my fantasy, but now I'm going chicken, is my next thought.

Dee Dee, using her authoritative voice, snapped out, "Teddy, give me your hands."

"What? . . . Why? . . . What do you want to do with my hands?" I stammered.

"I said give me your hands, and I mean right now. Your hands, Teddy," ordered Dee Dee.

So I sheepishly stood up and stuck my hands out in front of me, thinking, What in the devil does she want me to do with my hands?

She grabbed my wrists with her cold, icy hands, and pushed them down. Then with her hands clutching the top of my hands she moved them up under her baggy sweater and right on top of her cold, large, sexy, jiggling, fantastic breasts. There was nothing else underneath the sweater except those great breasts.

My hands were resting on top of those cold, ripe, cantaloupe size breasts and I'm thinking, I'm going to faint. I had always wondered just how big Dee Dee's breasts were and how they would look and feel. Then I could feel hard protrusions in the center of my palms and I'm thinking, What is this? Then I remembered they were called nipples.

Yeah, that's it. Her nipples were pressed hard against the center of my palms and I could feel them. She pushed my hands harder against her cool breasts.

Since I entered high school I'd been curious about women's breasts. The girls in our freshman classes just didn't have breasts like Dee Dee's then, although some appeared they might develop them later on.

Right then, I couldn't believe what I was experiencing, and what she was doing to me. My knees began to wilt.

"Stand still, Teddy," Dee Dee commanded.

I knew I should pull away, but I didn't because all my wildest fantasies, my desires, my dreams, and my thoughts were right there in my hands. Suddenly those once unobtainable breasts were now mine that morning, my warm hands under her sweater cradling those cool things as her hands hold my palms tight against her big tits.

Dee Dee murmured softly, "These are freezing honey and I need some warmth. Hold them tight. Yes, just like that, just hold them."

"What . . . what . . . what about Cookie?" I stuttered. I could just see our morning cook walking through the back door and into the kitchen and seeing what I have in my hands.

"Suppose Cookie comes in now?" I stuttered again.

"She will not be here for an hour, relax. This won't take long," Dee Dee answered.

Easy for her to say, I thought.

"But 'Cowboy' MacGarth might come in now." I said, giving the back door a quick glance.

"Cowboy will not be in here for thirty minutes, if at all," Dee Dee commanded, again. "He has the afternoon shift this week. Then Dee Dee murmured, "Just stand still, don't back away honey."

Then she suddenly released my hands and turned around which caused me to loose my hold on her breasts. With her back to me she reached back and regrabbed my hands bringing them back under her sweater to cover her breasts again. Now her back was against my stomach, my hands cupping her cold breasts. Wow!

Dee Dee, using her hips, pushed me backwards by about two steps, pinning my butt against the edge of the cold steam table, but I didn't complain.

Her hands grasped my wrists, moving my hands around those full breasts and I'm thinking, I have in my hands those fantastic things I have admired, bouncing around when she walks, especially when she is in a hurry and Holy Mackerel, those things are fantastic.

Dee Dee's head went back against my shoulder and her ruby red lips had never seemed to glow like they did this morning. I was nearly a foot taller and I watched her mouth open slightly and heard her inhale and exhale.

She slowly rubbed her tongue around her glossy, scarlet lipstick coated lips while rotating her hips against me.

She released her hands from my wrists, but my hands remained on her breasts, massaging those choices, yet firm, once thought to be unattainable goals.

I thought, What a feeling.

"Not so hard honey, go easy like," she told me.

I had about a minute to feel up her breasts before Dee Dee pulled my hands down and away from her.

Then she quickly turned around to face me. Looking up to me her face appeared to glow and she smiled. Then she grabbed my rear end and pulled me hard against her moving hips. Dee Dee continued to gyrate and pushed her hips against my front. I was still wedged against our cold steam table with nowhere to go.

I was guessing, She was giving me a real teasing with all the seductive movements.

I remember thinking, She was doing a 'dry job' coined by the big boys in the gym describing some of the older girls.

I'm thinking, What should I do? I lowered my hands to her rotating rear end. It was sort of firm, but real soft, like kind of just right. Here I'm guessing, 'Just right' because I had no experience concerning the feel of the female body.

Dee Dee brought her hands to both sides of my head and pulled my head down to her face and kissed me hard, her tongue pushing between my lips, her hands gliding to the back of my head.

I'd also heard 'from the big boys' about French kissing. Before that morning, I'd always thought French Kissing was kissing a girl on the neck or ears, or maybe licking the girl's neck with the tongue. Now I knew what Dee Dee was doing with her tongue deep in my mouth. That was French Kissing. Wow!

Dee Dee, broke away from the kiss and leaned back. She gave me a long look with her light blue eyes and wide, red lips smile. Her hands were still behind my head and she again pulled my head back to her face beginning another full, oral examination with her tongue. I entered the tongue wrestling contest with vigor.

"Swallow, don't slobber, Teddy," murmured Dee Dee. Her hips were moving hard against me.

My hands began to squeeze and massage that moving rear end of her's because I had also heard from the big boys, "Try squeezing the rear end of girls, that usually does the trick."

While I was feeling and grabbing all over, she was breathing faster. I slowly began to pull up her long wool dress.

Dee Dee, still smiling, leaned back. Then she released her hands from around my head and removed my hands from her rear end, straightened her skirt and sweater. She took a deep breath, smiled, and looked me in the eyes. "Honey, any more lessons like this and we'll have to find a better place than this kitchen."

"One more," I begged.

"No way, you're off to school."

"Please Dee Dee, just a minute or two more?"

"Another time and another place, maybe. Let me check you out."

Dee Dee grabbed one of Cookie's clean towels and went over my face quickly rubbing any lipstick off using her salvia. Smiling at me, she tossed the towel with lipstick into our large kitchen sink. She said, "I'll have to tell Cookie some story why I got lipstick on her clean towel.

Dee Dee turned to leave and one of her hands lightly patted me on my crotch where a bulge was poking out of the front of my Levi's.

"Very good," she said, then quickly turned and walked as if she was going to the front of the store.

Standing next to our kitchen's sink she stopped and turned to face me. She brought her hands up underneath her sweater, cupping those firm, yet soft breasts that I had just felt, and she lifted them up. "These are warm now Teddy, thanks."

With a wide smile and her white teeth flashing she turned and wiggled off to the front of the store.

I was left standing, watching the swinging doors slowly return to their normal position, but now I know what big girl's breasts feel like and what French Kissing was. This was certainly not like my first experience with a girl when I was in the seventh grade.

CHAPTER 2

GOING BACK TO THE time in seventh grade when I first kissed a girl, I was just twelve. Ruthie O'Neil invited me to my first boy-girl party at her parent's house.

There were eight of us, four girls and four boys. We were classmates at Emmet Markovich Grammar School.

Early in the evening the gang decided to play a game called, 'Spin the Bottle'. I thought I might have heard something about this at the time, but I don't remember what.

I guess I wasn't that interested in girls then. All they did were tell secrets and laugh at the boys trying to make asses out of themselves.

When our party group settled down in Ruthie's family living room, sitting on the floor in a boy and girl circle, I had to ask, "What's going on?"

"You'll have to wait and find out," laughed my school friends.

*   *   *

I told Dee Dee later, "We sat in a dumb circle on the floor with a boy then a girl."

"Was Nancy Blake the doctor's daughter there, Teddy?" Dee Dee asked.

"Yeah, she was sitting right next to me, but her mom came to pick her up," I answered. "I think Nancy was glad to leave. Maybe I should have gone home with her?"

"Well, what happened to you, Teddy?" Dee Dee was smiling.

"Well, someone would spin the empty coke bottle in the center, and we were supposed to take turns. Ruthie had earlier told us something about these stupid rules. I think the rules went like this: 'If a girl spins the bottle and if the bottle stops spinning and the narrow end points to a boy, then those two stand up and go into our closet in the hallway. The same for the boys if the narrow end points to a girl. Remember, it must point to an opposite sex or you lose your turn.'"

"Well, Anne Lacey was the first girl, and the spinning bottle pointed to Chuck Gomes and those two went into the closet. In a minute or so they came out smiling and blushing, rejoining us in the circle."

"Then Charlie Foxx spun the bottle and the bottle stopped, pointing to Mary Ann Kelly. Well, these two were kinda going steady, coming and going from school, walking around holding hands. They got up real quick and went into the closet. It was way more than a couple of minutes before they came out giggling. Both of them were blushing, smiling, and still holding hands."

"What did they do in the closet, Teddy?" asked Dee Dee.

"I didn't know? Nobody told me what I should do in the closet."

"Well, what happened to you, Teddy?" Dee Dee had a wide smile on her red lips and she's looking me straight in the eyes.

I told her, "You know that Blossom Ann Henry? The lumbering, loud mouth that lives in the Heights right next to Dr. Smith. Blossom Ann is the one with all the pimples on her forehead. You know her Dee Dee. She always comes into the store after school. She's the one that walks like a plow horse."

"Sure, who doesn't know Blossom Ann?" Dee Dee chuckled, her whole body shaking. "Hasn't Blossom always had a crush on you, Teddy?"

"No way Dee Dee!" I returned quickly. "Who would want to go out with a horse like Blossom Ann? Well, anyway, she spun the bottle and it pointed to Oscar Shumaker. Blossom Ann yelled out, 'The bottle is pointing at Teddy!'"

"Then what?" Dee Dee was holding back a laugh.

"I didn't know what to do, honest. I'd never heard much about this dumb game. Oscar, my best friend, is doubled over laughing, when that fat, loud mouth Blossom Ann grabbed me and pulled me up and said, 'Lets go Teddy.'"

"I asked her, 'What is going on Blossom?' because I had no idea what I was supposed to do in that closet, honest Dee Dee."

"Everyone in the circle hollers out: 'It was for me to find out.'"

"Oscar was laughing so hard he had tears in his eyes. He yells out, 'Teddy, you just won the prize.'"

"I didn't know what he meant, honest."

Dee Dee had a smile, then she asked, "Then what happened, Teddy?"

"That darn Blossom Ann is still holding my hand, hard like, and she tows me into the closet, and closes the door.

There's no light inside the closet, and I can't see anything so I tried to look around for a light switch. We're standing in the dark in this small closet, bumping into overcoats, rain coats, stepping on shoes, boots, and other stuff.

It was hard for me to move around because I kept stepping on those shoes, and somehow I keep bumping into Blossom. No matter where I turned, I bumped into Blossom Ann."

"Blossom asked me, 'Do you want the light on or off?'"

"I said, 'Whatever. I just want to see.'"

"So she opens the door part way so we can see each other, slightly."

"And then?" Dee Dee asked as she held her hand over her mouth. I think she was choking back a laugh.

"Well, that Blossom Ann says to me, 'You have to kiss me.'"

"And I sure didn't want to do that. I asked her, 'Why should I kiss you Blossom Ann?'"

"But, she said something like, 'If you don't kiss me, I'll hit you so hard, you'll wake up in the middle of next month.'"

Dee Dee asked me, "Did you kiss Blossom Ann after that threat?"

"Yeah, kinda, sort of. I know she might be a girl, but I also know she can hit hard. So I tried to kiss her on her cheek, but darn her, she turned her head, and I got part of her lips. Then Blossom really got mad at me."

"Why did Blossom get mad at you? You did kiss her, didn't you?" Dee Dee chuckled.

"She got mad because I tried to wipe off my lips with the back of my hand. What did I do wrong, Dee Dee?"

Dee Dee laughed and with tears in her dark blue eyes, she grabbed me and gave me a big hug. "Some time it helps to have some experience with girls."

"Like what?"

"Let's wait a couple of years, until you begin high school. Just stay the way you are now."

That was easy for her to say because back there in the seventh grade I began to wonder about girls. What makes them think they're so darn different and so perfect over boys?

*   *   *

"Hey, guys, got something to show you." This call came from Wee Willie Williams. His first name was Weldon, but we changed to Wee Willie. He had just transferred into Emmet Markovich Grammar School and our seventh grade.

Willie was one of the shortest boys in our class, but he become our magazine supplier; to aide us because of our lack of knowledge of girls and women. He must have had a hundred magazines with pictures of nude or nearly nude women.

I wondered back then, Where did he get them?

So we would crowd around to check out his latest issues loaded with women in various undressed posses.

"They sure look like Miss Yockovich, but not like our girls," said Fats Slavich.

Willie gave Fats a long look then answered, "Of course not you dummy because these are called mature women. Our girls are a ways off from these pictures. It will be a while before they will look like the ones you have in your hand, Fats."

Fats replied, "I want to see pictures of girls our age, not them old ones."

"Who wants to see pictures of skinny girls? They don't have nothing up top," replied Rex MacGee.

For some dumb reason, it seemed, Fats was more interested in our seventh grade girls.

"Yeah, who wants to look at a Nancy Blake," piped up Wee Willie, "the doctor's daughter, with nothing sticking out. She ain't got nothing to show."

I butted in, protective like, "As long as I am in the class, you won't talk about Nancy Blake like that, any of you, understand?"

Someone piped up, "Man, Teddy, you sure support Nancy. You two going together, and we don't know it? She's always the first one you pick for your team. You two got something going on?"

"No. We're just friends, turn the page, Willie," I said to change the subject.

Until Wee Willie Williams joined our seventh grade class, many of the boys only had stories of girls undressed or nearly undressed. These stories they related to the rest of us, we the sexual dense, uninformed group. So our so-called knowledgeable classmates would tell us about girls they had heard of or pretended to know. Then Wee Willie arrived in our class.

My friends and myself wanted to know more about girls; what they might look like, and why they think they are different from boys. We have tried all kinds of ways to find out more about girls with no luck.

Jed O'Brien, one of the few in our class who had accurate sexual knowledge smiled at us and proudly said, "I know how we can find out what Miss Yockovich wears under her dress."

"You can?" asked six or eight voices eager to find out something about girls or women with their own eyes.

"You guys just don't know nutten," exclaimed Jed. "We are all assigned desk places in her room, right?"

A big 'yes' came from us, followed by someone asking, "How is that going to work?"

"Well, let's see," continued Jed. "Four boys have the choice seats in the front rows, right?"

"Right," four of us answered.

I was one of the four, and Nancy Blake sat right behind me.

"Okay," instructed Jed, "you four guys will watch Miss Yockovich when she sits down at her desk, and watch her legs to see if she crosses them. We did that at my old school, and it works most of the time. Many times we saw the teacher's underwear."

"What about the rest of us," wailed a boy not in the exalted front row.

Jed smiled. "They will tell us what they seen."

Then comes a chorus of, "Good idea, Jed, you gotta another one?"

"Yeah, ever heard about dropping a pencil on the classroom floor?"

"So what?" replied Smiley, the happiest kid in our class.

"Okay, all of you get in a circle, you too Smiley," continued Jed.

Jed got in the middle with one knee on the gravel in the playground yard, looked at us, his eyes searching out all eight faces. He made sure no one was near our circle and then in a low voice he said, "Now listen. One of you will drop your pencil on the floor."

"What's that got to do with seeing the girls?" asked Oscar Shumaker.

"Oscar, you dip, pay attention," snapped Jed. "Who ever is sitting in the third row from the window will drop his pencil on the floor."

"Thats me!" shouted our Wee Willie.

"Okay, that's you," agreed Jed, then continued. "Now, the little blond gal who has the desk third from the window, in the back row, always sits with her legs apart."

"Hey," said Wee Willie excited. "That's Nikkei Lestervic. Yeah, you're right, she always sits with her legs apart."

"The rest us will not look at Wee when he bends down to pickup his pencil," said Jed, then turned to Wee, "This will give you a straight shot to look up her dress."

Everyone chimed in, "Wow, great idea."

*　　*　　*

Our school bell rang telling us recess was over and we walked to our classroom, all of us guys were smiling and laughing.

Nancy Blake, the doctor's daughter, walked up beside me and tapped me on the shoulder, "What are you guys planning, twin?"

"Nothing, Nancy. Jed was telling us jokes, why do you ask?"

"Well, you had better tell them the first one that tries to look under my dress will get his nose busted."

"Is that a warning to me, Twin?"

"No, no, not you, Teddy, I trust you. Remember what I said."

How the heck did she figure out what we were up to? I pondered, mystified.

*   *   *

Wee Willie is the center of attention as he drops his pencil and reaches down to retrieve it. He takes a quick look back down the desk line.

*   *   *

After school, we boys gathered in a small huddle and almost in one voice asked Willie, who was beaming with pride, being the man of the hour. "What did you see?"

"I don't know, I couldn't see much except something underneath her dress."

"What did it look like?" snarled Jed. "We need an answer."

"I don't know."

Then the admiration turned to anxiety.

"What do you mean, you don't know?" wailed one of the boys.

"Was it something like clothes, or something else, like skin?" asked another.

"What is underneath her dress?" squawked a third. Willie has let us all down.

Jed jumped in again. "You sure took your time to look at Nikkei? Are you holding something back from us?"

"No . . . Yeah . . . I could see right up Nikkei's dress," Willie replied, now under pressure.

Then almost in unison, "You looked up her dress and saw nothing? You must have shut your eyes."

Jed jumped in with, "I know you weren't trying to look away, and you saw nothing?"

"I just don't know," Willie sniveled, now a complete disappointment. "Could've been just some type of, well, something underneath. Maybe, I guess, it might been part of her dress, or underwear. I swear that's all I saw, cross my heart. Next time you look," Willie yelled at all of us, stomping off, now a complete failure.

*   *   *

Next morning the plan again centered on finding out what was under Miss Yockovich's dress? We four boys in the front seats were supposed to wait for one of us to drop a paper on the floor. I had suggested, "The best way would be when we return from the blackboard exercises." And wouldn't you know it, I had the first chance in our afternoon class.

Miss Yockovich was wearing her green dress with a square cut below her neck line. It's was a pretty dress, but my mind can't get past what is under it.

So, coming back from the blackboard, passing right in front of Miss Yockovich, I just let a paper fall to the floor and try to appear not seeing it drop.

I took just two steps before Nancy spoke up, "Teddy, you just dropped a paper, it's behind you." I heard a little fist pound a desk, and well there went my chance.

With Nancy sitting behind me and smacking me in the back every time she thought I was about to do something I shouldn't, I was essentially out of the loop to find out what girls wore under their dresses.

The rest of the guys and their debauchery were also thwarted by Nancy.

She told me, "Twin, I'm going to talk to Miss Yockovich about the boys trying to look under the girls dresses."

I quickly answered. "Really, Nancy, some of the boys are doing that?"

"They sure are, and before some big trouble shows up, I'm going to tell Miss Yockovich. I'm not concerned about you because you're to polite and gentlemanly to do some ugly, dumb thing like that."

"Well, thank you Nancy," I replied, knowing full well that I had just been worked, but let off the hook and my best behavior was now guaranteed.

Nancy continued with, "Oh, I just talked to Nikki and told her to keep her legs together, and she asked me why? I told her a lie. I said, that, "Teddy told me to tell you to keep your legs together in class because some boys are trying to see under your dress."

Now Nikki looked to me like I was infallible.

*   *   *

I also heard the playground was the place to look under the girls dresses, but at Emmet Markovich Grammar

School the boys were never allowed to play on the rings, the swings, or the monkey bars with the girls. The girls always had Monday, Wednesday, and Friday and we boys, had only Tuesdays and Thursdays to use the playground equipment.

On our off days we played baseball, football, or something we called Bouncy Soccer Ball, a game between soccer, football, rugby, and a touch of mayhem, unless the ground was too wet from rain or snow.

Before school in the mornings and after lunch we boys might have use of the playground equipment unless the girls wanted them.

Those darn girls would always say to us, "Get off our equipment right now or we'll tell." Usually they did it just to keep us off the playground equipment.

Now knowledge of women's underwear grew as we occupied ourselves in examining more risqué photos of women. Some of the women in the photos had breasts just like Dee Dee's or Rosie Kallich's, a well known, good looking, single lady that always came in our store. We decided the only girl in school that could come close to matching Rosie's breasts could be Jeannie Weatherspoon who had big ones and couldn't run at all with those things flopping all over the place.

*   *   *

We never did find out what the girls wore under their dresses using our visual tricks. We continued to try though, even through the seventh and eighth grades and some even into high school, but this was about the time my inquisitiveness turned from thinking voyeur, to thinking actual contact.

*   *   *

Nancy Blake, the doctor's daughter, was two days older than I and our families celebrated our birthdays together.

As I mention before, Nancy didn't have much to see yet, actually she had the flattest chest in our grammar school.

*   *   *

I was one of the tallest kids in my class and the best athlete so I was usually one of the captains in our school ground events and I always picked Nancy to be on my team, first. I mentioned this earlier, and I didn't do it because her and I had something going, but because Nancy was just plain good at sports. That included football, basketball, baseball, or our stupid made up soccer. She could run fast and had long fingers to catch a football or basketball. When she played soccer her kicking abilities kept the opponents away from her. Nancy's elbows were sharp and wicked and could cause bruises on the boys, and one of her kicks to the shins, and they steered clear of her. In basketball she was a good feeder who could toss the ball to a clear player, and she wasn't bad in her basket shooting. She was the ultimate tomboy and she was tough. She told me often, "I love your games because I don't think there is a boy that is not afraid of me."

For example, Nancy once caught Jeb O'Brien in his right eye with one of her elbows when he tried to take the basketball away from her, but, maybe, he unintentionally grabbed somewhere around her breasts.

Nancy swung around so fast she knocked Jeb right on his back and her boney elbow gave him a black eye. Then she calmly reached down and took the ball out of his hands. Nancy then stood over the crying Jeb, digging her toe into his ribs and told him, "Keep your hands off me, and the elbow is for you trying to look up my dress in class."

Our teachers continually said to Nancy Blake, "Stay out of the boy's games. It's not lady like, and you should leave the boys alone."

Nancy's reply was always, "Teddy is like a brother to me and he invites me to play. I like to be on his teams and I can't stand rings, swings, and that one bounce and shoot basketball that girls must play."

*   *   *

People continually told us we look like twins but Nancy said, "No, we aren't twins, as I am much older than Teddy." Again, Nancy was only two days older than I was. She never let me forget she was older, therefore, she knew what was best and she thought she was smarter than I. However, our grades were almost identical.

My folks and Nancy's parents were long time friends. That's why the two families always celebrated Nancy and my birthday together. This had been going on since we were one year old.

I asked Mom one day, "How long have you and Dad known the Blakes?"

"Well, let's see?" she answered, "Your father and Dr. Blake went to school together in Parish Junction and they hunted and fished together while in grammar school and through high school. After World War II they came home, and Dr. Blake and Glyniss moved here, and they picked up from high school, still friends, still hunting and fishing together."

"Mom, did you know Mrs. Blake before she married Dr. Blake?"

She chuckled, "Oh my yes. I was in an Army hospital when Mrs. Blake, Glyniss O'Brien then, came into the picture. She was a nurse and came to my hospital for some advanced training. We became friends, and I introduced her to a brand new, young doctor working in our hospital and we have been friends ever since. You and Nancy have been friends before you two could walk. Ted, one thing about you two, you have remarkably close, alike thinking, alike ideas, and alike talking and posture. Glyniss and I laugh about how two non twins can pass for twins."

CHAPTER 3

From grade school right on through high school we had new boys and girls from varied backgrounds and some with different skin color entering our school.

Every classroom had a World Atlas we could use to find out where one of our new classmates came from. It was amazing how many different names some of the counties had throughout history. Miss Yockovich, our sixth and seventh grade home teacher, would talk about the area our new classmates came from and it was her that peaked my and others interest in geography.

Racial prejudice did exist in our area to varying degrees, but for me, because of my parents and grandparents teachings it was a silly way to think. Dad would preach, "Any sign of racial intolerance is absolutely unacceptable. I mean entirely and no questions about it."

Mom was a little more pragmatic, saying, "They all bleed red just like us, or us like them."

Grandpa never failed to tell me, "Those people are as good as we are, and don't you ever forget it. I know what racial intolerance is because I experienced it when your grandmother and I landed in New York years ago. When your grandmother and I arrived we thought we were finally free in a new country. Then we were told, by other Slavs where to live, where Slavs should buy groceries. Where Slavs do not go.

Grandpa told them, "That's a lot of old horse shit ideas, and you can all go to hell. We will not to be told where to shop or live. That is exactly why we came to this country, to be free."

"Teddy my boy," Grandpa would advise, "you'll be a lot richer when you accept all people despite their color, nationality, religion, and language. We all started the same way. We came to this country not speaking English, or rather the American English. Now we all do. Have I made myself clear with you, Son?"

Grandpa continued, "I entered United States as an immigrant in 1910 with my wife, Grandma Olena and joined the US army in World War I because I wanted to learn English quick. I learned my English during my trench time during that War."

Today he is able to use every swear word in English, German, French, Spanish, and, of course his native Balkan Slovenian words. In Daisy Junction Grandpa Egor's use and knowledge of those swear words were considered a rare gift.

"I joined the American Army before World War I when they were looking for volunteers," continued Grandpa. "After that hellish war was finally over, your grandmother and I came to Daisy Junction and entered the community life. Now, I can speak good English, and good Slav, a little German, and even some Spanish. When I want to, I can, if it's important, swear in just about any language used in this town. Of course, for some reason, your grandmother becomes a little upset with my choice of words when I want to get a point across correctly," he ended with a chuckle.

*   *   *

Grandpa had a knack for people and their languages and it rubbed off on me. I would be told many times, "Teddy, you have an ear for languages, you're just like your Grandpa."

If I happen to be in our store, and Gramps was not close by I would get the call.

Grandma had a different take, advising, "Teddy, knows every swear word in every language we have in Daisy Junction, but don't encourage him."

When people immigrated they counted on their children learning and speak English because children assimilate into new surroundings faster. Many ended up being interpreters for their parents when they came into our store.

*   *   *

Grandpa Egor liked to stalk the sidelines watching any game I might be playing in. Any official making a call that Gramps thought was not right or against our team resulted in a torrent of swear words. All the officials knew Grandpa Egor. He was always there wearing his ancient leather hat crammed with various pinned on buttons and medals.

Usually, early in the game, Grandpa Egor was ruled off the field or court by one of the officials who got fed up and yelled, "Grandpa Egor, you just can't use those words here."

Grandpa always yelled back, "You Blind Jackasses, you haven't the slightest idea what I said."

"Oh yes I do," returned the official, then it's usually off to the press box for Egor.

"There was always a chair waiting for Grandpa Egor. We thought Grandpa was too stubborn to go up to the press box before the game started so he used the altercations to be ordered. Anyone who went to his assistance got a chewing out in one of his choice languages.

*   *   *

I first found out about racial intolerance when I was in the sixth grade. Some the boys in my class were laughing at the black twins, Lincoln and Washington Roosevelt. This was on their first day in our school. At lunch time the twins came outside with all of us to have lunch. In our class boys and girls usually sat together during lunch period at three of the four long tables, trading parts of their lunches.

The problem started when the twins came outside carrying their lunch in brown paper bags, looking for a spot to sit.

Three classmates hollered out to the twins: "You can't eat with us, eat over there by yourselves at that empty table."

The two Roosevelt brothers just stood silent, looking confused.

Then one of the three boys spoke out, "We don't care where you go, but go somewhere away from our table, you're not going to spoil our lunch."

Then the three laughed.

The twins looked sad, being told not to sit with the rest of the class when there was room for them. It was obvious from the remarks by the three boys that being black was the problem.

I stood up, not saying a word to anyone, left my seat, taking my lunch with me and went over to the twins as they were standing to one side and told them, "I'm sitting with you two. Come with me and no one will bother you."

Oscar Shumaker looked at me, and I motioned with my head for him to join me. He left his seat to join us.

Nancy Blake had tears in her eyes from what these cruel boys had said to Lincoln and Washington. Seeing what I did for Linc and Wash, she gave me a nod and a smile and then turned her attention to the three boys. I know Nancy, and she would fight any boy or girl that crossed her and she'll fight boy's style if she thought her rights were being challenged.

Nancy stood up and glared at the three boys, and I'm concerned.

Those three guys were the Olson twins, big Scandinavian boys, but not too smart, and Lester Conrad, another dullard, with more mass than brains.

"Nancy!" I snapped.

She looked at me again, and I shook my head to let her know, don't get into a fight.

Nancy, still standing with her hands clenched into fists and with tears running down her face turned to the three boys. I knew she was close to exploding and somebody was going to get hurt and it would probably be one of them.

Nancy stepped toward them, and they leaned back, not willing to tangle with a girl and especially not Nancy Blake.

Nancy walked right up to the three boys and snarled at them.

"You three guys are in trouble with me. You have no right to talk to anyone like that and give those kids those kind of orders. Who do you think you are?

*   *   *

Nancy told our teacher what happened after lunch.

Miss Yockovich spent part of the afternoon discussing race, color, and creed. She had the three boys that caused the problem stand up and apologize to Lincoln and Washington.

From then on the twins sat next to me, Oscar, and Nancy. Gradually more and more kids sat with us, and soon the three boys were eating alone.

*   *   *

Finally, before the month was over, Linc and Wash spoke to the three outcasts as we sat down for lunch. "Why don't you three guys join us for lunch?" From then on nothing more was said regarding any racial talk.

There was Sammy Otsuki, Jan Singer, Frank Chin, and Jose Torres to name a few, new kids that were different and Nancy and I welcomed them to our school. We always welcomed any one new to the long tables, had lunch together, and traded sandwiches. Trading food was an amazing equalizer.

Every nationality was welcome at all my parties out by the lake where we lived, and if no transportation was available to them, Mom or Dad would say, "No transportation, no problem because we'll pick you up and take you home."

So Nancy and I became the protector of the minorities clear through our senior year in high school.

*　　*　　*

When I was in the seventh and eighth grade, I really developed my ear for languages, and with the varied colors of skin we had in school, I had the opportunity to learn a little of many languages. When I'd be over to someone's house to play or have dinner I'd try to speak in their native language. The parents would coach me on certain words. Everyone would laugh as I tried to get the accent correct. I was even able to speak the deep south droll style with the help of the Roosevelts.

Mrs. Roosevelt would tell me, "Teddy boy, you speak it just like my Daddy and you eat them fish cakes and grits like your Mom or Dad never feed you, and you people got a restaurant."

When we all rode our bicycles to our favorite fishing place, next to Chester's Dairy on the Swinjoscie River and we caught fish, Mrs. Roosevelt always made us stay for a fish fry dinner.

She'd say, "Teddy, get your white tail over here Son and give me a hand in fixing them fish. You're the only one around here that knows how fix and cook them fish and ain't lazy like those sitting over there. They is just a sitting and a waiting to be fed. Look at them Teddy, ain't that a picture as they got their mouths open just like baby birds."

I learned how to cook a fish Southern style from Cookie down at the restaurant.

"Rupert," she would say to her husband. "Looky here. We got a Mexican, a Jew, a German, a Chinese, a Japanese, and a Slovenian all sitting at our table eating our fish as if they'd been eating with us for years."

Mr. Roosevelt would say, "You're right Mama. Only in America and especially right here in Daisy Junction could this happen."

Mrs. Roosevelt would laugh and tell us, "You boys can bring them fish here and you can sit at our table anytime. If we ain't got room I'll move those two," she pointed at Linc and Wash, "outside."

Mr. Roosevelt would laugh, "Me thinks Teddy is better than those two young roosters that live with us. I wonder if Mr. Radovich will trade one for two?" Then he would laugh and slap his hand hard against his leg.

*   *   *

When I entered high school as a freshman my athletic activities and knowing some various words in every language probably helped me. I'd assisted those who were having difficulty in certain subjects, especially with our language. We would get together during study hall period to go over their lessons.

Out in the athletic field I would exercise with Lincoln and Washington, Sam Otsuki, Jan Singer, Jose Torres, and Frank Chin. I was sort of the leader and coerced everyone into trying their hardest. I knew they all wanted to be as fast and athletic as I was so it wasn't difficult. I even got lazy Oscar Shumaker to join us in wind sprints.

Oscar was square built like a fire plug, and his forte was shot putter, discus thrower, and a javelin tosser. He was stationary muscle and he didn't see any reason to run, but he did with me and the twins because I had his number. I would tell him, "Okay you Dutchman or German or whatever the hell you are, you have to run wind sprints with us or we're not going to tell you what our weekend plans are."

When any of the kids of various nationalities would come into our store they were treated exactly as the others.

Mom and Dad were great with all the boys and girls. The girls would always receive a hug from Mom and Mom instituted a charge account for the high school customers and kept the charges in her little brown book. No one ever saw that book except her, even my nosy and gossipy Aunt Helen that worked in the store.

Whether a girl or boy could charge or not, came from a nod or a slight shake of Mom's head. Charging depended on the balance left in Mom's black book. She never let the student's bill go beyond five dollars. Most parents never realized their child had a charge account in Radovich's Confectionery and All American Cafe.

Dad would give the boys a handshake or a pat on the back. The girls, he would tell them how great they looked and if they played sports he would comment about that.

Any girl with problems, Mom, once a Major in the army and the head superintendent of nurses at an army hospital was always available to talk to the girls when they came into our store.

If the store was filled with customers that didn't bother her at all. She would take a girl that wanted to talk to an empty booth.

If any of the boys or the girls were involved in some type of athletic program, Dad always took time to watch practices and many of the school home games or events they entered. Not every day, but once or twice a week he would take time off from the store just to watch their practices or local events. This gave him an opportunity to enjoy sports, something he felt cheated about because he didn't get the chance to play, having to grow up so fast.

Dad's advice, "You looked good. One suggestion. When you have that person in your advantage, take them apart. It is important for you to know what you can do."

One thing about my parents. Any advice was always on the positive side, directed dedication to one's goals.

On of my dad's favorite motivational speeches was, "You certainly can do better than that. You gave that person a break, don't do it in competition, take them out. It's a lesson for them, and a lesson for you knowing what you can do."

*   *   *

It was fun to go to Mr. and Mrs. Chin's restaurant, or the Otsuki's house, or Torres Mexican restaurant and eat their family specialties. The first time the gang ate at the Torres we all thought our tongues would never stop burning.

We all became big fans of the various fare each family served us, the ethnicity was fun, like eating with chop sticks at Frankie Chin's, The Golden Dragon, or Tommy Otsuki's house where eating Sushi was a special treat. We'd sit on our knees in their large restaurant kitchen.

When Mom and Dad with Grandma Olena and Grandpa Egor would have dinner in the Golden Dragon, I would demonstrate my expertise with chop stick technique.

Dad was always better than I with the sticks. He must have picked it up somewhere in his Army travels. He never told me about his travels or where he went on his assignments.

*　　*　　*

Every week, we boys would gather at someone's house for dinner. I would ask Nancy if she wanted to join us in a dinner, but Mrs. Blake would not let. The reason; Nancy would be the only girl with six or so boys.

*　　*　　*

Oscar, with his large thighs and being squatty and square, had problems getting down on his knees at Sammy Otsuki's or Frank Chin's. Oscar usually sat with his legs out in front of him.

Mr. Otsuki would kid Oscar, "You sit just like a Kraut."

Mrs. Chin would tease Oscar about being a typical German; built to only drink beer, eat liverwurst, and sauerkraut. The rest of us wondered about our knees because we were not slim and slight like the Otsuki's and Chin's and were used to sitting at a table with chairs.

Sammy Otsuki's house was way out in the country, but not too far for an occasional Japanese dinner. The family raised carnation flowers for the wholesale markets all up and down the East Coast.

* * *

When we started high school Grandma and Grandpa would still have the boys over for some of their boiled beef and cabbage and we all would listen to Gramp tell his stories of living in the old country, or his fighting in the trenches during World War I. Our gang learned to sing a few of Gramp's songs in Slovenian, but Grandma Olena put her foot down. "Egor," she'd say with her hands on her hips, "you know better than treat the boys to a cup of your beer and sing those off color songs."

When we all became older Gramp would sneak in a couple of bar songs and two cups of his homemade, dark heady beer.

Grandpa Egor would laugh and tell anyone eating there, "You guys would make great Slavs the way you scarf up Olena's dinners, Yeah, you guys stuff the food away just like you're straight from goat hills of the Southern Transylvanian Alps."

CHAPTER 4

I WAS TEN YEARS OLD when Dad retired from the Army in 1948 with twenty-one years in uniform. He remained in the Active Army Reserve for many years. With his discharge money and what he saved he bought the cafe from his father and mother, Grandpa Egor and Grandma Olena.

Along with the sale came the store's delivery truck. A 1931 Model A Ford Panel, my family called the 'Goosey Truck', but nobody knew why. Twenty some years of sitting out in snow, freezing rain, and heat, and it was a mass of rust and patches of dull black paint. However the windows worked and so did the engine.

* * *

When I turned fifteen it was my vehicle to drive and take care of, and I learned to drive on a learner's permit, making deliveries, driving carefully. I couldn't take an unlicensed passenger with me, leave town, or drive at night, although I did sneak a few night drives, alone. I quit bicycling at night so the old Ford was my only transportation, but I had to go straight home after work. I was also now working as a 'soda jerk' in the afternoons and evenings.

* * *

Goosey sometimes seemed to run on gas fumes as the tank gauge would roll into the red empty mark long before I would the fill the gas tank at Whitey's. I never once ran out of gas.

One day, I stopped for gas at Whitey's and Whitey was talking to me as he was washing the front and side windows. "I don't know how to figure it, Ted, but your tank holds exactly ten gallons of regular gas and yet you take ten point eight gallons. Impossible Teddy."

"I don't know why, Whitey. I wait till the red rolls up on the gas gauge and then wait a couple of days before I bring it in for a refill."

"Dammit Teddy, I started working on these A's when Henry first brought them out, and I know them front, and back, and sideways."

"Maybe it's your meters, Whitey?"

"Crap. My meters are checked every two months, and I have the stats on these machines and they have new meters and when they say ten gallons it's ten gallons, but your truck takes more."

The only seats in Goosey were in the front and both had springs ready to come through the old black leather seats. Just one spring was trying to erupt from the driver's side, but on the passenger side a whole bunch were just about ready to explode through the old cracked leather, but it didn't concern me because I didn't sit on that side, ever.

"You are going out for football this fall?" asked Whitey.

"Yep, been working out at home running up and those two hills behind our house in the morning and evening. Then doing all kinds of exercises. Dad has me working out, kinda army like. I'll be really ready for the second week in August, I'll be darn ready and I'm looking forward to a better season than last year, Whitey."

"Listen kid, I've known you when Mimi carried you in a wicker basket. Last season you were better than anyone on the field, and Val tells me your still growing. I don't think I'd want to tackle you head on and coming from the side you'd just show me your speed. You were good last year, but man with those bigger muscles this year you're going to be great with your size, weight, and your sprinter speed you showed this spring in track. Teddy, I'll see you on your first game even if I have to close the store. Good luck Ted."

*   *   *

I measured myself later that day and I'd grown to five-eleven, weighing 185. I'm was fifteen and would be a sophomore in Daisy Junction High School that fall.

*   *   *

Besides working in the store on summer weekends, I'd life guard on the Swinoisce River. Working in the restaurant and life guarding gave me more than a nodding acquaintance with the local prostitutes from the end of Virginia Street. Their houses butted right up next to the Swinoisce River and in the summer they were no stranger to the river beach. The girls also came into the store a lot.

These ladies were not much different than any other customers except they were always dressed smartly in the newest fashions. Mimi, my mother, always told her friends,

"If you want to know what the newest fashions are, just see what those girls are wearing."

They were always cheerful and nice to me. When the girls came in, and I was at the counter, they'd sit on the green swivel chairs across the counter from me and I'd make the fountain orders for them. These ladies always left me a better tip than most of our counter customers.

When the girls came in, it was, "Hi Teddy how's school?" or, "I read about your game last Saturday," or, "you did a great job in the last track meet."

Dee Dee, if she was working that shift, would question me later; "Why were those whores so friendly to you?"

"I don't know Dee Dee. The only time I see them is when they are in the store. Honest. I would never go to those houses."

"If you ever go in any of those houses, for whatever, you'll pick up some disease that will stay with you forever. Do you understand?" The look she then gave me was a warning that I quickly understood. I was determined no to visit any of those houses.

This did not stop my imagination from running the gauntlet of what really went on in those houses, Did the girls really just do it with just anyone, and how much did they charge? Yeah, just how do they really do it? Golly, those girls were so good looking.

"One of the girls, very young looking, always wore a silver bracelet and a fancy diamond ring on her middle finger with a silver strap between them. On the strap between the middle finger and her wrist she had a diamond studded watch; it rested on the back of her hand connected to her wrist and her ring finger.

I asked her if I could see it up close. She showed me then asked, "Want to get one for your girl friend, Teddy?"

"I don't have one," I responded, not even considering what the items might cost.

All these ladies, at one time or the other, gave me a hint that it was time for me to start thinking about a girlfriend.

I was content to have the ladies come to me, but one day Dad threw me a curve by asking me to make a delivery.

"Okay Dad, where?" I responded, eager to take any assignment that let me drive.

"Teddy, I need you to make a delivery to 52 Virginia Street at four this afternoon," he instructed.

"Where?" I stumbled, hesitating. "There?" I knew the address, and it was one of those 'houses'.

"I'm not going in one of those houses, Dad," I answered quickly, not really meaning what I just said, but Dee Dee and Rudy, our dishwasher and handy man, were present.

"Son," he slowly replied and looked at me with a smirk. I knew that look. Dad knew my previous declaration was a load of crap. He knew I was curious as hell about the inside of one of the houses. "You are making a deliver and only a delivery, that's all." He was still smirking. "Take these boxes of candy and ice cream to 52 Virginia."

"Send Rudy," I offered, still feigning rigorousness.

"Not me," proclaimed Rudy, "I'm saving my money." Rudy then explained that he had sworn off 52 Virginia Street. He claimed the last time he went, about six months ago, Carlotta, he though that was her name, took everything in his wallet plus what he had in his shoe.

"And how long were you in there?" Dad asked.

"It wasn't all that long," Rudy exclaimed defensively.

"Rudy." Dad stared him down. "I know for a fact that Maude always tries to get you home before all your money is gone, but it never works."

Rudy's face turned red, but he offered up his excuse, "It was a good thing I had the next day off because I couldn't move a muscle for a whole day. I was as limp as yesterday's used toilet paper, but they will sure never forget me."

Dee Dee spat out, "You men think you're always giving a woman a good time, but the only good time is in your mind and pants. Those whores could care less what you're doing or how well you're doing it. It's the money they want." Dee Dee continued, looking at me. "It's just the money. Every thing else they do is just plan fakes and window dressing. Don't listen to Rudy, Teddy. Just make the delivery and be quick about it. Just consider them actresses.

"Speaking of money Teddy," said Dad, "Mrs. Maude Angel, she will be the tall, fiftyish lady with dyed red hair and she will pay you in cash."

Now Dad smiled. "Here's the bill. Don't bother to count the money when Mrs. Angel hands it to you. She's honest, and not like some of our customers."

"Gee, Dad what am I supposed to do when I am in . . . in? Ah . . . that, uh, place?" I was trying to play it cool, like I was really concerned, but I was eager as hell.

"My gosh, I cannot believe this?" chuckled Dad. "Son, just listen up."

When Dad used his military term, "Listen up," I listened because it meant, 'No more conversation, just follow my orders and get to work."

"Teddy you will deliver the order and wait for the money. You've done this a hundred times on other deliveries and this one is no different. Be sure to say, 'thank you'. That should be easy to remember, so load up and get going. We are running a business. Number 52 Virgin is the two story house with the yellow side door on the right going toward the river?"

"Yes, Sir Mr. R," piped up Rudy, "that yellow door is their service entrance.

Sure is." Rudy hesitated, looking around proudly. "I use the front door. That's for paying customers and I've more than paid my share."

Dad gave Rudy a stern look, then turned to me and continued, "Okay Teddy, pay attention. Knock three times, that's three times only, on that yellow side door. You'll deliver everything you have, the candies and ice cream, that is, inside. Wait for your money and hurry back here. I would suggest you refrain from accepting any samples, please."

"But Dad, those people are prostitutes or whores."

"Here we go again. You are exactly right, but they are also our customers and we will always treat them as customers, just like everyone else. Understand? They come into our store and pay us. You have waited on those girls. Nothing is different except we are making a delivery. Is this hard for you to understand?"

"No but . . ."

"No butts Teddy. Nothing will happen to you. They will not jump out at you. Get going lad."

"Watch out for that Spanish gal," chimed in Rudy, "I think her name is Carlotta. Wow! She is one good looking, hot number."

*　　*　　*

I loaded my old trusty, rusty, Model A Ford Panel truck Goosey and drove off to 52 Virgin Street. Man-oh-man it was cold outside. There was a heater, of sorts, in the old Model A, but it needed more than six blocks before it would work, yet I was sweating. It had to be where I was driving that made me sweat because I was never nervous like that in sports.

"Well," I said to myself, "they do come into the store and pay cash, and they are honest and not like some of the others that just forget to pay, usually saying, 'Sorry. I was busy and was thinking of something else.'"

Those six city blocks were longer that I remembered because I just knew everyone I saw was looking at me and they knew exactly where I was going. I tried to hunch over not wanting to be obvious to anyone who might recognize me making this delivery.

*   *   *

I turned down Virginia Street, two blocks past our Police Station. I wondered how the Police Department can be so close to the whore houses and gambling places and not recognize what they are doing?

Outside, along the street and sidewalk some white, but mostly dirty, gray snow had been pushed off the streets on to the sidewalks. This street, or better yet, this last block of Virginia goes right to the Swinjoscie River and was the last street to be plowed out after any snow storm.

Daisy Junction's street crews didn't hurry to clean off the sidewalks in this end of town. I guess their backs hurt by the time they get down this far, so a lot of times the customers made their own trail from the street to their house of choice. In really bad weather the whole of Daisy Junction could be shut down, but this area was always bustling. One thing about it, the ice cream I was delivering sure wouldn't melt in this weather.

I parked right in front of 52 Virginia and looked around. It was still pretty early in the day so there were no cars, and no one walking or standing. A well-beaten track, left in the old snow from last weeks storm, went from the street to the front door of the house.

There were four small row boats tied up on the porch. They were used when we got two or three straight, rainy days.

The trail to the yellow side door had just a few tracks. So, in my tennis shoes, I waded through the one foot of old, dirty, crunchy snow. I hurried to carry all the packages up the porch steps on the side of the house.

Man-oh-man was it cold outside? Each step I took required me to kick the snow to make a trail, and my tennis shoes weren't exactly made for snow kicking.

It took me three trips to get all the delivery stacked on the last step to the door. I had the last package, a heavy one, in my hands. I was holding the ice cream container when up drove Captain Otto Shumaker of the Parish County Sheriff's Department. He was Oscar's father and coach of our hockey team, and he was a blabber mouth.

"Hi Teddy need some help?" he called out his open window.

Oh shit, I thought, Now everybody's going to know.

"No sir. Got it almost delivered, 'for Dad'." I over emphasized Dad.

"Must be a big party tonight, Teddy?"

"Gee Mr. Shumaker, I don't really know. I'm just following 'Dad's' orders on a delivery." I was shaking, but thankful there were delivery items right there in front of me.

"Going to be at the practice game at the hockey rink tonight, Teddy?"

I exhaled my breath. "Sure am. I saved some money and bought myself a new Easton Senior Shaft hockey stick and it's autographed."

"Thanks Teddy. Thanks a lot. Now I'll have to get one for Oscar or I'll never hear the end of it. He will owe me for a year the way he pays back his debts."

I added, "Captain Shumaker, tell Oscar I'll anchor the right side tonight."

"Great Ted, see you tonight. Oh, be careful, and not too many samples before practice. You don't want to be worn out for tonight's practice."

Captain Otto Shumaker grinned and then he drove away.

*   *   *

I turned my attention to the yellow door and I could hear talking and laughing on the other side.

I took a big breath and knocked three times, the special signal.

Suddenly, the door was not simply opened, but flung wide open.

There, standing in a nearly transparent, blue, short, something or other, was Miss L'Affaire, one of the customers of the All American Cafe.

There she was, blonde hair, bright blue eyes, clear complexion, and looking very young with no makeup on. Miss L'Affaire was about five-one and weighed perhaps near one-hundred pounds. Right then she could pass for a junior or senior in my high school, if she had clothes on. There she stood, legs apart, well outlined and everything on her white body was slightly visible. Miss L'Affaire was perhaps one of the best dressed ladies from Virginia Street who came into the cafe every Saturday afternoon for her chocolate-fudge-malted sundae, called a Dusty Road.

She was the only one that would always order that expensive fancy sundae, the others usually ordered ice cream sodas. Miss L'Affaire always told me, "Teddy, Honey, you make the most delicious Dusty Road I have ever had."

This afternoon she greeted me with, "Teddy, it's you. What a welcomed surprise. Sorry I can't help you. You can see I'm really not dressed to walk outside in this cold weather."

Miss L'Affaire was not even dressed at all. I could see right through the shear blue short, something or other and she had nothing on underneath, what so ever, but white skin from chin to toes.

She had no dark hairs at her crotch area, like those women in the pictures that were passed around in my six and seventh grades. I focused my eyes, confused by the absence of the triangle I thought all woman had.

Now I saw her breasts. Man-oh-man, those things pointed straight out. Probably not as full as Dee Dee's, but they're straight out. I'm reminded of the big boy's talk when they refer to Lisa Robert's, Pastor Robert's oldest daughter's breasts as 'watch fob hangers'.

I remembered why I was there and averted my eyes, quickly, bring in all the orders. Man-oh-man, inside I was met by four more scantily dressed young ladies all squealing and acting like teenagers as they greeted me by name.

More customers from the cafe, Carlotta, Rosalinda, Angelica, and Lily. All these girls look not much older than teenagers.

Miss L'Affaire told me, "Honey, put the boxes on the floor over there, and the girls will sort out the candies. Please bring the ice cream into our kitchen. I'll show you where to put it."

The four girls bounced back and forth between the kitchen and parlor with bowls for the candy and began a slow sorting out of the sweets. They were all wearing something like baby doll pajamas, or short dresses, or just pajama tops, but not as sheer as what Miss L'Affaire was wearing.

Because of my limited knowledge from looking and reading certain magazines for women or those special nude magazines for men, I was not sure how to properly analyze what I was witnessing. Pictures do tell a thousand words, but this was something new and exciting. I knew I was seeing the real thing and my thought was, The magazines don't really compare with what I'm seeing now.

I was uncomfortable as I stood in the parlor with the girls bending over to sort out the candy. In my position I could see right down the front of their pajamas or clear down to their painted toe nails. That was, if my eyes didn't stop somewhere in between, and I'm thinking, Man-oh-man, if I ever looked at Nancy Blake like that, she would blacken both my eyes.

Well, Nancy Blake was nowhere close, I was thinking, when Miss L'Affaire bounced back to the parlor and told me, "The money is coming, so just sit down. Honey. Do you want a coke or something?"

My throat was so dry I could only shake my head. Finally, I squeaked out a, "No thank you."

"I'll get you one anyway. Sweetie, sit on that blue couch. I'll be right back."

So, I'm seated on the end of this leather couch with my left arm stretched out on the top of the couch. What I'm trying to do is demonstrate a calm and unconcerned position, but I'm far from being unconcerned and calm.

Miss L'Affaire giggled when she came back with a coke and sat right next to me, kind of in touching distance.

We started talking sports, which I was surprised to learn Miss L'Affaire was quite knowledgeable about, but I couldn't figure out why. The whole time I'm sneaking many glances at Miss L'Affaire. She was sitting so close to me, any of her body movements kinda rubbed against me, and the physical reaction I was starting to experience was not one I cared to share.

If I'd of had the guts, I would've liked to put my arm around her shoulders and let my hand flop down to one of her breasts. Those things stuck straight out, kind of like some of those natives I'd seen in National Geographic Magazine pictures.

The four girls, Carlotta, Rosalinda, Lilly, and Angelica smiled as they give me looks. Then they nudged each other and laughed about the free show I'm getting.

One of them whispered to the other three as she looked directly at my crotch that I'm trying to cover. I think it was the one Rudy referred to in the store's kitchen before I left on delivery. Did he say Charlotte or Rosalinda?

Perhaps, I think, if I look somewhere else maybe my erection will go away.

But it didn't work very long because the girls took the candy to a long table next to the door leading to a long hallway, and I'm able to see their scantily covered rear ends as they bewitchingly and twitchingly walked. I didn't remember any of the girls at school walking like that. Well, Lisa Robert's came close.

On the table were a number of egg timers with numbers painted on them from one to five. Now there was something I could talk to them about, fixing eggs.

So I said to the ladies, "You girls sure must eat a lot of eggs?"

The girls looked at me curiously and did not say anything for a moment or two. "Not really. Why do you ask, Teddy?" asked Angelica, a slight, brown eyed beauty.

"Well, I noticed all those egg timers on the table over there." I pointed to the table.

The girls erupted in laughter. Their breasts bounced as they giggle and laughed, holding their hands over their mouths.

Miss L'Affaire leaned all the way over to me from the waist up, coming against me with nearly nothing on and she was giggling.

A tall, older woman entered the room. Her hair had the red chromatic look of dyed, and she was heavily made up, with black eyelashes that stuck straight out. I'm wondering if they are false? The lady's cheeks are a rose color and she's wearing bright orange lipstick. She had on a green, velvet housecoat that came right down to the floor. Even with her high heel shoes she had a glide type of walk.

I started to stand up, but I hesitate because I had the erection. I'm thinking,

How silly I must look, trying to cover my crotch because there's a lump in my pants.

One of the girls, still laughing, tells the lady, I had asked about the egg timers.

The woman turned to me, as I struggled to look comfortable because I'm still half standing. "I'm Mrs. Maude Angel. You must be Mr. Radovich's boy, Ted? Please, don't get up for me."

I quickly sat down, relieved.

Mrs. Angle continued, "I have read about your accomplishments playing football and running track in the newspaper. You have done quite well. I know your mother and dad must be proud of you. Welcome to our home, Teddy," she continued, "What you see on the table, Ted, are egg timers, however, we do not use them as egg timers. They are to time our clients. We do not want our customers over extending their time without paying extra. We too, like your father and mother, are in the money making business and nothing is ever given away. Just a lousy habit we got into, working for money." She gave a slight chuckle.

Looking carefully at me, she continued, "You must take a tour of the house. L'Affaire, Carlotta, Rosalinda take this young man on a tour and when you return I will have his money for him. Come on girls, move."

Miss L'Affaire stood up and extended her hand to help lift me out of my chair.

I'm worried, thinking about my erection.

She bent slightly over right in front of me, ready to help pull me up. Now I can see down her whole naked body, clear to her knees. Of course, my eyes took in this scene and this scene was not helping reduce my problem. Miss L'Affaire tugged on me, and finally I'm on my feet, but standing slightly bent over.

She looked into my eyes and with a very serious tone of voice, asked, "Are you Okay Teddy? Can you walk?"

In a shaky voice I replied, "Oh sure, of course I can . . . I think.

Miss L'Affaire gave me a large smile and looked at my bulging crotch. With a light laugh, showing her white teeth, she said to Carlotta and Rosalinda, "Take his hands and lets go."

With two ladies on each side of me, we followed the white rear end of Miss L'Affaire as we walked down the wide long hallway. I'm really embarrassed as I poked out the front of my pants.

Rosalinda and Carlotta giggle and danced me down the hallway past four doors, all closed. They tugged me to the end of the hall, still following the tail end of Miss L'Affaire.

"Where are we going?" I asked, keeping my eyes on the twitching white buttocks of Miss L'Affaire.

"Teddy, Honey, we will give you a tour of a couple of our house's special rooms," Miss L'Affaire answered my question with her bright smile.

At the end of the hall way, Miss L'Affaire opened a door and we went into a room with a large wooden tub of water sitting on a high platform with steps going up to the edge of the tub.

"What's that?" I asked, looking around this room. I saw many unlit candles lining the round tub.

"A brand-new thing called a Jacuzzi. It came all the way from California," said Carlotta. "Let us all get in."

"What do you do in it?" I had never seen or heard anything about a Jacuzzi.

"It has warm perfumed water and blowing warm air to agitate the water to soothe sore muscles and relax people. Let's get in, Teddy." Carlotta was trying to pull me into the room.

"I think you need it," chuckled Rosalinda.

"With my clothes on?" I asked confused. "I don't understand."

"No silly, without clothes." Carlotta appeared to be serious. "Come on in and we will help you undress."

Miss L'Affaire then came to my rescue.

"Okay Carlotta, give Teddy a break. We are just going to show him those two room upstairs. Maybe another time Teddy. You might consider coming back after a football game to take a soothing bath. Great way to relax those leg muscles and ease away the bruises and sore spots. I've read that some colleges and pros are starting to use these for their players after games."

I'm most grateful to Miss L'Affaire for her suggestion to get me out of this room. So up the stairs we went, following the bouncing Miss L'Affaire with her white buttocks gyrating all the way. Reminded me of the deer in our area. They to twitch their white rear ends as they slide through the thick forest.

Now I'm pulled into the first room on the left at the top of the stairs. They tell me it's Carlotta's room. My first thoughts are, Why such a large room just to sleep in?

This room had a red, thick, soft rug going from one wall to another and pink wallpaper with touches of specks of gold. In the middle of the room was a gigantic round bed also in shades of red and pink.

I had never seen, or even imagined that a bed could ever be that large and round, and in the middle of a room. I wondered, How do they keep the sheets and blankets on this bed, and how does she keep the two pillows on the bed when she sleeps?"

The rug, when I stepped on it, seemed to be three inches deep and cushioned my tennis shoes.

Carlotta placed one arm around my shoulders and pushed one of her breasts hard against my arm. I sure could feel it, but I didn't know if I needed that right then. Using her other hand she tilted my head back, and I saw that the ceiling was completely covered with square mirrors. She pushed me next to the round bed. Still looking up, I could see the bed from every angle and I had an overhead view of the girls, again, down to their painted toe nails as they scampered into the room.

As I stared at the scene reflected in the ceiling this sight of flimsy clad, young ladies was giving me a dull, cramped feeling in my groin area, again.

"Well, Teddy, what do you think?" asked Miss L'Affaire.

"I think I should go. Maybe the money is ready?" I answered.

Miss L'Affaire said, "Not before you see my room, Honey. Come on Teddy as long as we are upstairs lets go. This room is Carlotta's. You will really like mine."

That said, Miss L'Affaire started out the room, and again the other two ladies took my hands. We followed Miss L'Affaire, still in her see through blue, short, nightgown. Miss L'Affaire's rear view still reminded me of the White Tailed deer in the woods around our house.

To her bedroom we went. Somewhere around my groin I have more of a cramp coming on.

The girls, still holding my hands, pulled me into Miss L'Affaire's room. My groin was hurting more from the prolonged erection. This bedroom had walls that were covered in gold and silver wall paper. Another huge bed was covered with a dark yellow blanket and gold colored sheets.

The ceiling had three large mirrors, much, much larger than the room we just left. Along the walls are mirrors slanted in such a way that I could see myself, and the girls from where I stood. The mirrors appeared to be angled to show Miss L'Affaire's generous size bed, no matter where I looked from.

"Check out the bed, Teddy." Carlotta motioned to me. "Pure silk sheets and pillow cases, and this is a waterbed."

"A what?" I exclaimed.

"Lie down on the bed, stretch out, then you'll know what I mean," Carlotta said.

I slowly sat on the bed, and the bed moved in a rolling movement.

"Feel it, isn't it great?" giggled Carlotta.

"Somebody turn on the vibrator, please," Carlotta asked the girls.

Miss L'Affaire's bed began to shake.

"Damn-it, What is it that I heard about these water beds?" I think, laying on my back on the moving and vibrating bed.

Now Carlotta stretched out next to me. My groin area was really hurting and gaining in intensity, but she smelled so nice.

Rosalinda then climbed on the bed and straddled me by sitting on my waist. Damn her. She began to move up and down with her body, and the bed's movement caused my cramping body to go up and down. She was rubbing her crotch against my crotch. This was too much for me.

Suddenly, I felt an extremely sharp pain down deep in my testicles or groin area as if someone had just kicked me there. The same thing happened once last year in a football game, but not as painful as I was now experiencing.

This pain made me forget about Rosalinda as I tried to roll into a ball, bringing my knees almost to my chin. I was hurting bad.

"What's the matter Honey?" inquired Rosalinda.

"I'm in trouble," I responded with clenched teeth, trying to sit up, but I couldn't. Now I was really in trouble.

Rosalinda was still trying to sit astride my hips. She grabbed my hands and was only able to place my right hand on her left hip. I was in such severe pain that I couldn't care less about what ever she was doing.

Rosalinda, I guess, finally noticed I was in pain, and laughingly left me on the bed.

Miss L'Affaire bent over me and tugged me upright. Now I was seated on the edge of the undulating waterbed, but bent over and groaning.

She reached her hands behind my head, put her mouth to my ear, and quietly told me, "Grab me around my waist."

I struggled to sit upright.

Miss L'Affaire, still bending over me, ordered, "Teddy sit up and stand. Pull me up, lift Teddy lift. You have to lift me. Please, Honey, grab me and pick me up as you begin to stand. Your hurt will go away, I promise. Now stand up the best you can."

I struggled up and sat on the edge of her bed. My legs were between Miss L'Affaire legs. Right then I didn't care where the legs were.

She grabbed me, tight, around my neck, and tried to press her body next to me. I could see her light blue eyes and clear complexion, and smell some type of perfume I had never smelled before.

"Stand up Teddy," she ordered.

"I can't. It hurts too much."

"I understand and trust me, lift me off the bed, and as soon as you do the pain will go away. Please."

I fought and struggled to stand upright with Miss L'Affaire's arms around my neck. I bent my knees and my hands found the white, butt cheeks of Miss L'Affaire. Slowly, I tried to stand upright.

"Honey, now lift me off the bed," this time her tone was a demand. I locked my hands under Miss L'Affaire's smooth, white buttocks, and she jumped up slightly, her white legs going around my body and she locked them tight around me.

I was surprised how small and light she was. Slowly, I began to lift Miss L'Affaire off the bed, while she's talking to me in my right ear,

"Honey keep lifting," she purred.

I struggled to remain erect, while the pain in my crotch area was subsiding, the pain slipping away.

I kept my hands locked under Miss L'Affaire's white, rear cheeks. Her legs remained tight around my body and her dainty white arms remain locked around my neck. With her mouth against my right ear, she murmured softly to me: "Say, big boy, next time put a little more chocolate fudge on my Dusty Road sundae, then I will owe you a real treat."

I don't know how, but I decided to lift her higher. I could smell her and I think I could feel her right nipple against my chin. My thoughts were, Get her just a little higher and I can get that breast in my mouth. Her body felt like she was melting against me, her legs still wrapped tight around my waist. Hurray, the pain had gone. I feel free and ready for Miss L'Affaire.

Keeping my grip on her bottom with her head and chest back, I could look into her bright light blue eyes and also see her breasts up close. I asked, "What happened, Miss L'Affaire?"

"You had what many young school boys get when they are first experiencing girls up close. It is called, 'The Blue Balls'. Your testicles or groin will cramp up as if someone hit you right there. You've had that happen in football, haven't you?"

"Yes, yes. This year I got hit right there, but not doing something like this."

Miss L'Affaire was still holding on to me and moved her head against the top of my head. One of her 'pointy' nipples was again pushing against my chin. She still had her arms tight around my neck. She spoke into my ear again,

"When that happens, Teddy, to relieve this pain, the boy must lift something heavy, and this stops the cramping or whatever is causing the pain. Maybe, if it happens again, try to lift the back of your car. Of course you can't, but the pain will go away."

"What if I'm in the car?"

"Get out, walk to the back. You should be able to figure that out. Of course there's another way to get relief, but I'll let it go for now, sweetie."

Not relaxing my grip on Miss L'Affaire's rear end, I'm still trying to figure out, How I can get one of her 'pointy' breasts into my mouth.

Miss L'Affaire kept on with her analysis of my symptoms, but my attention was elsewhere. "Maybe it will never happen to you again Teddy, and maybe it will, depending on the situation."

Still holding Miss L'Affaire, I'm not showing any interest in anything she is saying.

I now decided to see just how far I can go because I want to be like the big boys in the school gym when they talk about Lisa Robert's breasts. The fast boys that have experience with Lisa's well developed and well used body.

Miss L'Affaire's grip tightened around my neck, her legs squeezing harder around my hips, and one of her breasts is almost ready to be inhaled into my mouth. What strength she has. She was still talking to me, but I was not paying attention because I'm working so hard to get a nipple in my mouth.

I was thinking, If I can lift her just an inch I'll then have one in my mouth. I tried to drop my chin lower. With both hands griping her white, smooth, rear end, I tried to lift Miss L'Affaire just one inch higher.

She seemed to tighten around me. Miss L'Affaire was impossible to lift any higher, but I'm trying, I'm really trying.

Damn her. Now she licked my ear, and I let out a low groan because I had an organism. Then she moved her face directly in front of mine and with a husky voice she said, "Let me see how you kiss."

I was still holding Miss L'Affaire up. She slid slightly down a few inches, and our mouths met, just like Dee Dee's when we kiss. We are in a full, grinding mouth examination. Miss L'Affaire whispered to me: "I think you have done this before."

I heard Carlotta say to Rosalinda, "Maybe we should leave them alone."

Miss L'Affaire pulled her head away from me and looked me in the eyes, she said, "Wow, I'm nearly out of breath. Teddy, you have some strength. When you are ready, so am I, and it will be my treat."

"One more kiss, please," I pleaded.

She patted my face, saying, "Not now honey, lets get your money, sweetie.

Wash your face, and remove my lipstick. Maybe you should clean your shorts in my bathroom, I'm going down stairs and see if the money is there. Charlotte, take care of my Teddy, and no messing around with my man."

Talk about someone who is spaghetti limp, that's me when I walked into a gold colored bathroom with gold colored fixtures and full mirrors from ceiling to floor. Shutting the door, I washed my face and wiped off the inside of my pants and shorts.

Carlotta kept asking me whether I needed any help.

"No, no, I don't need help, but maybe some other time," I replied.

I left the luxurious bathroom, and Carlotta gave me a quick check of my face and neck for signs of lipstick. She took my face in both of her hands, and moved her head so close to me I could see her deep brown eyes and clear complexion. She searched my face and shirt making sure no trace of lipstick was left.

Then she ran her hand outside my pants and with a slight grab on my groin, Carlotta announced, "Okay, good job, no wetness came through."

I started for the door to leave Miss L'Affaire's room, but Carlotta stopped me. "I need one dance with you," she said.

She turned on the radio Miss L'Affaire had by her bed and fiddled with the knobs until she found some music that appealed to her, breasts close to the radio. "Okay Teddy, let's have just one dance before you leave.

Putting my arms out, she slipped right up to me, and we began to dance. Holding her, I could barely feel that flimsy dress she had on. It felt as though she was nothing but soft skin.

We did a couple of twirls, and she stayed right with me. I'm trying to figure out how I can feel her breasts with my hands.

I've got it. The next twirl, I spun her around and lightly drug my hand across her breasts as she turned. I think they are firmer than Dee Dee's. We do another slow spin, and I get an even a better feel.

She came right up to me and molded her body against me. "Give me another spin big boy, but slower," she instructed me.

This one is a very slow turn, and I'm able to run my hands around her breasts, then glide my hands down her body and cup her brown butt cheeks. I just have to pull her closer. Do I take her, or wait for Miss L'Affaire?

Carlotta held me tight. My hands dropped down and clutched Charlotte's light, chocolate colored, rear end cheeks. I'm massaging them, and she was purring. Then, looking up with those big brown eyes, she said, "Honey, we got to get down stairs, or there will be trouble in the house. I'd like to try you out, but Miss L'Affaire will not like it. She wants to be your first. Sorry. Lets go."

She took my hand and using her middle finger, she lightly scratched my palm as we walked hand in hand down the hall, then down the stairs to the parlor. I still had a tremendous urge to grab Carlotta, and see just how far she really would go with me.

Quickly, the parlor door opened, and waiting for me was Miss L'Affaire with a frown on her face as she stared at Carlotta. Next to Miss L'Affaire is Mrs. Maude Angel still in her green velvet housecoat. In one hand she had the money.

The girls, all smiling, not trying to cover anything up, said goodbye. They all shook my hand and said, "Good-bye Teddy, and come again. We hope we'll see you Saturday."

*   *   *

My drive back to the store with the money was slower than my going there.

Wow, this was some afternoon. I checked my watch and my fifteen minutes had been stretched to over forty-five. I rechecked the front of my pants, again, and they appeared dry. Whew.

My lateness might require an explanation, maybe to Dad, and of course to that damn Dee Dee. I considered a number of excuses of why I was late, but none of them were really acceptable.

What the devil, I finally decided, I just won't use an excuse, just let the issue remain untouched. If the money was slow in coming, that is that.

*   *   *

Walking into the back of the store, in the kitchen area, I saw Dee Dee sitting on a stool, doing her finger nails. She snapped at me, "You get lost, or find some entertainment along the way?"

"None of the above," I told her.

Dee Dee jumped up and grabbed me, and began sniffing around my face and neck. "Did you get your first lay, Teddy?"

"No way, I just had to wait a long time for the money in a parlor or something like that. I talked with some of the girls, waiting for the money, that's all. Well, some of them did sit close to me."

"My sweet ass," Dee Dee said. "I don't believe you. We'll see about that, maybe later."

With that said Dee Dee flounced away, switching her rear end, but nothing compared to Miss L'Affaire's.

Dad has never said anything about my tardiness after that delivery.

CHAPTER 5

Dᴇᴇ Dᴇᴇ ꜰɪʀꜱᴛ ᴛʀɪᴇᴅ to make me dance when I was around thirteen years old and in the eighth grade. If we were in the kitchen together, and she was off her shift she would grab me and try to dance with me.

I kept telling her, "I don't want to learn how to dance, Dee Dee."

She always came back with, "Oh yes you will, and a lot sooner than you think."

She would start dancing with me to the music coming out of our old Philco Magic Eye radio that was always on in the kitchen.

Dee Dee kept telling me, "If you want to date a girl, instead of hauling those chairs up and down those three flights of stairs for the Rainbow dances, you'll have to learn to dance. Now that next year you will be a sophomore in high school, this is the time to learn the various dance steps."

*   *   *

After the feeling up with Dee Dee and the wild experience of the girls at 52

Virginia street, it didn't take me long to change from a boy-boy to a boy-man.

I knew what a lady's breasts felt like, since I had Dee Dee's in my hands, and Miss L'Affaire's tits almost in my mouth, and a quick hand on Carlotta's. I think I'm getting smarter. Now I had a better idea of what French Kissing was, what real breasts feel like, and what rear ends are all about.

*   *   *

Now, with those special, sexual introductions, I tried to learn more about dancing. I stopped resisting Dee Dee, and begin to pay attention to the dance steps. With my makeshift dance lessons, I think I'm becoming somewhat of a proficient dancer. Now, who would I date?

CHAPTER 6

It was now spring, and I hadn't dated yet because: first, I haven't picked the girl, and second the transportation problem? I'm going to be sixteen this late fall so I'm still months away from a drivers license. With my learner's permit I can't take unlicensed riders with me, however, I'm slowly learning more about dancing.

Dee Dee pestered me to date one of the many young freshmen high school girls that frequented my mom and dad's store for cokes or sundaes after school. These freshman girls would crowd into the two front booths or sit at end of the counter to stare at me as I worked behind our long, green marble counter making fountain drinks and sandwiches, but hey, they certainly didn't have figures like Dee Dee's, Miss L'Affaire's or Carlotta's.

There seemed to be the high school pecking order in our store based on where to sit.

Freshman kids always sat in the first booths or tables up front, or on the stools at the end of the marble counter. The Seniors always sat in the back booths and tables, but never at the counter. I don't know how it started, but that's way it's done. The sophomores and juniors gather in certain booths and tables between the seniors and freshman according to class.

Dee Dee kept telling me, "Those cute freshman girls keep asking me if you are dating anyone? I tell them no. So why don't one of you young ladies ask him out to a movie, or how about your Rainbow Sadie Hawkins dance, but all I receive is giggles."

I thought about this, but because I was now driving the Goosey I decided that any date I got would be a driving date, but until I got my license I am only allowed to drive by myself to and from the store and for deliveries so I will have to wait to date the cute girls. Oh, and I could also drive by myself through the dry pasture lands that surround Mallard Lake, once called Lake of Mounts. Mallard Lake was where my family lived, about four or five miles from Daisy Junction.

Along side the lake are the two 500 foot high bumps named West Mount Mallard, and East Mount Mallard. They are the highest spots in Parish County. Mallard Lake sits at the base of the two mountains. This lake was originally called Lake of Mounts, supposedly by the early pioneers.

Ivan Stankorvich, my history teacher at Daisy Junction High School and the town's unpaid historian, relishes telling the story about The Lake of Mounts.

He always began this story with; "The name, Lake of Mounts, came from the early pioneers. They gave it the name because of the large number of migratory ducks and geese that lived on the lake year around. When they arrived, the migratory birds began to mate with the domestic waterfowl the pioneers brought with them."

Someone would always ask, "How can they live there year round with the rotten, cold winters here?"

Mr. Stankorvich's answer was, "It's the hot springs in the lake that keeps the lake from freezing completely over in the winter." He goes on to say, "Many of the early Daisy Junctions pioneers believed the dissolved minerals from the hot springs caused the year round breeding season and this is why the early settlers named it; The Lake of Mounts."

That remark usually stopped the questions as they appeared to mull over his answer trying to figure out the reasoning.

Then Mr. Stankorvich continued, "When this village became a town with more immigrants from Europe arriving of course churches subsequently followed. The early church leaders took a sudden and shocked notice of the continual mating of the waterfowl in and around the lake. So, the church people just assumed something was in the water so the lake water started selling for sexual reasons. Of course, these pious, early church leaders thought it was morally wrong to drink the lake water, and worried about their children drinking it. They blamed the water for young people acting the way they did. They changed the name of the lake from Lake of Mounts to Mallard Lake and forbade any of their church members from drinking it."

The same four churches that established themselves back then are still there and they are, Saint Francis Xavier, a Catholic Church, The Ellaho Anthony Methodist Church, The Mission of the Apostles Church, and the Conservation and Progressive Baptist Church.

Even today, the most staunch church people continue to believe, and sermonize, "It's the water in the lake that causes our people to be more sexual active. The churches continued to condemn the sins of our younger generation every Sunday, rain or shine, and of course the young keep drinking the lake water.

CHAPTER 7

Nancy Blake and I sang in the C and P Baptist Church choir. Like I said, she was two days older than I was, and kept reminding me about it. From kindergarten, and then in high school we still appeared to be twins.

In the Thomas E. Bakich Elementary School teachers would ask us, if they didn't know our last names, "Are you twins?"

Nancy would always reply with a flip of her blond pony tail, "No. I'm much older than Teddy."

"Yeah, but only by two days," I always said under my breath.

*   *   *

When we got to high school we were called those blond non-twins, or just the non-twins. We shared projects together and our grades were almost exact. We were at the top ten percent in our high school with grades, and we lettered every year in two sports. Nancy competed in swimming and field hockey, and I play football and track.

During the end of my freshman year in high school I had to write a composition about some part of our town, Daisy Junction. I thought, Ah ha, I will cover Daisy Junction's open gambling and prostitution.

Dad told me, "I can't believe that history teacher, Ivan Stankorvich, is allowing you to prowl through the gutters of our town and write about our illegal businesses. Are you sure this is your report you want to turn in?"

"Dad, all he said was, 'I want stories about our town not found in our newspaper, but they must be accurate.' He also said, 'Remember the six cardinal rules in writing news: who, what, where, when, why, and how. Get all those down and you have a story.'"

Dad nodded his head. "Well, okay. I just wish our local news organizations would follow those six simple rules."

"When I finish, Dad, I'll let you check my assignment before I turn it in, I promise." Then I asked, "What do you know about the two?"

"Good," he replied, then continued, "Now this is what I know about those issues. So far, there have been no problems in or around the gambling or prostitution houses. As you know, they stay in the lower part of town and make sure the business stays there also.

"Why is that Dad?"

"Officer, 'Cowboy' McGrath will tell you it is well known that Lee Wong, I went through high school with Lee, now runs the gambling and prostitution. His family has been doing that since the beginning and they don't allow any foolishness down at the Waterfront. You know Lee, everyone calls him, 'High Pockets Wong' because you can see his socks below the cuffs of his pants.

Normally you see him wearing white socks, but if he is wearing red that indicates the houses and gambling are closed. Yellow socks indicate new girls are in town, and white, the houses and gambling are open."

High Pockets always dresses in a black suit, a black shirt, and white tie. Moshe, our local haberdasher, supplies High Pockets with his clothes. You know him Teddy, you go to school with his son Sammy.

Moshe told me once, 'I keep a good stock of Wong's cloths, black suits, black shirts, white ties, and of course, his red, white, and yellow socks. I have never sold him any other colors, and High Pockets never has anything cleaned, just buys new clothes. He calls me constantly and orders many of whatever he wants. Easy customer to have, Val.'"

Dad continued, still talking about Wong. "During our local ticket selling drives by the service clubs or churches, High Pockets Wong always asks me, 'Val, it's ticket selling time so how many tickets do you have you to sell this time, about the same as last year?'

Lee Wong then always pulls out a roll of money and buys all my tickets. It never makes any difference what organization I'm selling tickets for, High Pocket's always buys me out, and I'm sure he has done the same for other ticket sellers.

Many silent prayers are said by the religious citizens that benefit from the causes. Of course, Lee High Pockets Wong's name is never mentioned in the prayers, and of course, each church knows the system."

"You're right Dad," I said, shaking my head. "I've never heard Pastor Roberts mention his name, or anything below the Watermark."

The Watermark defined the high water point when the Swinjoscie River flooded. The homes and business down close had two colors inside on their walls. The dark colors from the floor up were black or brown stained by the flood waters. Nothing on the floor is permanent. Not even the linoleum is ever glued down. When the river starts to rise everything moveable was stacked above the high water, including the linoleum. They planned well down there.

* * *

Mr. Stankorvich told me after I submitted my article. "I thoroughly enjoyed your article, Ted. However, your topic and the excellent job you did might not be suitable for the school's newspaper. Teddy, it was well written, neatly balanced, and would be most interesting, especially with some school trustees. I think 'some' of them may have a financial interest in your subject. You and your sources exposed some things about our town that is normally kept among only a few people. I will give you a high A for your in-depth writing, but I'll keep your article under raps. These papers you handed me are the only copy?"

"Yes, Sir, I made only one copy."

"What about your source?"

"I never told anyone where I got the information."

"Good, keep it to yourself. Too many people could get hurt if someone wants to make an expose out of this. Eventually the businesses may die out, but let's let the authorities at the state level handle the problem."

CHAPTER 8

IT WAS A SUMMER day, over two years after my 'feeling up' experience with Dee Dee, and months past the bedroom tour from the girls in big yellow house on 52 Virgin Street and I am getting close to sixteen years of age. Of course, I had been thinking more about girls after my sessions with Dee Dee, Charlotte and Miss L'Affaire.

Dee Dee had not made any direct moves on me recently. She would caress my rear end when she was able and unseen as she passed behind me while I worked the fountain counter. A few times she lightly ran her hand over my crotch when she had to squeeze in front of me.

Miss L'Affaire, Carlotta, Rosalinda, and Lilly still came into the store frequently. Miss L'Affaire always received an extra ladle of hot chocolate fudge and more malt on top of her Dusty Road so she always gave me a nice smile and a generous tip. Oh, I sure would've liked to grab her.

*　　*　　*

With Dee Dee's instructions, my dancing had become smoother and of course I did enjoy holding her close while we danced to the slow music.

When we danced together in the kitchen, other employees would sing out, "There's the Ginger Rogers and Fred Astaire of Daisy Junction."

When we danced the Samba, a Brazilian dance of African origin, and the Jitter-Bug, we confined it to the candy making area, when it was not in use, due to the swinging and kicking.

*　　*　　*

Now that I was close to supposedly getting my drivers license and would get to have a real date I asked Dad one day, "When I start to date do I get to drive the family car?"

Dad replied, "No, use the Ford."

"But it is so old and the seats are not good for sitting any length of time," I whined. "It may also break down."

"Why would you want to sit in the Ford a long time anyway, Teddy?" My Dad asked nonchalant.

"Well, gee whiz, I don't know right now, but sometime I might want to."

"You have someone already picked out to sit with you in the Ford?

"Well, not yet, but maybe soon."

Dad leaned back against his desk, "Listen my friend," he said, "you have a ways to go before you get your license and can have passengers. That is if I sign on, and don't go asking your mother as she feels the same way. Until then, you always have your bicycle."

"Wait a minute, Dad. I will be sixteen in a few months and allowed to have a real driver's license.

"It's three and half months to be exact, and time is only a guide. It will be your maturity that will be the determining factor. Your mother and I will make the decision, when you will be ready to receive your license."

I was really downcast and mumbled out, "Well, I better find a girl that likes to bicycle when she is all dressed up."

"That is a good idea Ted, find a girl that likes to bicycle?"

"Well, Dad, the only girl I know that even owns a bicycle and still uses it is good old Nancy Blake."

"Well, now, you two have been close for a long time so I'd look into it if I was you. You two would make a great looking couple."

"I've never considered Nancy a date," I grumbled again.

* * *

So with by best friend Oscar Shumaker, I discussed asking Nancy for date.

"Sure Oscar, I've know Nancy all my life," I told him when we are considering the problem.

Oscar snapped back. "Yeah, I know that, and you've always protected her too."

"What are you getting at, Oscar?"

"It might be tough going out with her because you're more like a brother."

"What I can't understand, Oscar, is why she won't call me up for one of the Rainbow dances because she 'has' her license?"

"I just told you why," said Oscar.

"Well, when I get my license I'm going to invite her to one of the dances."

"In the Goosey?" laughed Oscar. "I don't even like sitting in that wreck because it smells like a horse with diarrhea."

"It's not that bad," I squawked. "Oscar, if she would ask me to one of her Rainbow Girl's formal dances, I'd even go out and buy a good suit."

"Teddy, you just can't wish to get Nancy to ask you, you have to ask her."

"I can't think of any way because of that damn trumpet player Roberto that is always around her between classes and after school. What could she see in him; except he has a car?"

"Teddy, just ask her."

"I don't know?" I said uncertain. "You're right though, we've always been just friends, like a brother and sister."

"Maybe you haven't shown enough personal interest in Nancy?" added Oscar.

"Like what?"

"Picnic's, a walk to the Dream House for a movie. Go to the park and bum around. Show some interest in her besides just the choir and sports. Try talking about other things, and hold hands while you talk and walk."

"Oscar, you are some smart man on girls. How are you coming along with your date?"

"Mine is different," now he squawked. "After all the church things she learns, like why she shouldn't kiss boys or show them any attention, I think she will end up a nun."

"Never," I interjected. "she's too good looking to end up like that!"

"Oh yeah, you don't know," scoffed Oscar. "At least your biggest problem with Nancy is transportation."

"It's more than that Oscar, right now Nancy dates Roberto who plays in the school band and orchestra, and has that damn car. I hope it's not serious. They do go together, but not on a real steady basis, I think."

"I know it's tough competition because Roberto can use the family car. Why don't you just ask her for a date? What is keeping you? I would ask her out, but she is to tall for me," joked Oscar. "Dammit, just ask her out."

"But I don't have any wheels, Oscar."

"You dummy, you have a bike."

"You been talking to my Dad?"

"No. Listen friend, that trumpet player is no match for you. Just ask Nancy out for a movie, and you two can walk to the Dream House."

"Yeah, you're right. I will ask Nancy out, sometime."

"Sometime my aching butt. Ask her out this week. Okay? You want me to ask her for you?"

"That will be the day. I'll do it. I promise."

"She has a license, why don't you ask her to drive?"

"I can't do that!" I exclaim mortified.

"We can double date," offered Oscar, but I can't do that because my parents said no double dating with anyone they don't trust, and that would be Oscar. Besides, Oscar is 'campused' most of the time for one reason or the other.

*   *   *

After home games, I always tried to work behind the fountain in our store. Our soda fountain had about twenty stools along a green, marble counter. There were six booths on the sides of the walls and four tables in the middle. Then there was the swinging doors to the kitchens, both the candy and food kitchens.

On the green marble counter, on the furthermost end from the front door, was an overhang where the sandwiches were made. In the back corner of this overhang I kept a bottle of castor oil I purchased next door at Jimmy Johnson's Pharmacy.

When certain high school couples came in I could add a tablespoon of castor oil to the boy's order, but not enough to taste.

Our night waitress would giggle and say to me, "You dirty little bastard," but she never told on me.

Should Nancy Blake come in with a date, especially if she was with that trumpet player, he would receive an extra dose of castor oil and a double shot of syrup. I always wondered what happen if they decided to park in one of the many apple orchards that surround Daisy Junction. I could almost see the scene. Lights out in the car, the radio on to some slow music and the kissing would begin.

By the time the car windows began to start fogging over, the boy should have a sudden urge and need relief in a hurry. I was always wondering if my dosages for Roberto were correct and he would no sooner have the car parked when he would receive that urgent call. Really, all I was doing was protecting Nancy.

I had tested my castor oil treatment on myself before I tried it on the boys. I did it four separate times before I was ready to implement my protection plan for the girls. One tablespoon usually stayed in me for one hour and the double shot of castor oil was never over forty-five minutes.

About two weeks later after my first inauguration with castor oil, Dee Dee asked me, "Why is there a bottle of castor oil in the corner of the counter overhang?"

"It's for me Dee Dee. I've been slightly constipated, and it helps."

"Have you talked to your mother about your problem?" Dee Dee laughed. "You know she was once a nurse?"

"I know that very well. Thank you anyway."

"Yeah, well, you be careful you don't get caught and you had better not pull that stunt on me."

"I'm not doing it for myself," I told Dee Dee because after all, I assured myself, I'm doing it to protect the girls.

CHAPTER 9

Nᴀɴᴄʏ Bʟᴀᴋᴇ ᴡᴀꜱ ᴀ tall girl, about five nine or ten with slim body and long legs. Her eyes were as blue as the corn flowers. Nancy's long, natural blonde hair went halfway down her back. She usually wore it in a pony tail. I thought she could pass for a Viking Goddess. She had that athletic figure and a slinky, sensual model's walk.

Nancy was extremely competitive and a well coordinated athlete as many a new field hockey opponent would quickly discover, should they decide to test that tall defensive player with the long blond pony tail. Gaining an advantage on her was not an easy proposition.

Dad and I usually watched the home field hockey games, and he told me once. "It's difficult for opposing girls to come down Nancy's side of the field and try to play chicken with her if they value their face or shins. I've never seen a girl play with such fierce determination. She is definitely college material."

Nancy's sport activities, being extremely smart, and her height kept her home on many Friday and Saturday nights until her junior year. Then that trumpet blower Roberto, with the acne on his face, came into her life.

The damn trumpet player irked me. He was tall, but didn't play sports, even in PE where we have the same period.

I'd holler over to him, "Come on Roberto, we need one more player." Hoping to take him on one to one.

He always shook his head and said something like his ankle hurt or he had a headache.

I would've give him a good headache, he could've remembered for a long time, if he had ever entered any game against me.

I think he only enjoyed playing his trumpet and taking Nancy out on dances.

Roberto was a mommy's boy, and mommy gave her 'little boy' a Mercury convertible. A convertible in Daisy Junction with the lousy weather? But, if wasn't raining or snowing, the girls enjoyed riding in his Merc with the top down and their hair blowing.

Nancy was a member and an officer in the Daisy Junction Rainbow Girls club. She never attended the once a month formal Rainbow dances, unless she had a date. When she did come to the dances she was always with that damn trumpet player.

I just could not bring myself to ask Nancy for a date to the Rainbow dances because I didn't have a car and I sure wasn't going to ask her to drive, period.

*　　*　　*

My mother Mimi, as she is called by everyone except Dad and me, was the Mother Advisor to the Rainbow Girls. When the Saturday formal dance with a live band was held, many girls and moms volunteered to arrange the dance floor walls and ceiling with rolls of crepe paper to sparkle up the old dreary and plain Masonic dining room.

On the third floor of the Lodge was their game room with pool tables, card tables, and lots of chairs.

My job, thanks to Mom who insisted I volunteer, was to haul fifty chairs from the game room to the bottom floor, then line the hall with the chairs, all by Saturday noon. I did this two chairs at a time, and after the dances I hauled the darn chairs back.

Oscar usually helped me after the dances. A hamburger and a milkshake at our All American Cafe was his reward.

During the dances, I had to stay close to Mother. Mom watched and would notice any girl without any dances. Mother would instruct, "Teddy, I want you to dance with that little freshman girl with the dark brown hair sitting in the corner. Now get to it, and I went and danced with her.

Using my wide smile, I'd slowly walk across the dance floor and right up to the usually very timid girl. Then I would bend low and place my face right up to the girl and quietly say, "I have been watching you this evening, and may I have the pleasure of signing your dance card for this dance?"

The dances came in three to a set.

Of course this girl would be thrilled, I assumed because I am a popular student and athlete, and have just asked her for a dance.

If she had not been told by the other girls or this was her first time dancing with me, she certainly did not realize I had had just selected another innocent victim.

If she had been warned, then she might say, "Are you going to pull that stunt on me? The one you have done to some of the other girls? You'd better not because I will march right over to Mimi and tell her what her son did to me while we were dancing."

Sometimes they were intrigued and asked," Teddy, are you going to do that stunt with your stomach?"

I would appear surprised and so innocent, replying, "Do what with what?"

One girl remarked, "Damn you Teddy Radovich, one of these days."

I'd take the girl's hand and lead her out to the dance floor, then wait for Freddy's band to begin his new set of three dances. When the down beat started, if it was a slow piece, I'd bring the girl close to me.

We danced that way, face to face, chest to chest, stomach to stomach, hips to hips, and sometimes even thigh to thigh. One can't get much closer than that and still be allowed on the dance floor.

From early childhood, I guess I was about nine or ten years old, I learned to do tricks with my stomach. It started when I watched the female carnival performers do things with their stomachs while they stood on a high platform outside their big tent. There were two or three carnivals a year in Daisy Junction, from spring to early fall, and this was the best part. They could roll their stomach muscles fast or slow, some even rolling their stomachs side to side to the canned music while they tried to lure the big spenders into their tent with the seductive movements. They wore tops similar to two piece bathing suits. The bottoms were grass skirts, worn low on their hips. I was too young to appreciate what those solo dance movements represented, I was only impressed with the ability they demonstrated.

Unfortunately, I was never allowed inside the tent, and I knew better than try.

In my bedroom, standing in front of my large mirror, I copied and eventually perfected the stomach maneuvers. I could do the all the stomach tricks and continue them for some time.

I could pull my stomach way in, then push it quickly out, way out. I was able to roll my stomach from one side to the other. Even today, I really believe I have better stomach muscle control than the ladies that performed on the outdoor stage. So, what could I do with this seemingly worthless talent? Ah, back to the dances of course. If the band didn't started with a slow dance, I'd just dance normally, but as soon as a slow dance started I'd bring the girl close to me using my right hand to push firmly on her back keeping her tight against me. My left hand would hold her right hand out and away.

The sweet, innocent, young girl, her eyes closed and her head on my chest or shoulder would be enjoying this lovely dance with me and wouldn't know about my tricky stomach. Then at the opportune time I'd give her my slow stomach roll. Maybe she couldn't imagine anything other than the beginning of a possible high school romance feeling a slow creeping, rolling movement against her stomach because she knew something was caressing her body.

My eyes appeared to be closed and my hands were in place.

"What is going on?" one young girl wondered because she felt something rubbing against her certain places. I could see her face through my nearly closed eyelids, and she appeared appalled. Then she pulled back, our dancing coming to a stop. She tried to look me in the eyes, but my eyes appear to be still closed, but I could see her face and expression. I was trying to be oblivious to whatever she thought she felt, now wide eyed, with firm lips.

Opening my eyes I asked politely, "Is there something wrong?"

"No, no, sorry," she replied, still looking confused. Then I pulled her close to me again and went back to the close dancing.

I waited awhile to start the creeping, rolling movement again. This time I did the fast roll with my stomach and broke the romantic spell, again. Man-o-man was it broken?

She abruptly stopped dancing, pulled away, and looked me in the eyes with her little fists clenched on her hips, and she snapped, "You stop whatever you are doing, right now, Mister Teddy Radovich, or I am going to tell Mimi what you just did to me."

She never told my mother, but if she had, I'm sure Mother would have given me a very serious talking to because It wasn't the first time I'd pulled this stunt.

*　　*　　*

Whenever I would be dancing with Mother's selected partners, and Nancy Blake with that damn trumpet player, I would seek her out, pucker up, and blow her a kiss. Most of the time she ignored me, but every once in a while she would return the gesture, and I would reaffirm my decision to ask her for a date.

If Oscar Shumaker came without a date, which was most of the time because his girlfriend would not go to any dances at the Masonic Hall because of something about her religion, Mom would also recruit him for dancing with the wall flowers.

Even a boy just standing around would get Mom's attention and be enlisted in dancing and signing the girl's dance cards. Mother also insisted that every girl have a corsage. These were Mom's unbreakable rules, and we had to stay after the dances for cleanup. Of course, Oscar always got his hamburger and milkshake for his efforts. I think he didn't really push his girlfriend to come to the dance because he was always broke and he loved the free food. His father would say, "Oscar spends money like a drunken sailor returning from a twenty-four month cruise to Antarctica."

I had, on occasions, gotten asked to the Rainbow dances by girls I though I might have wanted to date, but always refused? I remember Greta Haas, a popular freshman in our high school, asked me once, but I was too embarrassed because I didn't have any wheels and I just couldn't accept.

I always hopped Nancy would ask me, but for some reason she never did, or even hinted, yet we shared the same chemistry table and worked on many assignments together in school. One would think the dances were secret, considering how little information Nancy handed out to me.

However, Nancy was always quick to inform and then correct me if she thought I made any type of mistake, in anything. "Teddy, older people know better. Remember, I'm older than you are."

Yeah, by just two days.

Each month there was a Saturday night formal dance, and the boys did a lot of trading of dances during the week before. The boys would gather in the gym and discuss who they were taking to the dance; next the negotiations would begin.

"Okay, I'll give you two dances with my date if you give me two with yours," was an offer."

"No, one for one is all I'm willing to go," someone would counter.

Another guy might say, "I promise I won't try to take her away from you, so just give me one dance, well maybe two, or, "How come you want two dances with my sister, but you're only giving up one dance with your date?'

So the horse trading went on for the entire week before the dance.

One Saturday night Nancy arrived with that trumpet player, Roberto, and I asked her if I could help fill out her dance card. He tells me, "I'm sorry Teddy, but Nancy's card has been filled up for some time."

After that, that damn Roberto danced continually with Nancy. I realized he had lied to me, but there was nothing I could do.

I comforted myself with the knowledge that Dee Dee had taught me the new South American dance steps. The Tango was my favorite. Dee Dee told me that it was 'The Dance of Love'. I could hardly wait for the Hansen Dance Band to learn Latin dance music and especially the Tango beat, so I could show Nancy and that Roberto a step or two.

CHAPTER 10

On a warm spring, Sunday afternoon I was helping dad with some moving around the store. When we finally finish the project, I asked him, "Dad, when will I be ready to take my full driver's license test, so I can take a date to a dance?"

"So, now you feel that you are ready to date, Teddy?"

"Well, yes, I have been studying the state vehicle rules for a year now, and I'm a good driver and I can park. In September I'll be a junior in high school, and I can legally drive."

He nodded to a booth, and we slid in and sat opposite each other. "You have someone in mind, to date, Teddy?"

"Well, not exactly, yet, but I'm thinking of asking Nancy Blake."

"Good choice, son. You two have known each other from before kindergarten days."

"Yes, but, she only dates that guy Roberto because I don't have the wheels because I don't have a license, what can I do?"

"Teddy, if you're talking about a date, why not a picnic for a first date?"

"How can I take a Nancy to a picnic without a car?"

"Teddy, I see her bicycling now and then, and you, young man, you bicycle. Why not a bicycle date for starters?"

"Well, yeah, but she likes to ride in Roberto's 'Merc', that new, green convertible his mother gave him for his birthday. All the girls like to ride in it with the top down. He never takes any boys for a ride, just girls, but I wouldn't ride withhim anyway."

"You said his mother gave him that new Mercury?"

"That's what everyone says, Dad."

"Well, she married good the second time around. Try the bicycle for the first time date, Teddy, it's a lot easier with just one on one and no pretensions. Give her a call and pick out a Sunday, see what happens. Make sure you get a rain check, just in case."

*　　*　　*

With that and Oscar's constant urging, I finally decided to take a chance and call Nancy for a bicycle date.

"It's about time, Teddy," Oscar said. "Don't chicken out though, or I might ask her out because Patty was a little cool toward me the last time we went out."

"It's no wonder Oscar because you're always out of money. I'm going to ask Nancy on a picnic date. Where can we go?"

"Holy cow, Teddy, you pass Chester's Dairy every morning bicycling from your house to the restaurant. Every morning you bicycle past that open spot on the knoll, just up from the river where the gang fishes. You know, it's between the two forested areas."

"Oh yeah Oscar, the spot the county is talking about making into a park. It's pretty there."

"Right, nobody is ever there on Saturdays when I go back and forth to work cleaning Chester's dairy barns."

"Good idea. I'll call her, I promise, I'll call her."

Now that I'd finally decided to call Nancy, I carefully wrote out what I would say. I used many practice runs going over my request for a picnic date. I tried to formulate in my mind how Nancy might reply. After many tries, I was not happy with any of my openings.

One more problem I had to overcome was making the phone call. In Daisy Junction a call still required going through a telephone operator because dial telephones had not arrived yet, but we knew about them. And Daisy Junction telephone operators were notorious for very good voice identification. Most of the telephone operators knew me because I delivered sodas or ice cream sundaes, on hot summer days, to the telephone office.

So I placed my carefully composed note next to the telephone stand where I could see it and I'm sure my voice was trembling when I gave Nancy's number to the operator.

She said to me, "She's home Teddy, she just got off the phone with that Roberto fellow. I'll dial her for you now."

I almost hung up the phone.

Dr. Blake later told my father, "When I told Nancy that Ted Radovich was on the phone, her heart must have skipped a beat because she appeared to be in shock. She always wonders why your son never calls, and now he's on the phone. She asked me, 'What does he want Daddy? What can I say to him?'"

"Why don't you get on the phone, and maybe you will find out why he called?"

"I don't know what to say, Daddy?"

"Well, you could start with a nice hello?

I could hear some conversation and knew Nancy was talking to someone. I wondered if it could be that damn Roberto? Then my darn note slipped off the telephone stand, and I couldn't reach it.

"Teddy, is this really you?" Nancy asked so sweetly that my heart skipped a beat.

I'm trying desperately to drag my note back with my foot, but just can't reach it.

"Ah, let's see, uh, yeah, in the living flesh, uh, darn it, Nancy, my Dad," I choked it out, then went completely blank, not saying anything. I'm still trying to get my notes, but the phone cord was stretched to the limit, and my toe only brushed the piece of paper.

After ten-seconds of my silence, Nancy finally rescued me. "I know you didn't call me to talk about him. Are you all right? I hear some grunting on your end of the line. You okay?"

"Who?" I finally answer.

"Who . . . what?" Now I've got Nancy confused.

"I was talking about someone?" I continued.

"You mentioned your Dad. Is everything all right because you're grunting Teddy Joseph Radovich."

"Must be the line, not me," I said with an annoyed tone. Now I'm really on my own and again tongue tied.

Another ten-seconds of silence went by.

Nancy, again has to break the silence. "What do you want Teddy Joseph Radovich?"

"I thought you had forgotten my middle name, Nancy Olivia Blake, NOB, for short?"

"Okay Teddy, fair is fair. Why did you call me? I'm just in the middle of finishing my paper for chemistry. Have you finished your assignment or do you need my assistance, as always?"

"Hey twin, I finished mine, sealed it, and delivered three days ago." I hesitated again, not sure how to proceed. Finally, I got the courage to jump in. "Hey twin, if you can finish your paper by this Sunday, I thought, maybe, we can have a bicycle date, if it doesn't rain. If it rains maybe we can make it the next Sunday."

"I'm sorry Teddy. Did I hear you say a bicycle date this coming Sunday? A bicycle date? Do bicycles really date?"

"Very funny Nancy. I'm sure I can call someone else, but since I have you on the phone, and you are the only girl who's telephone number I know, listen, please. If it doesn't rain, and you have nothing better to do, I thought we might pack up a lunch and ride our bicycles out to Swinjoscie River and have a picnic and maybe talk, or even go for a swim."

"Am I the only girl in school that rides a bicycle that will go on a bicycle date with you?"

"Come on Nancy, we have known each other too long for you to start that type of game with me."

Nancy quickly switched gears and her voice softened. "How far is it to the place you want to go, twin?"

"From your house, oh about three or four miles to the cove. It's just before Chester's Dairy, and about one mile from our house. Oh, don't forget to bring a towel."

"Sounds great, except the way I figure it, I believe the mileage comes closer to six or eight miles."

"Yes, I suppose so, if you have to bicycle back."

"I can handle it. This is the first time you've asked me out on a date, and we've known each other for how many years, around fifteen, closer to sixteen? Am I the only girl you know that rides a bicycle?"

"Now that you mentioned it, I never considered that thought. Why did you ask Nancy? Do you know other girl that rides a bicycle and would like to have a date with me? Do you want to go with me to the river or not?"

"Okay, okay, forget my dumb remark. I'll bring the food, and you bring something to drink and a blanket to sit on. What time Sunday, Teddy?"

"How about right after church? Say, why don't we bicycle to church together and leave from there?"

"Got you twin. Pick me up at ten and I'll be ready. I'll see you at choir practice Thursday night just to remind you what you should bring. Thank you for calling Teddy. I've got to get back to my chemistry paper. See you in class."

I hung up the phone and wondered what I had done.

According to her father, she said, "Can you believe this? I have a date with Teddy Radovich, even if it is only a bicycle date. He really called me for a date. Maybe he is finally growing up? About time."

* * *

It turned out, Sunday morning was clear and sunny. It was in the spring so there will be no suffering, sweltering heat to make the bike date unbearable.

Daisy Junction had only four months of really good weather: two months in late spring and a couple of months in the early fall. The rest of the year, Daisy Junction was either cold and windy or hot and baking.

So on Sunday I bicycled from my house, at Mallard Lake, six miles outside of town, to Nancy Blake's home in the Heights area of Daisy Junction. The Heights area was for people with money and that was where the Blake's live. The Heights are not really much higher in elevation, maybe forty or fifty feet higher, than the main area of town. The homes are more expensive and they receive a cooling breeze during the suffering, summer months. Also, no water from the Swinjoscie River will ever reach this part of town if it floods. Nancy reminded me more than once that week what I was supposed to bring. Peddling happily down the road my two rear panniers were jammed with cold, iced, soft drinks, Gram's homemade pickles, my mother's stuffed comforter, a towel, and my bathing suit.

She also reminded me to be at her house at 10:00 sharp. Also telling me, "I really detest forgetfulness and lateness."

As if I didn't already know.

As I neared her house I see that damn green convertible Merc parked out front with the top down. No one is in it so Roberto must be in the house.

I'm just climbing off my bicycle when Roberto walked out from the Blake's front door and he didn't look too happy.

I greeted him with, "Hi Roberto, going on the picnic with Nancy and me? We're bicycling out to the Swinjoscie."

"What picnic?" he grumbled, hurrying by me as I got off my bike. "It was nice talking to you, 'Teddy'.

Nancy had her pink, boy's bicycle ready outside on the sidewalk. It was sitting in front of the brick walkway to her folks white two story house. Attached on her handle bar was a pink wicker basket. About six months ago Nancy told me, "I painted my bicycle and the basket pink last weekend with no outside help."

So I suggested, "Maybe you can paint mine sometime?"

With a flip of her blond pony tail, she remarked, "Mr. Radovich, I paint only girls bicycles."

I asked her, "Aren't all bicycles the same, two wheels, two pedals, requiring two feet, and a place to sit?"

"My word do you have a problem?" Nancy asked. "Did you sleep through your health and sex class?"

"Nancy, nothing was ever said about bicycles."

"Well, Teddy, I have a project to work on."

Our lunch, I assume, is in the pink basket because I can see many wrapped items carefully packed in it. I start to look over the items to see what Nancy was bringing.

Suddenly from her bedroom window, over the garage, comes her familiar voice, "Get your hands off my food, Mr. Radovich. Can't you wait until we get to the river, twin?"

I quickly looked up. "Good morning Nancy. I was just wondering what delightful lunch you made for us. Is Roberto having lunch with us today? It sure looks as if you made enough for three?"

"Careful buddy, that remark puts you right on the edge," she shouted down to me. "Just you and I are having lunch, or have you invited Blossom to come with us? It had better be just the two of us. What's in my basket? Well, twin, you'll have to wait till we eat. Did you bring the cokes and a blanket like I asked?"

"Don't you trust me, Nancy?"

"I'll wait and see. This is our first date so you'll have to come in and talk to the folks while I finish getting ready."

"We are only going to the river, Nancy. I'm in shorts and a tee shirt."

"That's okay, now come into the house and visit, Teddy."

I walked into the house and stood in front of a straight back chair in the living room. Dr. and Mrs. Blake were sitting on a couch, smiling and had the Sunday paper on their laps.

After saying my, "Good Morning," I noticed a bouquet of flowers on the piano. I thought I knew where the bouquet came from, and it made me happy to think I might have ruined one of Roberto's deals.

"Nice flowers Mrs. Blake." I nodded toward the piano.

"Yes, they are nice, but I didn't expect them," replied Mrs. Blake.

The subject quickly changed because they began to ask me about my family, school, and sports. This appeared to be a general quiz on how well I could handle myself. It's a snap because I knew they already knew the answers.

I told the Blake's how proud of Nancy I was for her having five sports letters already and getting her sixth this May. I added, "With her four years in swimming and field hockey she will have eight letters by the end of her senior year. That will be a first in the history of Daisy Junction?"

"Yes, Teddy," agreed Dr. Blake, "I think the most any girl received was something like three or four." Dr. Blake continued, "Your father, Valmar, was the first student in the history of Daisy Junction to letter in two varsity sports, football and basketball. We didn't have a swimming pool or a track field, back then, just a rocky, unleveled piece of dirt for the track. Your father was a fine athlete and student when we were in school. Too bad the depression came on and prevented your father from continuing on to college. That was the reason your Dad joined the Army and became a career soldier. Do you know what your dad did during World War Two, Teddy?"

"No Sir, Dad has never told me, but I think he did some undercover thing, similar to what Grandpa Egor did, and that's all I know."

"Well, I'll let Val tell you. You should be very proud of your father's military record. What Val did in the army was beyond belief."

Then he asked about my mother and grandparents?

I told him they are doing fine.

Then he asked me how I was doing?

I told him my grades were near the top, and I should make the Daisy Junction Honor Society, for three years now. Last year I was just one decimal point under Nancy's grade point and this year my grades were better. I also received my third letter in football, and I hoped to win my third in track this spring. This will also give me six in three years, with my Senior year left.

Dr. Blake continued, "By the way Ted, where are you two going today for your picnic?"

"Just out to the river next to Chester's Dairy, at that open area just south of the dairy. The one that has that grassy knoll where the county is talking about a park."

"How far from the island?"

"Oh, gee, the island is a good mile or a mile and half down the river."

"Oh yes, I know it. Good fishing area down there with unusually clear water.

There are a number of trees under the water in that area? Many lures have been lost there, but the fishing is worth the lost equipment. Just the two of you?"

"Yes, Nancy is the only girl I know that bicycles."

Nancy entered the living room and commented, "There are many ways to get a first date and bicycling can be a start. Ready Mr. Radovich?"

"Are we going to take 'your' flowers with us, Miss Nancy Blake?"

"No, they are my 'mother's' flowers, Teddy Radovich," she tells me in a slow tone of voice indicating, don't pursue that subject any more." I glanced back at the Blake's and Dr. Blake gave me a wink.

As we headed toward the door Dr. Blake asked me, "What time shall we expect you two back this afternoon?"

"Is five okay?"

"That's fine. Figure on having dinner with us tonight, Ted. I'll take you home, if it gets too dark."

Nancy was wearing shorts and a tee shirt, same as I, except she had on pink tennis shoes. She took my arm, and we walked out of her house. She stopped me at the door, then asked, "Ever try washing those dirty tennis shoes, twin?"

"Never have considered it. Is it important big sister? Will it make me run any faster?"

"For looks, only. Leave them at our house tonight, and I'll wash them for you."

"How will I get home with no shoes?"

"I'll wash them while we're having dinner tonight. They might be a little damp to wear home, but they will be clean for school tomorrow and the horse barn fragrance will be gone."

"Our first date, and you're already giving me orders."

"Remember, I'm older and therefore, wiser."

"Well, I guess so, since you've had more time to learn from your mistakes." I returned with a serious tone. "Thank you for your constant guidance, twin."

"Next time, Mr. Radovich, we'll work on your English."

We left her house and began to walk down the brick walkway. From the open front door came a call from Mrs. Blake, "Nancy Olivia Blake, young lady, are you going to church dressed in shorts and a tee shirt?"

"Mom, we wear choir robes over our clothes."

"You know how Pastor Robert's feels about dressing for church?"

"Mom, maybe he should begin with his oldest daughter, Lisa, and check out what she wears and how she acts?"

"Enough of that, young lady. Have a good time kids, and see you two back at five."

*   *   *

We two, tall blondes, with blue eyes, fair complexion, and athletic bodies got on our bicycles and pedaled away for our first actual date. We laughed and talked as we bicycled, side by side, off to church. I'm confident we made a striking couple.

Many people were walking to church on this warm morning and they gave us, hellos, smiles and waves as we passed them.

Everyone in Daisy Junction knew us, and I speculated, If they might have wondered why we have never dated. Finally, we are together, and I hope this day we will always remember as our first date.

"Nancy, is there something about the flowers on the piano that you can tell me?"

Nancy looked at me annoyed. "Roberto came by with the flowers and wanted me to go driving with him. I told him I had a date with you today. He hinted that he thought we were going steady, but I told him I never considered 'that' possibility. I have told him time and time again, 'Roberto, we are only friends, and going steady with you is out of the question,' so he gave Mom the flowers and left."

See looked away, but added. "And, I thought your gloating to Roberto about our picnic was mean, twin, so don't act like that again."

"Boy, you must have great ears to have heard me from up in your bedroom."

"Don't forget it twin," she said, then added, "Oh damn, today is the fourth Sunday and Pastor Roberts will begin with the usual beating up of our generation. Let's skip church today."

"We'd better not Nancy because they need our voices and besides, 'Gerald Boy' Roberts will wonder where we were, and then everyone else will too."

"Yeah, you're right, the righteous snoop he is."

*   *   *

Nancy and I sing in our church for one reason, we like to sing, but give each other wide eyed, comical looks when

Pastor Roberts climbs on his 'Holy, High Horse'. One Sunday a month he rallies his crusade, trying to destroy the Devil that is in every young adult's mind. The Devil, according to Pastor Roberts, lurks in every teenager's mind.

*   *   *

This Sunday the church choir was magnificent, then Pastor Roberts reaching for his oratorical best started his sermonizing condemning all who do not accept or believe in his interpretations of 'The Book'.

This being the fourth Sunday of the month, Pastor Roberts, again, leaned heavy on the younger generations and their dating too young. He bemoaned about the loose sexual morals we 'young' ones had. It couldn't be me he was referring to as I'd never dated anyone and how would I know about loose morals? I didn't consider Dee Dee, or the Virgin Street gang as morally corrupting because they were older.

The only references I had came from the other guys talking about the loose girls, especially Lisa Roberts the Pastor's own daughter. Pastor Roberts guaranteed our generation were definitely on their way to Hell. He knew this because of 'The Word', he received straight from Heaven.

So once a month, his 'Going to Hell' speech was accompanied by voice modulating, wild arm waving, and sweat dripping from his bald head down to his nose, eventually dripping onto his sermon notes. He must have had the whole thing choreographed because never looked at the notes during his heavenly discourse.

He and his faithful congregation, by now, must have had his fourth Sunday spiel down pat because Nancy and I could almost recite it by heart.

Today, Nancy and I sat together under the watchful and suspicious eye of the choir master, 'Gerald Boy'. He was also a 'watcher of morality' like his older brother Horace the Pastor.

Gerald's self imposed assignment, other than directing the choir, was to keep a diligent watch over his younger generation singers. Especially, not to allow any act that may hint at the beginnings of a moral breakdown.

Gerald Boy knows, and knows for sure, that the younger generation is running toward a life of complete moral ruin. Obviously, the word came from his brother Old Hoarse Horace who always strains his voice sermonizing about, 'us', the decadent generation.

Under the folds of our choir gowns Nancy and I play finger games, then an occasional bump with our shoulders or elbows while the emoting pastor strikes another chord of attack on our generation.

Does Old Horse Horace the Pastor know that Lisa Roberts, his oldest daughter, is rumored to have the most fondled breasts and body in school?

Lisa is one of the most available girls in school, so any date needs to be knowledgeable in 'making out' or be completely overwhelmed. Most of the boys are not up to Lisa's 'hot pants standards', and are left out in the cold just wishing and wondering. Yes, I'm one of them, too.

This Sunday I'm squirming and so is Nancy. All we want to do is get out of church and bicycle to our picnic. Gerald Boy is giving us his stop what ever you two are doing stern look, and his brother is having difficulty ending his sermon.

I thought the Pastor was lost his closing 'kicker' as he kept going on and on. Even the congregation was moving around in the pews. This is one day I want to remember because of the first date with Nancy, not because of an overblown, ridiculous sermon.

* * *

Finally, church was over, and we say all the proper things as we greet the many parishioners. Everyone told us we made a striking couple. As we started to leave Nancy said, "Everyone is especially friendly this fine day, and aren't you glad they have no idea just how smelly your tennis shoes are?"

"Well, I think the people are glad it's me you're with, and not that guy with the green convertible."

"Teddy you're moving close to trouble, so get off the subject."

We were prepared to bicycle away, but not before receiving frowns and a statement from Pastor Roberts. He tells us, "I firmly believe one should stay home and pray and read 'The Book.'"

Yeah I thought, That sure doesn't concern hot pants Lisa Roberts. She could write some book, herself."

* * *

Nancy and I rode side by side on the flat, rural country road, singing school and church songs, trying to trip each other up on words we both know.

Singing and laughing, the four or five miles slipped by fast. There was a slight breeze to keep us refreshed, and the sun was just warm enough.

On our right is the Swinjoscie River, its line of trees mostly hiding the river, but there are a few open spaces so the river can sometimes be seen from the road. On our left are grassy meadows with dairy cows munching on the verdant green pastures.

This promised to be a special day for Nancy and me on our first date together. No one was on the road today, and we had a quiet bicycle ride just for us.

About a quarter-mile before my selected picnic site, Nancy pointed out an old yellow Buick with the rear nearly covered with brush. This was the only car we had seen that day.

Nancy noted, "Must be fishermen, Teddy?"

"Well, they are down stream from us and where we will be swimming. We're far enough up from them not to scare the fish. Where we will be the water is clearer and not as swift as down stream where they are."

"Have you fished here before, Teddy?"

"Of course, Oscar and the gang fish here often, and so has your Dad."

"How come you've never taken me fishing?"

"Take you fishing?" I replied surprised. "I didn't know girls fished. I always thought girls just walked around with their arms over each other's shoulders, telling secrets, or riding in convertibles"

"Teddy! You have a lot to learn about girls. Correct things. Maybe this afternoon you'll finally learn something intelligent about women, more than your school yard information."

"I can hardly wait," I say pulling off the road. "Stop here, we can park our bicycles because our picnic spot is that slight knoll on the left, near the line of trees."

* * *

We placed our bicycles alongside a barbed wire fence that bordered the county road and unload them. I stepped on the bottom barbed wire strand of the fence and pushed it down. With one hand I held up the middle wire, allowing Nancy plenty of room to climb through without a problem.

Nancy started to walk away, and I hollered, "Hey Miss Blake, aren't you going to hold the wire up for me?"

"I've got the food Mr. Radovich so what else do I need?"

"Nancy, you need me, unless you plan to picnic alone?"

Nancy turned around and smiled, placing the picnic basket on the ground. With her hands on her slim hips she remarked, "Do I really need you?"

Standing outside the fence I was thinking, I have to say something profound, something intelligent so I announce, "Nancy, I am so happy we are finally together on such a great day, and I consider myself incredibly lucky?"

"That's not bad, twin," she answered, returning to the fence with a smile and helped me through. "I surely can't let that speech pass, so after you've tasted my picnic lunch I made especially for you I'll expect many more accolades."

"Is that what's required to make a date with a girl go smoothly?" I chuckled.

"You surely don't know much about girls do you, Teddy Radovich?"

"Well, you should know because you do have more experience in dating."

"Don't push your luck, Teddy. This is our first date, so the count starts today. Come on, let's get to that spot you picked out."

*   *   *

I spread out the large blanket Mother lent me on the knoll, one hundred yards from the river where it entered a long, sweeping bend. We could see the river, but we couldn't see the fishermen, That part of the river flowed deep, with slow current. Oscar and I considered this area best for fishing because of the water clarity, and variety of fish. As the river continued around the bend, the current changed and picked up speed, moving out at three or four miles per hour.

Nancy asked me, "Why not go closer to the river, Teddy?"

"Lots of mud flies live in the muddy banks along the river. Besides, we won't bother the fishermen, up here."

"I'm glad you asked me to this picnic, Teddy. Have you ever brought any girl to this spot for a picnic or anything else?"

"I never even thought of bringing any other girl here, or anywhere. Only you, Nancy."

"Where can we change into our suits because I want to go swimming?" Nancy asked.

I told her, pointing "Not over there where the fishermen are. We'll go to our left, to those woods. More forest cover, but watch out for the Poison Ivy and the Sumac."

"I know that much!" Nancy scolded me. "I'll go first, and you stay put and keep out of the lunch, twin."

Nancy and I took turns changing into our swim suits. Nancy had last year's high school swimming team suit on. The blue, one piece suit shows off her long graceful, tanned legs, but appears to flatten her small breasts. Well, racing suits are not for show, but results.

*   *   *

We swam together, splashing water on each other, then came out to dry off. Settling down on Mother's comforter, we enjoyed the picnic lunch Nancy had made. We had fried chicken, potato salad, deviled eggs, and potato chips, soon followed by two large slices of a dark German Chocolate Cake. My contribution was the cokes, homemade dill pickles, and Gram's potato chips. We agreed, this lunch was the best.

We were stuffed as we stretched out on the comforter on our stomachs side by side, but not touching, just looking at each other. Nancy removed her dark glasses, then reached over and removed my dark glasses.

"I want to see your eyes, twin," she said, then suggested. "Teddy, we should do this more often."

"Better than riding in a green convertible?"

"Another dig? You certainly know how to stay on a subject."

Looking at my date with her blue eyes, her long blond hair still wet, I had a feeling never experienced before. I thought, This lady is a keeper, so why has it taken me so long to ask her for a date because we have known each other forever?"

I moved closer to Nancy, and she edged and inch or two toward me. We are both on our sides as we slowly experience our first kiss. No groping, just kisses. The kisses eventually gained intensity, then she rolled over on her back and admonished me, "Not below the shoulders, please." Then she added, out of breath, "Wow! How did you learn to kiss like that? This is your first date?" she asked suspiciously.

I was smiling at Nancy, then I replied, "Must've been those movies I've watched."

"They don't kiss like that in the movies, Teddy."

I reached around her neck to draw her closer, and she turned, and we began kissing again. Her mouth opened, and my tongue searched for Nancy's. She began to respond.

Again, she pulled back and rolled on to her side, facing me. "Mr. Radovich," she said with a provocative voice, "why did it take you so long to ask me out, when I wanted to date you as a freshman?"

"Nancy, I wasn't ready to date, and you spent your time playing with dolls and sports."

Nancy looked at me sternly. "Remember, I'm two days older than you and more mature, and I quit playing with dolls years before, when you were still trying to look up girls dresses. However, twin, your kisses certainly indicate to me, you know more about kissing than any boy I have ever known, but I'm no expert. Have you been playing around with Lisa Roberts on the sly, or how about Blossom Ann?"

"No way! You trying to get me sick to my stomach?"

She scooted closer to me, resting her head on one hand. "Teddy, do you realize how many dances we could have gone to if you had only asked me? By the way Mr. Radovich, speaking about dates, I have a very personal question to ask you?"

"Well, don't make it too personal."

"I've been wondering, did you have anything to do with Roberto taking me right home from the Rainbow dances or the basketball games? Right after we left your store, when 'you' were working behind the counter?"

"You mean, you two never stopped to park and let the car windows fog up from all the kissing? Doesn't everybody do that? Man-oh-man, talk about two cold people dating."

Hot damn, my castor oil plan worked.

"Again, my question. Did you have anything to do with Roberto not wanting to park?"

"I don't know what you mean, Nancy?"

"Well, I think you do, but I'm glad our first date is here. If we were parked in an apple orchard, and your kisses, well I don't know?"

Now, Nancy nearly rolled on top of me and we were back to some heavy kissing. She murmured, "Just stay above the shoulders. I still don't know why it has taken you so long to take me out on a date, Teddy? I could just stay here all day kissing you. Darn you, I missed dancing with you so much. We could have danced two years earlier at the Rainbow dances, if you had only asked me."

"Well, lovely one, you could have asked me, but I guess the lure of a convertible out-weighted my 31 Ford Panel Truck."

"Maybe your scaring those little freshman girls with your stomach tricks was more important than asking me out?"

"My dear, I wanted a lot of practice before I was ready to ask you for a date."

"Well, I'm sure you didn't learn a thing from those young girls who would have given anything for a date with you. I know because I heard them talking about you, Hon."

When she was talking to me, her lips were nearly touching mine. Now she was kissing my ears, neck, forehead, and all over my face. Sometimes she would straddle me and other times she lied right on top of me. Her arms went under my head and her tongue and mine got into a dance.

Finally, she pulled away and with her bright blue eyes she stared at me with a very serious look on her face.

What was she thinking?

Now Nancy smiled. "I love his picnic honey. I've waited so long to get you in my arms. Do you know that?"

"No not before . . . but, I sure know it now."

"Teddy. I want to ask you a very important question. Please be honest with me, please."

"Anything you want Nancy."

I had no idea what she was aiming at. All I could say was, "Nancy, honey, any more kisses like those we just had, we had better be very careful."

"That's part of my question, Hon. We should be careful, but are you ready for this on our first date?"

I have no idea what she is driving at. "Okay, your question my dear?"

"Can we go steady, twin?"

"I was hoping you would say that. Of course we'll go steady. There is no other girl I would want for a steady partner than you."

She smothered me with her kisses then sat up, still straddling me, and pushed back her long blond hair and tied it into a pony tail. "This will keep my hair out of your face, Hon."

My two hands were on her hips, and I'm looking at this blond goddess. I'm thinking, What a beautiful girl she is, and how lucky I am.

Suddenly, Nancy became stiff and her eyes grew very large. She bent down close to my face. I think she's going to kiss me again so I'm ready and began to pucker up. Instead, she whispered in my ear, "There are two men over in the woods where that yellow car we saw earlier is parked, in the edge of the forest with some bushes stacked next to it. Those men are looking at us."

I never turned to look. "Don't pull away Nancy, pretend to kiss me, but watch them. They're probably only fishermen. I'll think of something, so act normal. Just two?"

"Yes . . . no . . . there's three. One's a large man, and smaller man next to him, then about four feet away or more is a real small man. I'm really scared honey."

"Be calm Sweetheart," I tell her. I'm still thinking. Okay, what would Dad do in this situation?

I had to think of something, someway to protect Nancy if I had to. "Can you still see them?"

"Of course, they're standing in the shadows of the tree line."

I placed my hand against Nancy's head, bringing her head in complete contact with mine. I told her, "Now let's slowly stand up, and don't directly look at them. Keep one eye on them and put your arms around me and keep on kissing me, but watch those men."

"In front of those men? You want me to kiss you in front of those men?"

"Of course, we don't want them to think we've seen them. How far away are they, and what are they doing?"

"They're about 75 or 100 yards away. One man has a stick or club in his hand, it's the man in the middle, next to the big man. The third man, the little guy, is standing away from the other two. What are we going to do?"

"Do what I tell you. When I say go, you go. Run to the river and start swimming toward the center. I'll be right behind you. Don't worry, we can outrun and out swim those three easy."

"But they're closer to the river than we are. What about our bikes and picnic stuff?"

"Don't worry. We can pick them up later. I'll protect you. Just run as fast as you can and forget about the rocks and twigs."

Nancy and I rose as one person. My back was still to the men, but Nancy, with her face against my cheek, was keeping one eye on the men.

"Ted, I think they are coming toward us now. My God . . . they're starting to run toward us!"

"Okay! Go! Stay ahead of me. Nancy. Let's get to the river!"

As we ran toward the river, we forgot about any stickers or rocks that could hurt our feet because we never put our shoes back on.

I could see the men running, coming at a right angle to us, and I hear someone holler, "Head them off Jesse! I'll get the girl! Get the kid!"

Nancy and I raced toward the river, and from my right came the large man, some distance ahead of a shorter man who had a club or thick stick in his hand and appeared to be limping, slowing his running. My mind was racing. I had a plan. I slowed up to let Nancy be the bait.

Nancy neared the waters edge just as the big man reached for her and made a grab at her. He caught only a shoulder strap of her bathing suit, the top half of her bathing suit tearing down, exposing her breasts. Nancy fell to the ground, but immediately she was backup on her feet, her hands pulling the torn suit back up. Her face showed rage.

It was a short distance for me to reach Nancy.

Her blue eyes were wide open and she let go of the swimsuit and clenched her fists, waiting for the man to approach her. Her suit had slipped back down to her hips.

The big man hollered out, "I got the babe," and lunged at Nancy with his arms outstretched. Nancy met the man with one hell of a kick to his groin and, my god, she straightened him right up, quick. He yelled something and began to buckle over.

I was only feet from him moving at high speed and had my chance. I dropped my shoulders and launched my body like an arrow and hit the man as he stood bent over from Nancy's kick. I just slammed into him, right below his knees, with a perfectly illegal full body clip. He screamed out in pain. I knew I'd ruined his knees because I heard the crunching.

I rolled away from the yelling man and rose quickly just in time to see the other man a few feet away, half running, half limping toward me. He had his hand back, holding the club, and appeared ready to swing it.

I heard a splash and knew Nancy had made it to the water.

Taking about three quick steps, I dove into the river also and began to swim away from the bank. The man threw his club in my direction, but it splashed some distance in front of me. About thirty or forty feet out in the river, I stopped swimming and turn around to look back to shore. The man was striping off his dungarees and was going to continue to chase us in the water.

The dungarees . . . ? I knew those blue clothes were prisoner clothes. I could see the white lettering on the pants They had to be escaped prisoners from the prison upstate, damn it.

The man ran along in the shallow water at the river's edge until he was abreast of Nancy, then dove into the water and began to swim toward her. She was about twenty or thirty yards out in the river from this man who seemed to know something about swimming. He headed for her. Nancy stop swimming, turned around and shouted, "Are you coming Ted?"

I yelled out, "Keep going. Don't worry about me. Don't worry, I'll be righ there."

"Hurry Teddy, come out to the main stream where I am."

This man was swimming toward Nancy and his strokes looked good. I've got to protect Nancy. I know she can out swim this guy, but after a full lunch, one of us might suffer from cramps as the river water is cold. I have to do something quick.

With strong strokes, I pulled myself right at the man.

His head when swimming turned to his left, leaving me in his blind spot. I knew I could catch him on an angle, then swim under water and grab him as he swam over me.

Nancy yelled out. "Teddy, he's coming after me."

She turned around and with one hand, the other holding the torn suit, she tried to swim toward the center of the river.

On this curve of the river the water was fairly clear, and I swam hard to cross this prisoner's route as he headed toward Nancy. The river current was pushing us down stream.

I don't think he saw me as his head was still turned to his left to inhale air, and I was on his right and abreast of him.

I took a deep breath of air and dove down below the surface of the water, swimming under water into his route.

Staying deep in the water for a few seconds I saw the man swimming slightly on my right, and the current was pushing him right over the top of me. I let the sucker pass, then reached up and grabbed his right ankle with both of my hands and I pulled down hard.

His arms flailed the water and he tried to kick, with his free foot, what ever was grabbing him. I pulled down harder and twisted his leg, keeping him away from me. Man-o-man did he fight with his free leg, but I was on the other side of him. I knew I owned the sucker and kept away from his kicks.

I could feel a submerged tree limb under me and I was able to wrapped my legs around it. Usually, I could stay under water for two minutes and a few times, showing off in a pool I have gone two and half minutes. I grabbed him by the balls and jerked him completely under the water.

The man struggled to get back to the surface, but I had him tight. After about ten-seconds, I could hear him start to gag, then about ten more seconds the man stopped his fighting and was going limp. I could hear him gurgling under the water. I guessed his life was ending.

I pushed him down with my feet on his shoulders. His limp body sank deeper in the water, and I had to get to the surface for air.

When my head broke the surface, I grabbed another couple of breaths of air, then submerged again. This time I swam down to a limp and slow twisting body and pushed him deeper, down and away from me.

This time I stayed underwater until I felt I could stay no longer, watching this man slowly twist and sink away from my view.

I rose to the surface and inhaled the fresh sweet air. Now I was about twenty yards down stream from Nancy who was not swimming, just watching me.

My God, I've just drowned a man. How can I explain this to Nancy and everyone else? I've just flat ass murdered a prisoner who was after Nancy. I'll just keep this to my self. Okay smart boy, what are you going to tell everyone? It had better be a good thought out story. I know, I'll make it simple.

"You okay Nancy?" I asked as I gulped air.

She slowly, one handed, swam to me. "Oh my God, are you are all right?" she asked, gulping breathes . . . "I was so scared . . . . You disappeared . . . Where is that man? The last time I saw him, he appeared to have cramps and was splashing water with his hands, then he just went under . . . You didn't see him?"

"No." I quickly lied, sensing a way out of the dilemma. "I got my foot caught on a tree or something and had to fight my way out. Where did he go?"

Nancy swam up to me and touched my face. "You don't know what happened to that man?"

"No. What about the other fellow?"

"He's still along the bank, following us. Over there, there, in that little clearing. He has a stick in his hand, but he's so small I have to laugh at him threatening me. Do you see him now?"

"Yeah, little guy. You Okay? You can float, can't you?" I'm trying to smile.

"Yeah, I can float, except that first man tried to grab me and tore the top off my bathing suit and the damn thing won't say up. I almost lost it diving into the river. I was worried when that man came swimming after me and I was ready to give up my bathing suit, when he went under." Nancy continued, "Honey, I've got to drift along because I have to keep pulling up my bathing suit or it will come off. I'm so scared."

"Just stay calm, Nancy, we'll see the island soon." I had no reason to go any further with my drowning of the second man. The first man; I know I got him good.

"Teddy? The big man I kicked, and you hit in the legs. Where is he? What were those men trying to do? Why were they after us?" Nancy was pale, her blue eyes were open wider than I had ever seen and her teeth were starting to chatter because the water was cold.

"Easy Nancy, I think we took that man out of commission, for a while anyway. We'll float down stream and we should see the island as we clear this bend."

"How much further is the island we're going to?"

"The island is about a mile or so down river. With this current we'll reach it easily.

"Why don't we swim to shore, I'm getting really cold, Hon?"

"Right now we're safer in the water than on shore."

"I'm sure glad it's you with me today, honey."

*   *   *

We were out in the river drifting with the current, Nancy using her left hand to hold up her bathing suit, her right hand as a paddle to keep afloat.

"We are going, to the island? Can't we just go across the river, Teddy?"

"Do you remember the good lunch we had?"

"Yeah, I see what you mean, cramps, right? Mom shouldn't have made such a big lunch for us."

"And all this time, I thought you made the lunch."

"Well, I helped a little. Well, uh, uh, well you know what I mean."

As Nancy and I floated we talked. To keep her mind off the episode, I needed to keep her talking. She was continually pulling her suit up trying to cover her breasts with no luck.

"Teddy, keep your eyes on something else. This suit is so badly torn I can hardly keep it on."

"I'm just looking at you and your beautiful blue eyes."

"Oh yeah, well, my eyes are not just under the water?"

To keep Nancy's mind off what has happened, I decide to tell her a story. "Hey Nancy, did you ever hear about the Church War they had in Daisy Junction?"

"Yeah I think so, but I didn't think it was a true story," she said with her teeth chattering.

"It is true, Nancy, Grandpa Egor told me all about it." I'm also thinking, Telling this story should also help keep my mind off drowning that man.

"About forty years ago our town had a real Church War and it lasted about two months."

"Darn you Teddy Radovich, are you making this up?"

"No, I'm not, so just listen. This war was know as, 'The War of Bells', and it started on a Sunday morning in May. All four churches in town, at their eight and eleven o'clock service's, as you know, ring their bells five minutes before the service. On this particular Sunday, Saint Francis Xavier, the Catholic Church, decided to ring their bells an hour before, at seven, to announce to all sinners that they were more serious about saving all the wayward souls. Of course the town didn't know it then, but the 'War of Bells' had just started. It eventually made Daisy Junction famous and furious at the same time. Well, slightly famous in our state, but furious in our town."

"Teddy, can I believe you? Was Grandpa Egor sipping or gulping his homemade wine when he told you this story?

As long as we need to float along toward some island, please continue your wild story, but I'm getting tired of holding this top up, so can't you keep your eyes on something else besides my breasts . . . Ted?"

"Do you need another hand?"

Nancy was floating on the surface where the water was warmer, stretching out, her nipples hard and protruding.

"Yes, probably, but not your hand right now, just your story."

"Well, then, the Ellaho Anthony Methodist Church decided to ring their bell at ten the same morning, an hour before the eleven service. They figured they needed to promote themselves as well. It was all the town talked about for the whole week, so the next Sunday, the two remaining churches, The Mission of the Apostles Church and our Conservation and Progressive Baptist Church got in the game.

The four churches, as you know, are still only eight blocks apart, and it slowly escalated to church bells ringing on Sundays for about ten minutes on the hour starting at six in the morning. It actually worked though because more people were attending all the churches. Whether it was an upsurge in piety or just to be a part of the excitement was never determined.

Anyway, each church tried to out ring each other and it got out of hand. During this time of the 'Bells' many people began to refer to Daisy Junction as "The Holy Bell Town' or 'The Hell of a Town with them Holy Bells. Our Mayor at the time was Sam Brasovich who still owned The Apple Dryer on First Street and he referred to Daisy Junction in the local paper as 'The Center of a Damn Holy

Universe with them Damn Holy Bells making them Damn Holy Noises'.

Many Daisy Junction citizens thought the end of the world was about to happen, and of course Gabriel would be arriving with his Golden Horn."

Grandpa Edgar told me, 'You should've seen the people standing outside, looking up toward the sky. Many church going citizens thought they might have a religious conscious problem or problems with their morals so their attendance skyrocketed. Many non-church goers also made a quick dash to the closest church to seek immediate forgiveness.'

Grandpa said, 'Those churches were suddenly stuffed with more people than even their Christmas or Easter service's.'

The religious leaders got into their sudden new notoriety and talked about the 'Comet of Gabriel and his Golden Horn', and the obvious future of all the sinners in town—where they would be sent? So that's why every fourth Sunday, then as now, each church devotes its sermon on the assumption the end of the world is close at hand. So those who do not repent and repent right now will roast in hell while the repeters will rise up to heaven and live with the angles.'"

"I know that," Nancy complained. "We hear it every month ourselves. That's why Dad and Mom skipped church Sunday. They told me, 'We've heard that sermon so repeatedly we know by heart.'"

"I continued, 'Gabriel did not arrive in Daisy Junction, but the War of the Bells did. Then the ringing spread to the days in the week from seven in the morning to eight at night, ten minutes on the hour. For some reason, known only to God and perhaps to the local church leaders, the church clocks, somehow, became unsynchronized.'

Grandpa told me, 'Eventually the citizens of Daisy Junction became disgruntled with the bell ringing seeming to last forever.' Grandma Olena said, 'There were very loud bells, soft melodious bells, harsh bells, and high shrill bells. It sounded like Easter in Rome.'"

"Whoops!" Nancy interrupted. "Wow, my suit slipped off again. Excuse me. I got it back. Can you look somewhere until get it back on? That was close. Okay, continue Teddy."

I was watching Nancy tug the remaining part of her suit up. At times her breasts were visible.

I resumed my story, "Not until two things occurred did the ringing contention finally end; one was when the city counsel threatened to ban all ringing of bells, much to the churchs' dismay. The second, perhaps the more important of the two reasons, was when Captain Francisco Lopez of the semi-volunteer fire department, you know his grandson, Brandon Lopez, good basketball player, he's a year behind us in school."

"Yeah, a good looking boy. Too bad he's younger." Nancy gave me a raised eyebrow look.

"If I can have your attention on my subject and not on another I'm not interested in?" I asked.

"Go on twin," Nancy conceded.

"Captain Lopez pointed out, 'If a fire or emergency should occur when those bells are ringing, our loyal Fire Department volunteers may not respond as they would be unable to hear the town's siren summoning them.' The church bells were reduced to a melodious peel and only twice a day on Sundays just as it is today. Also, the city-fathers told the churches to get their clocks synchronized or get rid of their bells."

"Well, I don't know about your story, Ted, but I'll check it out when we get home, that's if and when we get home."

Nancy was just keeping her head above the water. We were now closing in on the island where the water was murky enough so I couldn't see much of anything below the water. "If you are getting tired I can give you the lifeguard assist, if you want, Nancy."

"Yes, I know what kind of grab you'll use, but it's not in the book. No thank you. Is that the island coming up?"

Ahead was the tree filled, sand, clay, and mud island.

Soon, our feet touch the muddy bottom.

I snap out, "Wait Nancy. Let's go around to the back of the island because the sand should be harder. I don't see that other man, but we don't want to take any chances."

*   *   *

Arriving on the far side of the island our feet touch gritty brown sandy mud that sloped out into the river. Green willows, Poison Sumac, and Poison Ivy covered this island about fifteen feet up from the muddy waters edge. Not a good place to hang around.

"Teddy, how did you know the bank was harder here than the front side?"

"Dad and I shoot ducks and geese here in the fall. Also, Oscar and I have hunted this area for the last two years.

"The rule, Oscar and I follow, is, the one who shoots the duck does not go in the water for it. The one that missed the duck or didn't shoot has to go in the water. Most of the time it's Oscar in the water. He complains constantly when he has to strip off his clothes and go for a swim. I tell him, 'You're a better retriever than a dog when you can see the duck, but in the brush your nose isn't too good."

"You two go swimming in the nude for ducks?"

"Someone has to get the ducks. This river is really cold in the winter, and it's hard to dry off, so we use our underwear as towels. I know because I had to make a few swims myself, that's why I know about this island."

"Okay, so I'm here with an outdoor man who swims nude after ducks. How long are we going to stay in this mud hole you have picked out, Mr. Duck Hunter?"

"Let's wait for a while and see what happens."

I have decided not to mention what I did to the man that was swimming after us. If she's convinced the man had cramps, she'll say that when we are found, so I'll leave it as that.

Nancy stood up to walk out of the water and the bottom part of her bathing suit slipped almost to her knees. She whirled around and dove back into the river, the suit getting pulled completely off by the drag of the water. Before she dove back into the water, I had a view of her small round bottom. I grabbed her sinking bathing suit.

Nancy slithered back to the muddy bank and stretched out on her stomach covered by the mirky water. She seemed to be feeling around in the mud for her suit, but I had it.

"Honey, I lost my suit. Can you help me find it. I'm not moving until it's found."

"Here it is," I said, holding the suit up. "Do you need it? Why bother because it keeps coming off. Are you in a hurry or going somewhere?"

"Yes, I need it and I'm not going anywhere. I'm staying with you. Come over here and just give me the suit, and no tossing and no feeling."

I waded over to her. She had only her head above the water.

"Don't be embarrassed Nancy. They are only fat and blood vessels," I quipped.

Nancy turned her back on me as she pulled the suit back on before returning to the shallow water. Lying on her stomach, Nancy retorted. "Then I don't have to worry about you trying to touch them. Let's get out of this muddy water. Teddy, how are we going to get home?"

"Nancy, I told your dad and mother where we were going and about this island. They know where we are. We are supposed to be at your house at five. If not, they will come looking for us. This I promise."

"What time is it now?"

I squinted at the sun and guessed because I wanted to keep Nancy calm. I told her, "About five, or a little after. We have been in the water for some time before reaching this island."

Nancy, on her stomach, turned to me and remarked, "Come closer to me."

I did, coming into almost touching distance to her. With her beautiful blue eyes looking at me she tells me, "I have two questions for you Mr. Radovich. This is our first date, and I believe it is your first date, right?"

I nodded.

"Already, you have seen more than any boy, and most of the girls I know? This damn suit won't stay up. This part of our story I don't want repeated.

What happened to that man swimming after me? I was worried he'd catch me if I tried to keep the suit up so I was about to let the darn thing go and give him a race down the river. Then all of sudden, he was waving his hands and hollering, then he just went under. You missed that part. Is that when you caught your foot on a sunken tree limb?"

Her story would mesh with mine about the drowning so I don't have to explain my side.

"Yes, I'm sorry I missed that part. You have two hands, use them to keep your suit up. Let's stay close to this island," I said, getting up. "I'll be right back."

"Where are you going?"

"Keep watching the woods and if you see anybody, holler."

"Teddy, don't leave me alone. Please."

"I'm going to check this downstream end of the island. I'll be right back."

When I was away from Nancy's sight I moved around in the waist deep water and ankle deep mud searching for a tree limb imbedded in the river.

I found this suitably submerged tree limb and rubbed the top of my right foot and ankle extremely hard on the sharp edge. Gritting my teeth, I kept rubbing until I knew I'd drawn blood. It hurts and I had a loose skin flap on the top of my foot. Looked good to me.

Then I limped while wading back in the shallows and joined Nancy as she sat in the muddy shore line with both hands cupping her small breasts. She watched my return from my exploratory mission.

"You're limping Ted, what happened?"

"It's my ankle or foot, where I got caught trying to swim away from that man. I wanted to keep him from getting you."

"You mean when that man swimming after us got the cramps? You didn't tell me about your ankle until now, why?"

"Yeah, it didn't seem to bother me until I started to walk to other side of this island. Maybe putting a little pressure on it caused me to limp."

"Let me see it."

I lifted my leg up, and Nancy bent over and moved her hands around the cut in my ankle forgetting about her bare breasts. I sure wasn't going to tell her.

"Why didn't you tell me about your ankle sooner, Teddy and why can't you look me in the eyes instead of my breasts?"

"You're such a lovely lady, Nancy."

"Keep your eyes up or keep them shut or look elsewhere. Maybe we can wrap your ankle and keep it clean."

"With what?"

"Well," Nancy took in a long pause then replied, "your bathing suit."

"That would be something. You have a problem with your suit, and we'll wrap my ankle using mine. If that happens we had better not be found by our parents."

"Okay, we will just leave it alone and let Dad clean it out and maybe stitch it up, if you don't lose your leg to infection before we get help.

"I can't keep covering my breasts and hold the bottom of my suit up at the same time," Nancy continued. "If you ever mention this part of our picnic, you will be in deep trouble, Teddy. Now look elsewhere. Checkout the sky or something."

*   *   *

We stretched out on our stomachs along the muddy river bank. We talked in low voices and watched the edge of the willow tree-line of the river and island for any sort of movement. We stayed on the edge of the island shore line talking quietly and wondering what had happened to the other man.

I still wanted to look around, but Nancy forbade it because she did not want to be left, again, especially with her swim suit situation.

After a short period of silence she turned to me and looked in my eyes, asking,

"Do you think you could spare another kiss Mr. Radovich?"

Nancy and I laid in the murky, silty water and the sticky mud and kissed. It wasn't long before our muddy chests touched together. Nancy murmured, "Stay above the shoulders.

So the kissing experience for us continued until Nancy rolled over on her back and exclaimed, "I don't know how long I can resist."

Turning on my side I looked at Nancy's muddy coated breasts and now her blond hair was a muddy brown. The first thought I had was, Damn they look nice. Much smaller than Miss L'Affaire's and certainly not as large or heavy as Dee Dee's.

Just then Nancy sat up and asked me, "Ted, what time do you think it is now. I'm still scared."

"Of my kisses or the man?"

"That man we saw in the water, you dummy. If he drowned, we might see his body float by. God what a miserable thought that is. And for you Mr. Radovich, none of your fancy moves on this island, I still have two hands, my two elbows, and my two feet, 'Buster'. What's the time, please?"

"I saw your kick. I don't have to we warned twice. The time is, I think, after six, closer to six-thirty. You have to go somewhere? What time is Roberto picking you up?"

"He's not. I told you he is history. Remember, I now have a steady boyfriend and it's you and it better remain you. I'm worried what my parents are thinking right now."

"Nancy, help will soon be here, I promise." I reached over to Nancy and gripped her hand hard and gave her a reassuring nod and smile. "You did a good job today, Nancy. You stayed very calm, and I am proud of you. Say, we make some team together. Lets work on it?"

"Not here on this island, Mr. Radovich. We have to go steady first. Then I'll pick the spot at my time and not yours. I have to know you a lot better and this island is not the place to find out especially with that little man somewhere and the other one missing. Then there is the man you hit who gave me this bathing suit problem, and this mud."

"Don' t forget the kick you gave him. You sure stopped him in his tracks."

Nancy quickly sat up, forgetting her breasts. "Teddy, what's that? Someone is hollering. It sounds like Dad. He's on shore. Get up, let's go, hurry honey, it's Dad."

She was on her feet forgetting about her bathing suit. She pulled me up and we headed for the front of the island, she barely holding the tattered bathing suit on. The suit was just hanging on her hips, slightly. With her other hand she tugged me through the sticky mud.

We sloshed up to the hard sand above the water line and ran. I was limping while being pulled by Nancy. We two muddy individuals hurried toward the pointed upstream end of the island. She kept saying. "I know it's Dad. I just know it's Dad. Please God, let it be Dad."

If it is Dr. Blake then Dad will be with him, and I must decide how to answer Dad's questions regarding the man I drowned going after Nancy.

* * *

Nancy and I were running, well I was limping, as she dragged me with one hand, her other hand trying to hold up the bottom of her bathing suit, but it kept slipping down her long tan legs. All I can see is her white rear end.

We were trying to run from the back of the island around to the front in the deep sticky mud. Nancy was hollering, "Daddy, Daddy, it's Teddy and me. We're safe."

We two muddy individuals arrived on the front side and wave and yell as we see someone paddling a small rowboat toward us. It's Dr. Blake.

His row boat hit the muddy bank and he stood up, starring at both of us. Nancy, bare top, dropped my hand and ran toward her father, as I limp behind her. Dr. Blake hugged Nancy oblivious to the mud Nancy brought with her.

I touched Dr. Blake on the shoulder and asked, "Is it possible for Nancy to borrow your shirt, she has been having nothing but problems with her suit."

Dr. Blake eyed me then hurriedly took of his hunting shirt and gave it to her. Nancy was fumbling as she tried to button up her father's shirt. Now I remember, men's shirts button on the different side from women's shirts.

Dr. Blake was watching his daughter fumble with the buttons of his shirt, "Tell me young lady, just how were you able to loose the top of a one piece bathing suit?"

Nancy turned and looked at me, then her father. "A big man tried to grab me and he pulled on the back of my bathing suit and I guess this old suit just ripped off. It was then that Teddy hit the man."

"Well, not exactly," I entered. "I think Nancy had already figure out what she was going to do. Right Nancy?"

Dr. Blake, trying to hold a stern look with little success waited for his daughter to answer.

Nancy narrowed her blue eyes at me then responded. "All I did, Dad, I kicked him in his groin just as you taught me, then Teddy hit him in the knees."

Dr. Blake shook his head then reached over to me and gave me a big hug. "You two are some team. As Val and I figured from the injuries that big man has, it had to be two athletic people to do that to that large man. Both us, your dad and I saw the results. The guy has two very blown out knees and one extremely serious groin injury. Let's get back and see our one prisoner and your dad, Ted. We can only account for two men. Where's the third man?"

I told Dr. Blake, "Don't know. Saw him enter the water and head for Nancy, then I got caught on a log under the water."

"Teddy's right, Dad, that other man was trying to swim out to me. Teddy got into a problem, then I saw that man struggling just like he got cramps and then go under. He never came back up. Teddy had already disappeared. I was worried about Teddy. Look at his ankle. Will he loose it to infection?"

Dr. Blake bent down and gave my ankle a quick look. "I'll clean it out when we get back to where Val is and then when we get to town we'll stop at the office, and you'll need a shot and a few stitches, Teddy. Let's get going."

*   *   *

We crossed back to shore where Dad waited with a small trembling man in prison denims. Dad gave me a hard hug and received a kiss from Nancy.

"You two look great considering what is left of your bathing suit, Nancy. Lucky we came along and not the local law enforcement people. You might have been charged with indecent exposure," dad chuckled. "Now, where is the other man?"

"The kids already explained what happened," Dr. Blake said. "I guess the guy got a cramp and drowned."

Nancy and I related our story, each interrupting each other as we told how we escaped to the river. I told Dad and Dr. Blake how the large man made a grab at Nancy, and that was what happened to her bathing suit. Then she kicked him in the groin and that stopped him in his tracks, and I took the opening to slam into his knees.

When we came to the next guy. "The last I saw him," Nancy continued, he was slapping the water with his hands like he was in trouble and then he just disappeared. When I got close to where I saw Teddy go under, Teddy suddenly came up and the man was gone. We never saw the man again, right Teddy?"

Whew, that statement from Nancy didn't require much more from me, I thought. "That's the way it happened," I said. "I was worried I was going to drown, stuck on a tree limb, but I guess he did instead."

I nodded and looked Dad in the eye. Neither one of us wavered in our stares.

We just stood looking at each other, until Dr. Blake asked me to lift up my foot for an examination.

Dad said, "Lets get back to town with the one prisoner and have Chet fix that ankle for you, son."

"Val," suggested Dr. Blake, "we'll bring the little guy with us in my car. The police will like to have him for breaking out of prison."

"We have to take him in, but with five people and two bicycles it will be tight in the car, besides he wet his pants," Dad reminded Dr. Blake.

"I don't think he'll need to ride in the car," Dr. Blake said with a sly grin on his face.

I asked, "Dad, how did you and Dr. Blake decide to come to where Nancy and I were?"

"I was working on my books and my radio was on when a news-flash was announcing a prison break," Dad said. "The station was broadcasting a warning that two prisoners had escaped with possible help from a third man who had escaped earlier from a work gang. The three were from the Anton Vitalenich State Penitentiary at Grayson Falls.

The radio broadcast was warning everyone, 'Be alert for three strangers, two are suspected to be dressed in their blue dungarees with large white block letters, VSP, on the backs of their coats and pants. The other man is thought to be wearing civilian clothes. They are believed to be driving an old yellow car, make unknown. They may be armed and must be considered dangerous.

One of the men is Rockland Forbes, a six-foot-eight, 285 pound man, convicted of brutally beating his mother and father and raping his younger sister. He was serving a life sentence. Forbes is originally from Parish Crossing, just twenty miles from Daisy Junction. He is also wanted in connection for raping a woman and the criminal assault on her husband, and the theft of couple's 1950 yellow Buick in Siders Crossing last Thursday evening. Why he was on a road gang rather than a solo cell, as sentenced, will be examined by authorities,' the warning broadcast continued. 'The other two men escaped from the State Prison in Grayson Falls. The prison authorities believe it was Saturday night, but their absence was not noticed until the second roll call at nine this morning.

One man, Jesse Ambrose, is described as six foot tall and 180 pounds. He's a drifter, and a convicted multiple rapist, also serving a life sentence.

The third escapee is Francis Story, five foot three, 125 pounds and a child molester with four convictions, now serving a life sentence. He is the cell mate of Jessie Ambrose. These three men are suspected to be together.

Do not try to apprehend them. Call your local authorities if you have any information regarding the escaped prisoners.'

"Then the radio broadcast warned everyone to be careful as Ambrose and Forbes are considered extremely dangerous and may be armed. This information bothered me," Dad said. "I knew you and Nancy were going on a picnic near Chester's Dairy alongside the Swinjoscie River and one of the three prisoners is from this area, so I telephoned Dr. Blake and informed him of my feelings."

"Chet told me, 'I just heard the announcement and will be right at the store and pick you up and we both will go to the picnic site.' He asked me, 'Do you have a gun at the store, Val?'

"I told him, 'Yeah in my safe, Chet. It's that old long barrel Western 45 left over from late thirties when I was first in the army. I think I have a few cartridges left. I'll bring it.'

"Good, I'll have my 10 gauge double Magnum with me and a box of buckshot load just in case. See you in ten minutes in front of the store. You want me to bring a shotgun for you?"

"No, this long barrel will do just fine, Chet."

*   *   *

Dr. Chester Blake, according to Dad, shot down Main Street driving a trifle fast and slid to a stop in front of the store, unnoticed because in Daisy Junction very few people are around on Sundays. There are no stores open because Daisy Junction's Blue Laws are strictly enforced, so the locals have nothing to do but go to church. Even the local movie theater, The Dream House, is closed on Sundays.

"Then we sped out of town going toward Chester's Dairy," Dad explained. "We both discussed if we should contact the local police or sheriff's department. Finally, we decided, we are only working on a hunch and we thought better of the idea.

As we neared the area where you told us you and Nancy would be having your picnic, we passed an old yellow Buick about a quarter of a mile away from the meadow. This car was parked in the edge of the wooded area and appeared to be partially covered with brush. Just ahead we could see the two bicycles leaning against the fence. Now we had warning signs.

We decided to go alone and not waste time trying to contact the sheriff as time was not on our side."

*   *   *

Dad appeared to be enjoying his story. "Chester stopped his car next to your two bicycles and we both left the car. Chet had his shotgun and I had my long barrel pistol stuck in my belt. We climbed over the fence and ran to the knoll where your blanket was still laid out, and the near empty picnic basket still in place. There was no sign of you and Nancy anywhere. We saw the clothes you two wore to church this morning.

Chester and I then ran toward the bank of the river. Alongside the bank were numerous footprints and a pair of blue dungarees with large white lettering lying close by.

We knew where the dungarees came from. I studied the numerous tracks and saw the one set of female tracks heading off to the river, along with two male sets following. I studied a set of peculiar tracks, like someone crawling and dragging something toward the woods south of your picnic site. Back where the dragging started, two sets of tracks intersected, one set intercepting the other from a right angle at high speed.

I suggested to Chet, 'Lets follow these. Looks like something may have been dragged toward the forest area ahead. Keep your gun ready.'

'Wait, Val.' Chet poked me. 'Look at that over there right by the river bank. That sure looks like . . . dammit it is, 'Son of a Bitch', I think that's part of Nancy's last year's swimming team swim suit? It sure and hell looks like the strap part of her suit,' Chet said running over and picking the material up. 'It's hers all right. Now there's going to be at least one bastard that won't have a trial. I'll kill that animal even if he just even touched one of the kids.'"

Dad continued, "Chester broke his gun and slipped two double-o shells into the twin barrels, then he whispered to me. 'I'm ready Val and our kids had better not be harmed,' he said shaking with fury. I have known Chet all my life and never have I seen him so worked up as he was this afternoon.'

'What's that?' I asked him, pointing to a small messy mound at the edge of the water.'

'Looks like vomit,' Chet replied. Chet poked it and nodded his head and said quietly, 'Yep, that's vomit, Val. Hot dogs and buns this guy 'wolfed' down without cooking the dogs and not much chewing. My guess, he was a hungry guy. Looks like he tried to follow the kids into the water. He'll need luck, those two can swim better than fishes."

"Now we are ready to follow those tracks," Dad said. "I tell him, 'Okay, Chet, no talking now. Just like we are deer hunting. Lets move. I'll take the lead and keep your double barrel ready. Just remember where I am and I'll do the same for you. I have five bullets in the cylinder of the 45. The sixth is open for safety.'"

I've hunted with Dr. Blake and Dad before. I know these two men can move with care and quietness in a forested area. These two friends have hunted deer, ducks, and quail since high school. Now the two hunting partners are on a serious hunting mission because Nancy and I are involved.

Dad told us, "When we entered the forest area, it was a cool and quiet. Willows, ash, birch, and tall, lush green grass greeted us. The trail I'm following was made in the foot high grass by something dragging.

We stood and slowly looked around. Side by side we searched the shadows, then Chet nudged me. He nodded toward an opening area facing the county road. Parked there is the old yellow Buick we had past on the way to the meadow.

Chet then pointed to our quarry. A body was in a fetal position on the ground about ten feet from the old yellow Buick. This person appeared to be a huge man sleeping."

Dad smiled. "Without a word we walked cautiously toward the man lying on his side. He didn't appear to be moving. We move along the mashed down path, obviously made by this guy as if he had pulled himself through the grass.

We stopped close to this man we both know is one of the escaped prisoners. This fellow is over six feet tall and very big, just like the one mentioned in the radio broadcast. No movement or sound came from this man. Then he let out a low groan. I moved close to the curled up body and kicked one of his legs. My God, a loud scream erupted from the huge figure man, followed by, 'Oh my legs! My legs! Don't, please don't do that to me. I'm hurting so bad.

That's when I notice his legs appeared to be in odd positions. He turned his head very slow, then blinked his eyes and tried to look up at us. His eyes had a blank stare look. He blinked a few more times as he tried, again, to focus his eyes.

Then he saw Chester pointing the double barreled shotgun at him, and turned to me and was looking down the barrel of my long barreled 45."

"Help me please. I've done nothing," he said in a weak, pleading voice just above a whisper. He's begging, "I'm hurt. Really hurt. Help me. Pleeeeease help me. Oh God I'm hurting."

"The man mumbled something," Dad continued, "then with a groan lapsed into an unconscious state, still in his fetal position."

Chester moved the shotgun barrel down next to the man's face and turned it toward us with the end. Tears had streaked down and across his dirt caked face and cheeks. His dilated black eyes stared back at us."

'He must have crawled and pulled himself along using the tall grass and bushes for help,' Chet said."

Dad went on, "The man's eyes maintained a dull listless look. His face had a pale appearance and perspiration drops stood out on his forehead. I was pretty sure he was in shock.

This guy was in deep trouble, his hands were muddy and what's left of his fingernails were jagged and two or three were hanging loose from the quick of his fingers.

Now he mummer, 'Water please. Who are you?' He appeared to be gasping for breath as he begged.'"

I asked him, 'Who are you?'

He just shook his head.

Looking him over, I told Chet, 'He doesn't look good to me.'

Chester broke his shotgun and handed it to me. Chet then bent over the man and began to assess this man's problems. As he started his assessment he filled me in on his medical observations."

'A weak fast pulse,' Chet explained. 'This guy's skin is clammy and cold. Very poor respiration, Good signs of shock, Val.' Then Chet continued, checking the man's head, arms, and the fingers with the damaged remaining finger nails. With a shake of his head, he added, 'A very slow capillary refill. Not a good sign.'

Now Chet pushed this large man on his back and probed the upper body with no response. When he pushed on the man's lower stomach area, the man groaned, but when Chet touched his groin area, this guy yelled out, 'Don't touch me there! Please. God all Mighty it hurts'!"

Dr. Blake took over the story from there. "I leaned back and looked at your dad. He nodded back with a smile. Now I continued toward the man's right knee. He groaned and with a very weak wave indicated something really hurt him around his knees. I felt around both knees and then look up to your dad, surprised as hell.

I tell Val, 'I'll be damned. Can you believe this, Val? Both of his knees are severely dislocated. I would guess, he was running hard and somebody got him with a viscous, illegal cross block. His groin injury appears to be very severe like someone kicked him right in the huevos. His lower abdominal area indicates extreme swelling, and indicates a vein or artery or even both appear to be leaking blood into his pelvic cavity. This is very unusual. This guy has been worked over by maybe one or two people we just might know. People who can react quick and cause these injuries.'"

Dad continued, "Chet asked the man, in his doctor's voice, 'What happened?'

The injured man tried to speak, but fumbled with the words.

It took a few moments, but we were able to get that someone kicked him in the groin and someone hurt his knees with a shoulder, and that was all he remembered.

Then Chet asked him, 'Was there a boy and girl involved?'

'Yeah. I guess, something like that,' he managed to stammer out.

'Where are they now?' I asked.

'I don't know I, I, I think in the water, I'm not sure,' the man answered. 'Help me please.'

I bent over the guy and poked him between the eyes with the 45 and asked, 'You involved with the prison break?'

Slowly he answer in a very weak, halting voice, 'Something like that.'

Where are the other two men?

He fumbled with the answer. Eventually he spoke, 'I don't know.'

I poked him with the 45, a little harder this time and he looked at me, like he's maybe thinking this is his way out from the pain.

'I think Jesse went in the water after the girl."

'Are you sure?'

He mumbled some more, 'We both wanted that blond girl and Jessie was going to catch her. I couldn't see because I couldn't stand up. This pain is like something I've never had before.' He said all this in a very low, slow halting voice and many of his sentences were incomplete and vague. His eyes had a blank look and he begged for water.

Where is the third man?"

'Francis?' he mumble.'

'You know him, I don't. Talk mister.'

Chester looked up at me. 'Val, he passed out again. You know, this sucker is going to die.'

'Right here?'

'Well, one thing for certain; he will die anyway. Either shock is going to kill him, or I will if he has laid just one finger on my daughter or your son, and I believe he has. He will be dead before the afternoon is over, this I promise."

*   *   *

Dad then continued with his side of the rescue. "Chester stood up and walked to the old car, reached in under the dash and pulled some wires loose. 'Just in case of a medical miracle, Val, but I don't think there will be one.'"

Dad suggested, "Chet let's go down stream, partner. There's an island and maybe the kids are there. You want to leave this guy here, alone, Chet?"

"No problem, he's as close to being dead as dead is dead. I'll put my money on him expiring in two or three hours with or without help. Lets go partner, I think our kids are okay and better off than we think. I think we have seen some of their efforts of staying alive."

*   *   *

"Your father," Dr. Blake related to me, "he moved along the bush covered river bank without snapping a twig or rustling a plant. He's following a faint track that would be invisible to most people and at times even to me.

We are two silent predators now stalking our prey. Occasionally the tracks became clear as the footprints sank deep into the mud bank. Your father slipped along the river bank without a sound, his head going from the grass or small bushes bent by shoes and then to what was up ahead that he should notice. I know what he did during the war time and now the past has returned to your dad. I'm sure his competitive juices are flowing in the cold anticipation of what may lay ahead and what will be his decision. I certainly did. I know what I'm going to do, right or wrong."

Neither one of us," Dr. Blake continued, "were too worried about you two. We quickly surmised you guys are safe right now. We know you and Nancy are excellent swimmers. Your escaping from the prisoner who left his clothes on the shore should be an easy chore for you two. They just don't have swimming pools in prisons and ten years in prison with no swimming does not make a swimmer, and I know he had eaten too many uncooked hot dogs, so maybe he got himself in trouble with cramps in the cold river water, but what about the unknown man ahead of us? We wondered; what are his intentions? Any prudent escapee would have left the area rather than continue the chase of two people with excellent athletic skills. Then the man who went into the water after Nancy. Where is he? I'm hoping he drowned."

Dr. Blake continued, "We would jog when a clear field of vision, free from trees, occurred. In the trees your dad stopped many times to listen, then smell the air. Silently, we slipped into the edge of a meadow alongside the river. A breeze was now in our faces and we know we had an advantage. Two does and a fawn trotted out into the meadow from the direction we're heading. The deer kept looking back from where they exited. Something was bothering those deer as they stomped their hooves and shook their heads and their tails waggled back and forth. A few birds then flew up and away from the brushy thicket across from the meadow from where Val and I stood silent. Now we both knew our prey was not far in front of us.

Suddenly, your dad stopped and bent over. He reached down and picked up a burnt match stick. He felt it then he handed the match stick to me. The match end was warm. Our target was not too far ahead. Cigarettes leave an odor and now we want to smell for a burning cigarette. We know our quarry is very close at hand. Slowly we two fathers walk along the bank. Val is in the lead searching for tracks and signs or marks.

For some reason, Ted, I hate to say this, but the fear, yet excitement of being on a chase with your dad did something to me. I was worried for Nancy and you, but I was ready to kill. A damnedest feeling came over me. Never felt that way before as I always wanted to save people, but today was different, scary for me. I've hunted with your dad enough times, but this strange feel of excitement flowed through me.

Val and I figure you two had escaped, but we didn't know the problems you two had using the river as the route."

Dr. Blake kept describing to me, "Your dad kept sniffing the air. Turning to me he nodded. I stared at your dad and I guess I frowned. Val brought a hand to his lip and pretended to smoke. Now I understood and nodded. He knows someone is smoking and is ahead of us and is close."

Dr. Blake smiled as he continued, "We had not gone more that twenty yards in this dark forested area next to the river when we both sight a short, slight built man with blue dungarees and large white initials on his pants legs. Here was the third man.

Val held his hand up as a signal for me to stop. We watch this man trying to unlatch a small rowboat with oars up on the bank and attached to a large tree. There's just a latch on the chain, not difficult to unsnap but he's having a problem.

The stranger tugged and swore as he tried to free the boat. Val motioned to me that he was going in alone, and for me to wait.

Silently, Val stepped up right behind this man, holding his long barreled pistol right at the back of this man's head, waiting until his presence is noticed.

The little man finally turned his head around and froze. Standing behind him, holding a large western style pistol was a tall broad-shouldered man with a rugged face and a sweeping and menacing looking black mustache.

I approached the scene and as I came closer I can see Val is smiling. I don't think his steady pale blue eyes ever wavered, and the barrel of the pistol never moved. For ten-seconds a deadly quiet prevailed.

Then Val broke the tension with, 'Are you prepared to die?'

'No! . . . I don't want to die!' the small man wailed. 'It was those other guys. Honest mister!' This little guy's high pitched voice was cracking, his hands trembling. I'm sure he had never seen a man like this one standing before him. He was shaking as if he felt death was coming and he is the chosen one.

The little guy slumped onto the old row boat seat with his hands in his lap and looked down and away from Val," Dr. Blake added. "Then he looked up and he saw me holding my shotgun with the two large open barrels pointing directly at his stomach.

Now he must have known he's probably going to die. He tries to talk. His throat is dry and nothing comes out of his mouth except a few squeaks.

I stepped closer to the small stranger and I poked him in his crotch with my shotgun. 'Fellow, want to see what a shotgun can do when I blow your nuts clear across to the island?'

'You won't do that. I'm a prisoner,' he whined.

'Oh? Not my prisoner though, right? Maybe not, but on the other hand maybe I will. Suppose I tell the law you tried to fight us and we just had to protect ourselves and I shot your nuts off as you charged us. Then you'll wear rubber diapers the rest of your rotten life. Do you understand me?'

'You just can't just shoot someone just like me?' he slobbered. 'I didn't do nothing.'

'Mister. I had to protect myself and when I did I cleaned out your ass. You'll wear diapers the rest of your stinking life. Of course, if I raise the double barrel a little higher then you're flat ass dead.'

'You can't do that to me,' he sniveled. 'What do you want me to do?'

'You sure and hell had better become a talkative prisoner or you're going to pay one bitter price of not being honest to us. Now, where is the boy and girl, or I'll pull the trigger? Remember this, when I am under some stress I have a nervous finger that twitches. Unfortunately it's my trigger finger and my gun is pointing at your balls. Now talk honest like to keep me not being too nervous.'

'I don't know. Please don't shoot me,' the little guy begged.

'Okay, you want it sitting down or standing up?' Then I poked the double barrels right into his pants and jabbed his groin area. Now this stranger jerked up and stood before us with his knees twitching and his hands tremble. The front of his pants are now wet and his whole body is now shaking vigorously. His face is pale and slobbering spit emerges from his mouth.'

The tips of my shotgun barrels were wet. I told your dad, 'Val did you see that. Now I have to clean my gun since he pissed on it so I might as well pull both triggers. Got to clean the shotgun anyway.'

Your dad tells me, 'Chet, it's your call if he won't talk. I'll walk away and leave you two alone.'

Now the little guy breaks down.

'Wait, wait. Don't go mister. Please don't go. I'll tell you. Get this crazy man away from me. I don't want to die.'

Then the stranger begins to cry, and I give him one more jab from the shotgun and he talks between sobs.

'My name is Francis.'

He tells us about a boy and girl that escaped and the names of the other two men. He thought the boy and girl were on the island.

Val asks him about the third man they haven't seen.

Francis tells us, 'I saw Rocky grab the blond girl's bathing suit and tear the top down.'"

Dad jumped in, "Chet got a real mean look, the shotgun moving a little closer to Francis's face, but then Francis held his hands up quickly, trying to explain something to benefit his well being. 'The girl kicked that son-of-a-bitch, Rocky, right square in his nuts, and I swear she lifted him right off the ground, and he is one big man. She sure kicked that bastard right in his most valuable jewels. As soon we saw the girl, Jessie's plan was to grab the girl and fuck her until she died. They were so goddamn horny they wanted a piece of ass in the worst way.'

'And what about you Francis, what did you want to do to my daughter?'

'Hey, look mister, I have two daughters and three nieces and they are precious.'

'Okay, Francis keep talking. What then?'

'Shit, when that gal kicked that bastard Rocky, he sure let out a yell, and that's when that kid, a big blond guy coming like a run-a-way freight train going down hill and out of control. Man-oh—man did he slam into Rocky. Damn, did he hit him? Caught that son-of-a-bitch Rocky right above the knees. He sure as hell snapped that asshole's head and body back. Christ did Rocky yell. Then that kid rolled over him and jumped up and dove into the river. Jesse has sort of a bum leg and couldn't get to the blond kid so he threw his club at the kid as he swam off. Jessie striped off his clothes to go after the girl, I expect, me knowing Jessie, he got himself a hard-on just watching the kids on that knoll and he was so excited be blew lunch down at the river. He said, when they first went after the kids, 'I got my best ever hard on to give to that blond girl.'"

"Was your friend ever a swimmer?" Dr. Blake asked.

"He always said he was. All I saw before I left was Jesse swimming after that girl. I lost track of the boy. I know he wasn't between Jessie and the blond girl. Yeah, I'm sure it had to be the girl that Jessie was after. As I told you, I don't think that big kid was anyway near the girl in the river. He just seemed to disappear in the water."

Dr. Blake continued, "I jabbed that shaking sucker again and he continued. 'I don't know what happened after that. I ran into the woods to get away. I saw the two kids later in the water, drifting down the river. That's all know. Please believe me.'"

"'Well,' I asked your dad, 'Val, do I stay here with this scum or do you? Five in the boat is one two many, your choice.'"

Dad answered, "I'll stay with Francis here if he promises no problems, Chet. Lets trade guns."

"Please Sir, stay here," begged the little guy looking at Val, while backing away from Dr. Blake.

Dr. Blake laughed, "I'm watching the pleading Francis and I had to smile. I told him, 'I think you made a poor choice.' Okay, I'll take the rowboat." I said to Val.

"Francis, what would you do if someone threatened those precious little girls you say you love?" Dad asked Francis.

"I . . . I would look for someone like you, someone with courage . . . like you, to protect them," he sniveled, trying to play politics.

Dr. Blake said in an off hand way, "If he moves, well you know what to do. You have done it before. He doesn't need his nuts."

Dad returned, "Yep, I hope he stays good and still. I think we may need a witness. Go, I'll wait here. Why don't you holler over to the island. Maybe the kids, if they are there, will hear you. You got a loud voice partner."

Dr. Blake said, "I walked to the rivers edge and hollered out, 'Nancy, Ted, do you hear me?' I hollered again. This time I heard voices coming from behind the wooded island.

"Val, I believe I hear Nancy. I still think I should have shot his nuts off," Dr. Blake looked at Francis, "but that bastard that pulled Nancy's bathing suit top off will be in deep trouble from me when we get back to where he is."

"Go on Chet, get the kids. Maybe I'll still shoot his nuts off for you while I'm alone with him then we don't have to coordinate any stories.

Dad laughed, "Francis's face went white with that one."

This is the way the two fathers pieced their story together for us.

*   *   *

Dad was smiling. "Yep, this was the best hunting we've done in years, Chet. Come on gang lets get back to the car. It's getting late and the mothers will worry."

Dr. Blake poked his prisoner, Francis, with the barrel of his shotgun. "Move fellow because this gun is still loaded and I still have a very nervous index finger that might unconsciously twitch a time or two and might do it now as my finger is resting on the trigger and the safety is off. Get going little man or I may get a nervous twitch."

We walked back to the meadow and along the way, Dad asked me to stop because he wanted to check my ankle wound again. "Chet how would you judge this ragged cut Ted has?"

Dr. Blake bent over to give my ankle a closer examination. He stood up and looked me in the eyes and smiled. "It's a good one. I think I can see some bark or slivers of wood stuck in the wound on top. I guess about four or six stitches will tie it up nice and neat," he continued as he examined the back of my ankle. "He'll be running track in four or five days." He slapped me on the back.

Looking at my ankle, I noticed; I have no injury on the back of my ankle indicating where I was caught by a limb branch. Just the top of my ankle shows injury. Well, no one said anything and maybe they didn't pay that much attention to my one sided injury.

* * *

We arrived back in the open area where we had our lunch. I helped Nancy pick up our stuff and limped to Dr. Blake's car.

"Chet, again, there are five people and two bicycles to get into your car," Dad reiterated.

Dr. Blake nodded. "As I said, Val, our prisoner will not be in the car. Val, strip their bikes and shove them in the trunk with the picnic stuff, but first pull out that chain I have by the spare tire so we can secure our prisoner. I'll just wander over to check on our man in the woods. Take care of our new friend until I get back. I want to see how the big man is doing."

He patted me on the shoulder as he walked by and then in a whisper said, "You stick to your story Son and I'll stick to mine." He took his medicine bag and headed toward the old Buick parked in the trees.

Nancy hollered to her father: "Can I watch you do the stitching on Ted's foot, please."

"It won't bother me," I said bravely, "but don't faint."

Nancy puckered up her lips: "I was going to hold your hand, but maybe I'll call Blossom or Lisa for that job."

The car's trunk was loaded with bicycles when Dr. Blake arrived back. Dad had pulled out the chain and had it laying on the ground. Dad looked at Chet and asked, "How's our man?"

Dr. Blake replied, "He didn't make it, just as I expected."

Dr. Blake motioned for Francis to come over to the car and patted the hood, indicating that Francis was to get up on it.

"But I can't ride there," Francis squealed. "It's going to be cold and not very safe.

Dr. Blake exploded, "'God damnit' you're a pedophile, I should have shot your nuts off when I had the chance."

Dr. Blake ordered Francis, who was still showing signs of being down right scared, to lay back on the hood of his car. Then Dr. Blake wrapped the chain around Francis's neck and snapped a latch to lock the chain tight. Then he attached the other end of the chain to the front bumper of his car.

"Now you don't have to worry, if you can't stay on the hood you'll still get back to town.

Dad laughed, "Gee Chet, that is some hood ornament you have. Might be hard to polish though. How about going through the car wash and then have his arms spread out as we drive through town?"

"Better yet. He is going to be chained to the Elm tree in our yard. That will give the neighbors something to talk about because they are running out of gossip," commented Dr. Blake as he slid into the front seat and then added, "Val, we have to call the sheriff and the coroner."

*   *   *

Riding back to Daisy Junction the car was full of talk. One question not completely answered yet was; what about the man in the woods that Nancy kicked and I hit? Dr. Blake, in an off hand, answered the question, "As a doctor, I would say he just expired." Dad gave Dr. Blake a quick look and Dr. Blake nodded his head.

"What did he die of Dad?" Nancy inquired.

Inside the car was quiet as we all waited for the answer.

"I guess his heart stopped pumping from his exertion. Maybe being kicked in his family jewels by a girl, then the followup by Ted who busted up his knees." Dr. Blake looked at me seriously. "Son, that cross block would have gotten your team fifteen yards and you ejected for the entire season. So he probably died from a culmination of being worked over by two athletes he did not expect to defend themselves. Of course I won't put that in the death certificate, it would only raise questions."

Nancy and I both let out a long sigh of relief.

I suggested to Dr. Blake, "Don't go too fast, I sure don't want to see your trophy messed up."

Francis was holding on tight, his arms spread wide, grasping the trim along the top of the hood.

Nancy was embarrassed, complaining, "I hope none of my friends see me in this car with that man sitting on the hood with a chain around his neck."

Dr. Blake came back with, "You are right. Okay daughter, I'll let you out and you can walk the rest of the way home, but give me my hunting shirt before you go."

We three men in the car erupted in laughter.

Nancy glared at me, then with a threatening tone to her voice, she mentioned, "We made a promise and you had better keep it."

"After I saw you kick that man, I will keep any promise because I don't ever want to be kicked like that."

Dr. Blake suggested, "I'll drop you off first Val, then I'll take Teddy to my office for treatment. Write out your observations while waiting for Mimi to get ready to come to our house. This dinner is not a dressy affair."

"Good thinking, Chet. We will need to be together when Captain Doug Shumaker comes by to fill out his papers."

"I'll have the kids take showers and then write their reports of what happened at the river. I'll stick them in different rooms so they won't be together.

*   *   *

One quick stop at the cafe to let Dad off and then to Dr. Blake's office and I'm stitched up without any pain medication. Nancy was watching the cleaning and stitching on my foot.

Dr. Blake told me, "Teddy, you are one tough kid and just as smart as your Dad."

I looked at Dr. Blake, "Include yourself in the group, now, Doctor?"

He leaned back, looked at me, and then smiled. "Might as well. I just joined a very exclusive fraternity." He ended his statement with a wink to me.

"What are you men talking about, I don't understand?" inquired Nancy.

"Man talk. Grown men talk, daughter. I have told you before, there's man talk and there is woman talk and let's hope their talks shall never meet."

"When I become President I will put a stop to all that man talk," snapped Nancy.

I ask. "What country can we all migrate to when that happens, Dr. Blake?"

"There's none I know about, Ted."

*   *   *

It's nearly dark when we pulled into the Blake's driveway. I helped unlatch our prisoner and Dr. Blake locked Francis to the big Elm tree that covered most of the lawn in front of the Blake's house.

I suggested to Dr. Blake, "You have a living statue in front of your house. If you can keep him, Francis will make an interesting Santa Claus this winter."

"Great idea, Ted. Yeah, I can have him appear like he's coming down the chimney or maybe riding on a sleigh. I'll put him right over Nancy's room."

"Are you two trying to embarrass me," she snarled.

"Well, daughter, first things first. Remember when you write out your report just stay with the facts. Nancy be sure to include, carefully, what you saw when that man disappeared swimming after you. After your quick showers write everything down as you remembered it and nothing else. Hop to it. Teddy use the guest bathroom and I'll have some clothes for you. Nancy, save some hot water for us, please."

Dr. Blake told me he had called Captain Shumaker and told him what had happened.

Captain Shumaker said he and Pat 'Cowboy' McGrath would go out to the meadow area. They'll take our Coroner, Ruben Greenfield, and bring back the dead man and have the old Buick towed in to a garage. Then they would come by the house, later in the evening, to finish their reports.

*   *   *

Our showers were over and we three, Dr. Blake, Nancy, and myself were diligently writing. Mrs. Blake was perturbed as she was unable to extract any information from any one of us.

"My dear," Dr. Blake said to her, "I don't believe I have ever given you a direct order in my life, but this afternoon is different. Oh, by the way we will have guests for dinner tonight. Val and Mimi will be joining us, also Captain Shumaker, Pat McGrath and Ruben Scofield, the coroner, will also be here."

With that last statement, Mrs. Blake dashed to the kitchen, but first told Nancy, "When you finish writing please give me a hand in the kitchen."

As Nancy hurried past me, heading to the kitchen, I asked, "Do you really know where the kitchen is in this house, Nancy?"

"One more crack liked that Mr. Radovich and I'll really air out my right foot on you, Sir. Oh I forgot, Ted, take off you tennis shoes and I'll toss them in the washing machine along with those gray or are they white socks. We are all cleaned up now and we don't need the smell of your tennis shoes permeating the house."

"Our first date and you are giving me orders already. What do you want, another bouquet of flowers?"

"Ted, you have gone far enough with the flower remarks." She grabbed my tennis shoes and socks, heading out of the room holding her one hand out away from her body, while the other hand pinched her nose.

Mrs. Blake called out to Nancy. "Honey, do the same with your shoes and socks, and remember to use lots of soap."

Just before she was through the door, Nancy turned to look at me. I sat still and tried to make a poker face. She blew me a kiss as she continued for the washing machine down the hall.

Mom and Dad arrived. Dad told Mom as they drove up to the Blake's, "Don't say a word about the man chained to the tree when we get inside the Blake's house."

Mother replied. "Don't worry, because you two guys always have something up your sleeves, and knowing our son, he's right with you two, but I can hardly wait to hear the story, why a man is chained to a tree?"

* * *

We were all in the Blake's living room, after dinner, talking, when Captain Shumaker, Officer Pat, 'Cowboy' McGrath, and Ruben Greenfield arrived. Before acknowledging any of us Captain Shumaker confronted Dr. Blake. "What in hell is that in your front yard, Chester? You didn't tell me you brought home a prisoner, or is that the way you treat the patients that can't pay the bill?"

"Oh, damn Otto, everything moved so fast and we were so happy to have the kids back with no one hurt, I must have forgot about him."

"Well, let's get him loose and in our car or someone will be checking those damn blue laws looking for violation, right Pat? Now he's your prisoner to handle."

"Oh nuts, I was going to write up Chester for a trash violation," Pat responded, getting up to take care of Francis.

* * *

Captain Otto Shumaker asked me, "Were there any unusual circumstances to these accidents?"

I told him that the event along and on the river were easily explainable.

Rubin Greenfield asked Dr. Blake, "Chet, I know you always have your medical bag with you. There was nothing you could have done for the big guy?"

"No, in my opinion he was too far gone and anything I might have done would have been to late and only prolonged his agony," Dr. Blake answered.

*   *   *

After questions from Captain Shumaker, and reading the reports each of us had written, Captain Shumaker, and Ruben Greenfield were satisfied. Then the two sat back and enjoyed the coffee and cookies Mrs. Blake had hurriedly baked for her company, however she gave Nancy credit for the cookies. Nancy stared at me waiting for a remark because I knew better.

Dad looked at me and said, "This week, Ted, let's get your driver's license taken care of."

This was the first time Dad had ever called me Ted.

Nancy was also surprised, then said, "There goes my bicycle dates. Thanks a lot Mr. Radovich."

I reached over and put my arm around Nancy and told her, "Don't worry Nancy, I'll try to save some time for you." Then ducked as Nancy's arm came around with a wide open-handed swing, not to hurt me, but to show me what she thought about my statement.

I told Nancy, "Our first four wheel date will be in my deluxe, rust colored Model A panel truck with the broken springs, but only on your side.

*   *   *

The next morning, Captain Otto, Cowboy McGrath and Rubin Greenfield strode into the All American cafe. Dr. Blake had come in for breakfast and was talking with Dad and I. "Val, Chet, Teddy," Cowboy announced, "we found the third man, Jesse Rile. He washed up alongside the Main Street Bridge in the trash catcher.

I took a deep breath and remained silent.

Dr. Blake asked, "Drowned of course?"

"No question about it," Rubin said. "His lungs were full of water and his stomach partly full of undigested hot dogs and buns. He must have just gulped his food down.

Rubin continued, "Drowning is a tough way to go. Drowning is a slow, agonizing death manifested by a desperate struggle to get air, but only getting liquid. Slow way to go, but that guy was over due and he should have been done away with years ago, but we don't have a death penalty in our state. Case is closed."

Looking at me, Captain Otto commented, "No Coroner's Hearing for you and Nancy. Oh, by the way, Francis is going into a real tough prison stretch, and will live a very solitary life. He did say, 'You, Chet. is one mean SOB.' I told him he was lucky that he didn't meet Val alone.'

Francis said, 'He never wants to see either one of you ever again.' What the devil did you do to the pervert?'"

"Don't know, we never laid a finger on him." Dr. Blake shrugged.

Captain Otto had one more piece of news. "The big man, Rolland Rockford, according to the corner's report, died of asphyxia. His knees were both busted and he had a lot of bleeding from his ruptured groin area and he was in such bad shape that he couldn't hold his face out of the mud.

No one looked Dr. Blake's way.

Otto Senior looked at me. "Ted you sure laid one clip on him. His knees were blown out and a couple of arteries ripped.

Otto then looked at Nancy. "He had a very severe groin injury with a great amount of excess internal bleeding. Our guess is it came from Nancy's kick. You two were definitely the wrong pair of tough cookies to tangle with."

Nancy jumped in with, "Teddy was just protecting me, that's all, and when that guy tore my suit I was darn mad."

I noticed Rubin Greenfield, my dad and Dr. Blake had moved off to the side and were conferring about something.

"Hells Bells," Otto Senior added, "you two young ones can really think fast. Most people would still be standing around with their fingers up their uh . . . uh, noses, deciding what to do next. Anyway it is all over, thanks to the you all. Oh. Ted, Otto Jr. wants to see you tomorrow for sure, He did not tell me what for."

*   *   *

After they left, I looked over to Dr. Blake. Dad had gone off to take care of something in another part of the store. Dr. Blake walked over to me. I stood up and he placed his arm around my shoulders.

In a low voice he said, "Rubin said that Jesse Rile had unusual bruises around his one ankle, and he has no idea what caused them. I know Val and Rubin suspect something from the both of us, but knowing them they will never ask. As of this week you are my patient and my lips are sealed. That said, now, Son, let's join the ladies for dinner."

*　　*　　*

The next five days were busy with reporters vying to get as much information as they could from Nancy and me. Dr. Blake's death certificate said the big man died from exertion, causing his heart to give out, but the mortuary said the guy looked like he was beaten to death, and died from affixation so there were questions.

Both Dad and Dr. Blake told the reporters, "Stick to the police report and leave the kids alone, it's accurate."

Still Nancy and I had to duck the nosey and prying ones. Our school administration was great to us. They ruled all reporters off the school grounds, and the city had a police car take us to school and back home. The police also picked me up at the store and returned me after track practice and Nancy to and from her swimming practice.

Dad had ordered all snooping reporters coming into the store to stay out.

One reporter didn't believe him and kept coming in to talk to anyone, employees and customers included. I know dad had had it with this short, cocky guy.

This reporter, according to Mom, had a loud voice and refused to follow Dad's instructions to just come in and eat but no questions.

Mom told me, "Today, this poor guy sure made a mistake not following Val's orders. This noon, during lunch, we had customers standing, waiting and this guy was at it again. Val lost it. He grabbed this obnoxious reporter and stuck him under his arm. The reporter hollered for the police and the lunch crowd cheered. Val then deposited the reporter out on the curb. He told the guy, "Come back in and make a disturbance again and you'll regret it.

Eventually the excitement died down both in town and in our school, and I was enjoying the legal aspect of driving. I took my drivers test in the Model A Ford with the passenger's seat with the spring problems. The man giving the driver's test sat down and had a look like, Whoops, something is trying to goose me, and my driving test didn't last long.

CHAPTER 11

WALKING DOWN OUR SCHOOL'S main hallway I saw Nancy ahead of me. I came up along side and asked, "If my best friend has Saturday open this week would she be interested in a horseback picnic lunch?"

She stopped.

I immediately thought, What a good looking young lady she is.

"I don't know," Nancy hesitated, contemplating. "The last time you invited me for a picnic we had a big problem,"

"Well, Nancy Blake, we are known for handling anything that comes our way. We'll ride up to the top of South Peak. About two or three miles. We'll take the round about way. Easier on your legs and rear end, and as a plus we may see some of the cattle drop.'

"Drop? What do you mean drop?"

"They are ready to calve."

"You mean we may see babies?"

"Definitely new born calves. I checked them the other day and there might be one or two even calving. Don't worry we'll leave them alone."

"Honey, as long as I don't have to get involved." Nancy looked at me with a look that made my knees go week. "Maybe we can continue where we left off at the river," she said in a sultry, seductive voice. "Oops, there's the bell, see you after school, my dear."

*   *   *

Saturday morning I drove the old Ford panel Goosey to pick up Nancy and I am met by one sleepy lady.

"The one day of the week I can sleep in and I don't," Nancy remarked at her door.

"If you're too sleepy, stay home, but I have to check the see if we have more calves and if they need help."

"Don't Vets do the job."

"Hey lady, those mountains take only horses. If you need sleep, I'll go alone. You can pick another day when you're awake." I turned to leave.

"Wait a minute cowboy. I'll grab something in the frig and be ready."

*   *   *

She came out in levies, a button down shirt, and tennis shoes. "Do I pass for a cow girl?" she asked and grabbed me.

I get an interesting morning kiss and say, "You'll pass."

"Honey, is it just you and I riding the range today?" she asked.

"Yep. I'll fix breakfast and a lunch and we'll spend the late morning and early afternoon riding the range. Oh, and grab your bathing suit."

"Ted, what about dinner?"

"I thought you would handle that. Lets go cowgirl because we have work to do."

*   *   *

Arriving at the ranch I fixed hot cakes and scrambled eggs for breakfast. Nancy finished her breakfast and then gave me a deep, serious look. "When we get married, you know, some time away, will you continue making breakfast for me."

"Certainly Nancy, but you will always handle the dishes."

"Ted honey, you made a mistake in that sentence."

"No, I didn't," I chuckled.

*   *   *

In the barn we saddled two horses, my thoroughbred Manana that I've had since it was colt and I named it. She's a tall chestnut horse standing 17 hands high.

Nancy's horse was shorter, 14 hands high.

"How come it's smaller than yours," she asked.

"Different bred, that mare is a quarter horse, very fast. Easier to climb on. Come over here and I'll help you up. Okay, put your left foot in the stirrup. Grab the horn and pull your self up and swing your right leg over. Go, I'll help you."

Nancy screamed out, "Teddy watch your hands!"

*   *   *

On South Mountain lunch was spread out in an oak grove and when it was finished the kissing began.

Nancy was on her back clutching me. I was almost on top of her, both kissing away. "Stay above the collar, honey. Your kisses are dangerous. I can't figure out how you learned to kiss like that without practice and you sure didn't learn from me, Mr. Radovich."

"I love this afternoon. No cars, no strange people around, just you and I. Give me more kisses, Nancy."

In the grove were some cows waiting to drop caves. I lifted up after some serious kissing and glanced around. There was a cow balling a different way. I sat up pulling my hand away from Nancy's shirt that I was slowly unbuttoning, her bra partly exposed.

I was watching the females cows and one was acting different and I know, immediately, something was wrong. I'm wasn't paying attention to Nancy as she unsnapped her bra.

"Stay here Hun," I said, leaving her half undressed. I walked toward the cow showing trouble. I'm thinking, Oh no, this cow has birthing problems and there is no time to get a Vet.

I hollered over to Nancy. "Bring my horse over here and hand me the rope that's on my saddle, please."

"I got to get dressed, first, Mr.Cowboy."

"Forget it. I need the rope now, hurry. This cow is having a problem. I think its calf is hung up."

"Shall I ride back to the house for help?" Nancy asked.

"Not enough time. Hand me the rope and hold the halter, keep the rope low and tight and don't let loose, I'm going after the calf or we'll lose two animals."

Nancy followed my instructions and quickly we had the cow tied to the horse. I was so intent with my mission,

I barely had time to look at Nancy, standing there with her shirt open, her bra unhooked enough to see a breast looking out.

I took off my shirt and started my hand into the cows uterus. Nancy was watching intently.

"Shit! The calf is a breach and hung up. Let's walk the cow to that Oak tree. I want the cow tight to the tree so wind the rope three or four times around it, then we'll get her head against the tree.

Nancy was following instructions. "One more turn and pull hard. Great job Nancy."

I reached in one of the saddle bags and brought out some thick clear liquid and rubbed it over my right hand and my arm.

"Okay, time to work," I said, as I walked behind the cow and then slowly pushed my right hand into her birth channel. Then I asked Nancy, "Honey, keep holding the rope and come over to me. Okay, push me from the back because I've got to get the calf turned around one way or the other. The cord is going to twist around the calf's neck unless I do something smart.

Nancy followed my instructions, her bra now so loose there were two breasts showing.

"Keep pushing me. It's moving, dig in and push."

I could feel the calf moving back and starting to turn inside the cow and I could feel Nancy's breasts on my bare back as she used her body to anchor me.

"Okay Lets bring out the calf backwards, the cord is not around the neck anymore. I sure hope it's alive.

"Easy Teddy, let the cow do the work," I said to myself.

"Are you watching Nancy. Here comes the little rear hooves. Come on baby. Ooops. I got one front leg caught under the body. Don't pull now. I have to straighten that leg.

Wow, now just be alive. Here comes the calf so release the rope from the mother. Nancy, the calf is alive. We won honey. Great job. Let's let the mother take over, and I have to wash off. I'll kiss you after I clean up."

"You had better," declared Nancy, re-hooking her bra. "Thank heavens for that calf. We almost went too far with our kissing. I was scared we were going to do it. I wanted you so bad. We had better keep the love making above the shoulders. Teddy, you were magnificent. Wait till I tell Dad what you did."

"It was two of us, Nancy. I couldn't have pushed that calf back alone, to save it.

"You're right, Ted. Where we were nearly headed was too fast and too close for us.

CHAPTER 12

It was now the summer of 1955, and I'm going on to be a senior in high school with two summer jobs: one in the store, and the other a life guard teaching swimming at the city pool or on the city's beach along the Swinjoscie River.

Our town offered swimming lessons free to all the kids in town and surrounding areas.

Nancy and I teach, both being excellent swimmers. That summer we were in demand because of the river incident. We were now both considered experts around the water.

That week Nancy was assigned to the pool, and I to the river. I dropped Nancy off at the pool.

"Be careful with all the young ladies, Hon. They may try to turn you on, and that's my job not theirs?" she giggled in my ear.

I drove the old Ford panel to the river beach area that had portable locker rooms, toilets, and a snack bar. They are pulled out from the river to high ground in the fall, before the winter rains. My 1930 Ford panel was a good vehicle to have as I have a place to change and leave my clothes.

That late morning, about ten, I'm assigned to work with a group of older girls that signed up for advanced swimming lessons. They were all about sixteen to eighteen years of age. I know most of them. I couldn't believe it. In my group was

Lisa Roberts. There she stood with her shoulders back, popping both breast out. She was smiling at me.

I immediately thought about the rumors: she is someone that really knows how to put out, she will definitely go all the way down on you, she is ready to screw as she wears nothing under her dress, and bring plenty of lubricated rubbers because she is sure tight.

Looking at Lisa that morning and knowing what she was capable of, I'm wondering if this is such a great break, I mean getting her in my group. Lisa was standing away from the group of girls assigned to my class. She was wearing the latest Bikini bathing suit like it might have just arrived from France or Argentina, and I realized the temptation she was going to throw my way.

I left the group of girls and hurried into the beach side office. I walked up to Miss Solari, our adult leader, and asked her to assign me to another class. Miss Solaria was also the girls gym teacher in our high school.

"What's wrong with your class, Teddy?"

I told her, "I just prefer not to work with those girls."

"You're our best swim teacher, and these girls want more advanced instruction and your it. Is Nancy concerned about you instructing certain girls?"

"No, she is not, but you have a couple of good teachers besides me?"

"I'm sorry Teddy but you're still it. Just be professional and it will work out. Your class begins in two minutes. I know Lisa may be a bother to you, but you can handle it. I'll keep an eye on you this morning." She checked her watch. "One minute, get going Ted."

I shook my head and left. I just know that damn Lisa will pull some stunt on me to attract my attention, someway, somehow.

I gathered the girls and told them, "Okay ladies, please stand in a line and one by one, dive off the pier and swim out to the raft, around the raft without stopping, and then back so I can see your swimming form. I'll start you off in thirty-second intervals. Go out on the right and stay wide returning so you don't run into a swimmer going out. Okay ladies, you Margie, you're first."

I noticed Lisa Roberts was last in line. I didn't think she could swim. I've always seen her soaking up a tan and never in the water. She was dark chocolate brown with her tan.

Lisa was about five-six and weighed, I guess, one hundred and thirty some pounds. She's a trifle chunky. Her two piece white bathing suit didn't leave much to the imagination. Lisa had a lot more skin showing than the other girls.

Now it's her turn for the swim. That damn girl walked over to me and stood close and then asked, "How do you like my new bathing suit, Ted?"

"Well, Lisa, I hope you don't scare the fish with what little covering you have on." I try not to look at her.

"Come on Teddy, Nancy is not here. Like the way my suit is cut?" Lisa said, pulling the tiny bottom away from her skin slightly, enough that if I would have had the right angle I would have seen something interesting.

"Hardly the bathing suit Pastor Robert's daughter should be wearing, Lisa. Is that what they call a Bikini?"

"Yes, it is named after a very small island in the South Pacific." She was smiling and arched her back to bring her breasts into a better view for me. Her nipples were on the edge of being exposed.

"I'll let you know, Teddy, that I made this suit myself. We have a full moon tonight, and I thought we could do a little swimming and practice my lessons here or somewhere else with no onlookers. Have you ever skinny dipped Ted?" Lisa was smiling and raised her eyes with that remark.

"No, uh, not around here, that is."

"Oh, you must have a better place we could go?"

"Lisa, it's getting close for your turn to hit the river. Let me see how well you do."

I wasn't too sure the top or bottom of that minuscule piece of cloth, called a bathing suit, would make the trip around the raft.

Her bathing suit top, such as it was, appeared to be seeking an escape from her captured but pointed breasts. That bathing suit didn't hide anything Lisa had. It just clung to her body, leaving every thing noticeable without much imagination.

Well, like a good trooper, she dove in the river and surprised me as she could dive well and swim correctly. Her bathing suit stayed with her, as I watched carefully.

She swam smartly around the raft and returned. All she needed was just a little work on her kick. I'm also thinking, That hot body would look great in the moonlight. But, I have Nancy and that is all I need," I say quietly to myself.

When Lisa emerged, her bathing suit didn't really cling to her, it stuck to her like another skin and was somewhat transparent.

She walked up to me and said, "How did I do?"

I had to tell her the truth. "Lisa, you did exceptionally well. Just a few adjustments and that's all you need."

"Anything else you would like to say Teddy?"

I looked at her and her suit, "Yeah Lisa. Have you ever checked out your suit in the shower? What you have on is now slightly transparent."

"That's kind of the way I was hopping it would look, Teddy, thank you for noticing. Every boy I know would like to see me in my new suit, but only you have. Now what about tonight?" She pulled the top part of her suit out and away from her breasts, exposing everything, and let it snap back. The fine details are less visible, but her shape is still very apparent.

Now she told me, "Maybe after my lessons we can just swim out to the raft and talk, eat our lunch. I'll be staying here all day.

I didn't know exactly what this teenage witch was up to. Either she was trying to woo me away from Nancy, or she was trying to get me into her pants, or both. One way or the other she wanted to mess with me. Probably to hang my jockstrap above her bed along with rest of her catches.

That was some tough decision for me, but I managed to keep the ball in my court. "Oh gee, Lisa, I do have a full day of lessons.

"Teddy, honey. I checked the swimming lessons list. You only have this morning for teaching. Now show me what I was doing wrong and we will see about lunch.

"Come on Lisa. Let's get over to the rest of the class."

I gathered the class and noticed the girls giving Lisa's bathing suit some long looks. It's hard to figure what they are thinking from the expressions on their faces. I almost hoped this might be some sort of inspiration for the others, but then I think about Nancy. I sure as hell don't want her wearing a suit like that because she is mine and mine alone.

We went over the mistakes or errors they made swimming. It's the swimming kick that all of them needed to work on.

So I take each girl into the river, chest high for me, and hold her using my outstretched arms under their stomach, and have them use their swimming kicks. I correct each girl as to her errors. If there was ever a chance for a feel now was the time.

That damn Lisa was last again, and just before our lunch break. By now most of my class has drifted away for lunch. I had Lisa waiting for me to hold her up in the water. I'm sweating because I know a feel is a feel, but not with her.

"Lets get out a little deeper, Teddy. You won't have to stoop over so much," purred this female hot pants number.

That seemed to be a good idea, going where the water was deeper, and the current would work great for the kick and the swimmer would not sag down in the water, so we moved.

She put one hand down and grabbed the top of my bathing suit to hang on to and she stretched out in the water.

I told her, "Lisa, remove your hand and just place them straight out." I'm standing alongside of Lisa. I placed my hands under her stomach, and all I felt is skin.

Where did the top and the bottom of her suit go? Her darn suit is there, I know it is, but it sure felt like skin. I tried to hold her slightly and told her, "Okay, use your kicks.

Just release that hand and stick both of them straight out in front, please."

"No," she said. "I'll hold on to you this way, and you tell me what I'm doing wrong."

There was enough river current, where we were, to keep a body out in a straight line. Lisa still had a grip on my bathing suit, only using one hand to hold herself into the current.

I tried to explain to her about her kick.

She's not paying any attention to my words. Now her free hand was coming under the pant leg of my suit and moving up higher. I'm surprised at what she is doing, but I couldn't move. Her hand was trying to get under my built in jock and she was about to have me in a, well, I guess it could be called a sensitive, stimulating situation.

I took one of my hands off her stomach to push her hand away, but she grabbed it and tried to shove it on one of her breasts as she was still digging to get under my jock inside my suit.

"Ted, I like this part of the lesson. Can we go for more lessons tonight?"

I looked around to see if anyone had taken an interest in what she was doing to me. So far everyone was in the shade eating their lunch, and I've got a 'hot pants' hanging on to me and I'm getting hard inside my jock.

There's only one thing I could think to do. I pulled my hand away from her breast, then shoved Lisa's head under the water and she let loose of me quick.

She came up sputtering. "What in hell are trying to do to me, drown me so you can count me as another girl you saved? Teddy, I want you to know I have boys hanging onto trees just for the chance to take me out. Do you know that?"

"Sure do. Go find yourself that tree, Lisa. I don't like to play these games with you. You are trouble, and I want nothing to do with you now, tonight, tomorrow, or ever. Get your well used hot body out of here and take a cold shower at home and cool off. I'm canceling your lessons with me. Head for shore and take that cock teasing bathing suit home with you, now."

She gave me a long look and with a smile she told me, "I'm still going to fuck you until your eyes fall out, come hell or high water. Don't you forget what I said."

Lisa wiggled to shore and grabbed her towel and never turned around to look at me.

I slowly returned to shore because I was still hard and I watch Lisa driving away. Damn, I'm mad. I walked into the make-shift office and Miss Solaria was sitting in an old scratched up office chair eating an apple.

"How did the swimming lessons go?" she asked slyly with a wide smile.

I noticed a pair of binoculars on her desk.

All right except for one person named Lisa Robert's. I don't want anything to do with her, ever, here or at the pool, or anywhere else. She is just bad news. Lisa thinks she can just wiggle her rear end or flop breasts around and boys will come running. Well, maybe they do, but not me."

"Ted. I saw what she did to you this morning," Miss Solaria confided. "I think you handled it correctly. I talked to Lisa, briefly, when she was leaving and told her, 'Young lady, you're history in this summer swimming classes. I don't want you back this year, and as long as I'm running this show, never show up wearing that bathing suit. Just one more stunt with one of our male lifeguards and I'll talk, eye ball to eye ball with your father and mother.'

As she left she told me, 'You can tell Teddy honey, I'm gonna get him in bed, yet.'"

"That's her all right. I don't want to have anything to do with her, Miss Solaria. I'm dating Nancy Blake and that is just great with me. Lisa has a figure and knows how to use it. All the boys know it, but I'm not interested in her one bit. How can I handle that problem?"

Miss Solaria leaned back and smiled. "Do you have any idea how many boys would like to have your problem with Lisa? My suggestion is; you tell Nancy the first opportunity you have. Lisa can alter her story to try and finish you off with Nancy, but any problems and you refer Nancy to me. Eat your lunch and I'll have another class for you in the afternoon. These kids are much younger so you're safe with them. Go eat your lunch and don't worry."

After my afternoon class I changed and went to pick up Nancy at the pool. She was waiting for me.

"High my love," I said to Nancy. "How's your swimming classes coming along?"

"No problems. I did have to push one smart-ass Freshman boy away from me as he tried to cop a feel. I told him, 'One more stunt like that and I'll kick you off the swimming lesson list and it won't be done with a pen or pencil.'

Now, how was your day, my sweet and steady love? No problems?" Nancy was giving me a smile that told me she knew.

"Well, Nancy, it was an advanced class and they did good except for one."

"Really? All those hot bodied, high school girls, and you had only one problem? You never let your hand wander around on some young girl's skin, feeling her up? Not just a time or two? Come on Ted, tell me the truth. I didn't know you could be that cool?"

"If you don't count Lisa Roberts's lesson, no, I had had no problems."

"Well, my dearest, Lisa stopped by and tried to talk to me about you. I wouldn't listen to her because Miss Solaria called me just before Lisa arrived. Don't worry, I got the full scoop so I was able to tell Lisa what she can do with flaunting her well used sex around my man. So you are now wondering; is Lisa worth the effort. Better say no way?"

"My lovely, blue-eyed Nancy, there was no need for you to worry about what Lisa has or thinks she has. No, Nancy, I'm with you."

That remark got me a series of kisses from Nancy. I'll bet Lisa doesn't kiss like Nancy, or does she?

CHAPTER 13

MY MOTHER INFORMED ME that my cousin, Samantha Prudence Drinkwater, from Florida will be coming to stay with us for a couple of weeks.

Mom outlined my responsibilities concerning Samantha, "You will show your cousin a good time and remember she is your cousin."

I don't understand Mom's statement until I look at Samantha's photos that came with her letter. After looking at Sam's eight pictures I decide to try to steer her clear of Nancy. Two photos looked like some model showing off a new line of dresses. Samantha appeared to be five-feet-six or seven, close to Nancy's height. Three other photos show her in tight shorts with a revealing top. The remaining three are of her in three different bikinis and has she got some figure. Not much cloth seems to there to hide her fully developed body. I immediately think of Lisa Roberts in her bikini. There seems to be the same scant amount of coverage, but Samantha seems to have a more athletic, more defined physique. I'm sure not going to show these bikini pictures to Nancy. Maybe to a few friends, but definitely not Miss Nancy Blake. I hope Nancy will not be too upset with Samantha staying here.

*   *   *

I show Nancy the two pictures of Samantha, apparently modeling, so Nancy can see what she looks like. Nancy takes her time looking at the two photos. "Pleasant looking girl, Ted. She looks as though she has a great figure, a little better than Lisa Roberts."

Man-oh-man, this is going to be a tough one. "But Nancy," I tell her, sounding defensive, "she is just a cousin and only fifteen years old, that's all."

"I'm aware of that, so I know you won't marry her, but you might find some other things you can do with her," Nancy said matter of factually, still looking at the photos, "that I won't know about," she added pointedly.

"What are you talking about? You haven't met her, my dear."

"Oh yes I have," Nancy said, flipping the photos on my lap. "Have you?"

"I saw her eight or ten years ago when they came up here to visit us."

"Do you have any more pictures of your cousin, and I don't mean baby photos?"

"Yes, in my pocket. I'll show you." I carefully brought out the three of the six photos of Samantha in her in shorts and halters. I tried to palm the three that have her in bikinis.

"See, here is a couple more she sent."

"Hmmm, she sure looks more grown up in these pictures."

"Nancy, her mother says her daughter is very mature."

"She looks it. Okay Ted, show me the photos you tried to hide from me. Honey, they're in your left pocket."

"Nancy, you're some observant gal and hard to understand."

"My dear Ted. You must learn this. Women are born that way. Remember when we studied about Sigmund Freud; I'll try to quote the master. 'The great question that has never been answered and which I have not yet been able to answer, despite my thirty years of research into the feminine soul, is, 'What does a woman want?'"

"Okay, okay, smarty, here's the pictures." I slowly pull the pictures out and give her the three photos with Samantha in her small and thin Bikinis.

"Holy cow, Ted! Do girls wear bathing suits like that in Florida? These pictures make Lisa Roberts overdressed."

"Remember, honey, this girl is only fifteen, Lisa Roberts is much older. I'm told, she is older than her age or thinks she is. Worldly I believe would be a better description."

Nancy shook her head. "Honey, Samantha will only be here two weeks, and you're going to show her around. I think she will show you, I mean show 'us' a few things. I have a feeling she can show us both what's around the block with that figure and red hair. I don't know, Hon?" Nancy said, still looking at the pictures.

"Nancy, I promise, years from now you will still be my steady girl and wife."

"Nancy grabbed me and said, "Better keep that in your mind, always, Ted. You're mine, especially for the next two weeks."

For the next couple of weeks I would have two women to pack around. To start with; Nancy wanted to eye ball Samantha when she arrived in town. Great! And now every boy in town wanted to see my cousin up close because word had gotten around. What are my chances? So this fifteen-year old girl would fly into our county airport with, according to her pictures, well appointed breasts, hips, and a figure of unbelievable portions. With the face and lips of a back seat 'necker' or worse, a 'puter' outer."

How can girls wear such skimpy bathing suits, yet complain about the stares they receive?

Nancy suggested I take Samantha around when she arrived. As I look at the photos again, I decide I'm not too thrilled about hauling this girl anywhere, considering how much trouble it could be.

Later, Nancy called me at the store. "Ted, honey, I talked to Mimi and she agreed it would be a good idea for me to meet Samantha when she arrives. At least I'll be able to see her before any of my girlfriends hit the telephone circuit and tie up our telephone for hours. You know Dad, he'll be upset, in grand style, with me on the phone with the whole student body of girls. Then I'll be mad at you because you'll be packing your sexy cousin around town for two weeks. I'm going to the airport with you and Mimi, end of subject," Nancy said emphatically.

*   *   *

Mom, Nancy, and I drove to meet Samantha at the county airport. We didn't see her at first as the plane emptied, but we knew she was coming off by the way people were leaving the plane. The departing passengers were turning to watch for someone coming down those steps behind them and not hustling to get their suitcases. Strange?

Then a fifteen-year old girl with flaming red hair and the figure of a well developed twenty-year old was the last off the airplane wearing a tight skirt and showing more seductive movements in her five-six or seven frame than I've ever seen before. Slowly, step by step, she descended the passenger stairs using her walk to show off her hips, legs and moving breasts. She didn't just walk down the plane's stairs, Samantha used slow, deliberate steps as though she was entering some elaborate function or meeting the queen.

This red-headed, short-shirted, sexual machine continued down, doing the silent introduction even better than Lisa Roberts could. She came off that plane with pomposity and dignity and she was only fifteen years old. How am I going to endure even one day with this cousin around our house and she will be with us for two weeks?

Mom mumbled to me, "God Almighty, that Samantha sure has changed in the six years since we last saw her. She's certainly changed into a traffic stopper.

Nancy stood open mouthed with wide eyes, staring at Samantha and her grand entrance. "Good heavens," she said, "is our quaint back-water town ready for this? I know I'm not, what ever she is.

Even the two pilots were now standing at the door of their airplane, looking, I guess, just to see her walk away.

I look around and saw people gathering at the protective fence between the airplane and the terminal all watching Samantha.

I put my arm around Nancy and told her, "It's no big deal, remember, she's just a cousin."

With Samantha as the cousin, what will I do for fourteen long days?

"Cousin trouble," Nancy said.

Mom received a, "High Aunt Marie," and a kiss from Samantha. Then this fifteen-year old bomb-shell turned to me and gave me a look. "You must be Teddy," she squealed with delight and flew into my arms, and I darn near fell over with this hot body in my possession. Then I received a kiss that even Nancy or Dee Dee could take lessons from.

Whew.

I extracted myself from her and saw Mom and Nancy both turning their backs to me and pretending to be blowing their noses. I know both of them are laughing.

"Hi Samantha," I stumbled, nervous as all get out. "Welcome to Daisy Junction and its eight-thousand people."

"Nice to see you again 'cousin' Teddy or is it Ted?" she asked me.

"Either one will do," I answered uncomfortably, not sure how to proceed. "Let me introduce you to my girl friend. Then I'll get your bags."

"Okay," her voice changed to sultry, "but do you know you are more handsome than your pictures you sent, and I didn't know you were so tall and good looking. You're surely not like the boys I know back home. You can call me Flash if you wish. Everybody calls me that because of my red hair."

The Florida Flash turned to Nancy. "So you are this good looking guy's steady?"

Nancy grabbed my left hand giving it a very hard squeeze. "Yes, we've been together a long time and care deeply about each other."

I'm thinking, There has to be more than just red hair to be called Flash.

Samantha grabbed my arm, "Say, cousin, I have three bags. I wanted to take more but Mom would not allow it."

Nancy squeezed my hand even harder.

* * *

There are only two daily flights in and out of our small regional airport, and people with nothing to do at the arrival times consider plane and passenger watching a viable recreational event. It's also a heads up as to someone important or interesting spending some time in Daisy Junction. This morning, the 'watchers' gathered close to the fence are exceedingly well rewarded.

Even the waitresses, cooks, and customers from Joe's Air Coffee Shop have been alerted and are now on the steps watching. I'm figuring one of the pilots radioed ahead, "Watch what gets off our plane this morning," or something like that so a bigger crowd than I've ever seen was watching 'The Florida Flash' do her thing.

Samantha grabbed my arm and pulled me toward the stacked bags from the flight.

I look around, and part of the local crowd seems to be following along side us from outside the fence, and Mom was talking to a couple of people she knew, but kept glancing my way. Nancy was really staring at us.

Flash grabbed my elbow and pushed a breast against my arm, then pointed. "That red bag on the bottom is mine. The yellowish one near the top looks like mine, and the big black bag all alone, mine. Grab them and lets go."

Three big bags, and she wanted me to carry them. The red and yellow bags I can handle, but that big black bag, I may need help.

A big, burley baggage handler came to our assistance. "Let me Miss."

"No!" replied Flash. "My dearest cousin will take care of them. I came all the way from Florida to visit with him and I'm sure he'll handle my every need." Flash gave me a seriously provocative look, and I suddenly realized how blue her eyes were.

Funny, I didn't notice that before.

"I thank you for offering," Flash brushed the disappointed looking man off.

Passengers were trying to find their bags, but they were delaying slightly as they took in Flash, the red head show stopper.

They were also giving me glances. I got some grins, some curious looks, some critical, and some, I think, are sympathetic.

I tell her, handing her the small red bag, "Take this one, and I'll handle the rest. Let's get going, I want to get out of here."

Her black bag felt like it was stuck to the tarmac. I didn't know what she had in this bag, but an anvil or a set of plow blades could be about right. "What's in this bag, Samantha? I can hardly lift it."

"Just my makeup, shoes, and some clothes. I met your girlfriend, doesn't she use makeup?"

"Nancy uses very little makeup."

"Is she your steady or do you have more than one girlfriend?"

"No, Nancy is my steady."

We walked toward Mom and Nancy. Both were giving Samantha a careful look. Samantha moved in close to me and whispered, "Good looking person like you with one plain girl that doesn't use makeup. My word Ted, you're going steady with a plain Jane? She must be your first?"

I nod my head as we walk up to Mom and Nancy. I broadcast, "The Florida Flash is ready to go."

Samantha looked at Nancy. "So you're the only one for Teddy?"

Nancy looked at Samantha. "You got it right. He's mine to spoil, mine to train, and mine to keep."

Samantha replied, "If I were you, I would think the exact same way. What a beginning you two had. I read the letter about your experience on the river. You were both so brave, a couple of real heros, and here I am with them. You pinned yet?"

"Not yet Samantha. I'll have that taking care of about graduation time, just a short year away because Teddy is still in training."

* * *

We left the airport, with Samantha and Mom in the front seat, and Nancy and I in the back. Nancy is almost sitting on my lap, squeezing my hand and rubbing my back.

We stopped first at Nancy's house to let her off, then to our cafe in for lunch. Dad took one look at Samantha coming into his store and he let out a loud, "Wow! So, Samantha, last time I saw you, you were just a scrawny kid. You are a dead ringer for your mother when she was in her teens. I understand you are sometimes called Flash?"

Flash walked up to Dad and gave him a hug and a kiss on the cheek.

"Do you remember anything about your last visit?" Dad asked her.

"I remember that you and Dad sure got into trouble with Mom and Aunt Marie when you two went to that football game and came home very late."

"As I remember, it was your father, and not me that kept us late."

"Not the story I heard because Mom lit into you for leading Dad astray."

"Well, Samantha, it wasn't exactly as you say, but close. Your dad and I generally can find some trouble when we get together. How was your trip? Enjoyable?"

"Yes, except some of those men aboard, I guess, never saw a girl before. Talk about giving me looks. I thought their eyeballs were going to fall out. I wonder if they do that to their daughters?"

Mother answered, "They shouldn't, but with other young women they are still little boys, men that haven't grown up. Well, Samantha, let us all grab a booth and have lunch."

I don't know how it always happens, but fate always plays a major role because, for some reason, many of my classmates just happened to come in the store. Every one of them had to stop by our booth for some silly question or talk about something very non-important.

I introduced Samantha to everyone, and she told them all, "My friends call me 'Flash', and you can to."

I saw more eyes sparkle from my friends than ever before. I'll bet Nancy's phone is ringing right now.

So I excused myself and used the store's phone and called Nancy. Two rings and she answered. That was quick!

"High sweet—" that was as far as I got.

"Well, Mr. Radovich you positively have the town buzzing."

"Me?"

"Well, not you, but that first-prize red head you brought into town. My mother says our phone has been ringing from the time she got off the plane. Should I be jealous?"

"Certainly not my dear, you're my only one. Promise you wont uncage your fingernails. I'll have to show her the town before I take her home. Want to ride with us?"

"We three in your Model A? Who gets the goosey-seat and who sits in the back on the horse blankets you have never washed or take out, dear?"

"I'll take the folk's car."

"Okay, but you have to kiss me."

"Don't I always?"

"Yes, always, but this time it has to be a bell ringer so Flash will get the real picture. Got it?"

* * *

After lunch Samantha and I drive over to Nancy's house. As we drive up, Samantha said, "Wow, some house, are they rich?"

"Her father is a doctor."

Sam tagged behind me as we headed up the sidewalk, and I saw Nancy's bedroom window curtain move.

Mrs. Blake opened the door, and I introduced Samantha to her. I'm trying not to use the word Flash.

I could hear Nancy coming down the stairs very slowly. She made her appearance and was really dressed up and had applied a little makeup.

"Hey sweet lady, you have a date tonight that I don't know about?" I jokingly asked.

"No, but a kiss from you, and I might change my mind." Nancy said, walking up and pressing her self tight to me.

So I received a very interesting, long kiss, as Nancy gave Flash a smile that said, "All mine."

Mrs. Blake was just coming back into the living room with a tray of some soft drinks and cookies.

Nancy looked at Samantha and asked her, "Does anyone call you Sam?

"Not really, I like to go by Flash, Nancy." It seemed to be instructions rather than an answer.

Mrs. Blake suddenly turned around and went back to the kitchen still carrying the tray with the cokes and cookies.

I'm sure the girls didn't see her enter the room or know she had turned around and left.

I excused myself and went into the kitchen.

Mrs. Blake had a shocked look on her face.

I asked her, "May I do the honors, Mrs. Blake?"

"Thank you Teddy." In a whisper she asked, "Is that her name, Flash?"

I nodded yes.

Mrs. Blake motioned for me to take the tray.

When I entered the living room, the girls were in deep discussion.

"Samantha, you are telling me you do not date, ever?" Nancy asked.

"That's right, Nancy. We have an excel program in school, and I want to keep my grades high so I study. I'm not allowed to socially date yet, my mother's idea. I guess it's okay by me. When did you start to date?"

"Really date?" Nancy answered. "When I was a sophomore some geek dated me for a while, then Ted asked me out for a picnic that we'll never forget as much as we try. That picnic did it, and we decided to go steady right then. He is the most perfect gentlemanly person I have ever known."

"Gee whiz Nancy, with his blond hair, blue eyes, and his height, I would think every girl in school would be trying to get a date with him."

"Don't forget his athletic endeavors and his high scholarship grades," Nancy was bragging me up. "He is also on an excel program, well, in fact, we are both in that program."

I'm still holding the tray with cokes and cookies. "When you two ladies get through dissecting me would you like cokes and cookies?"

"Set the tray down Honey, we're talking. See whether mother needs any help," suggested Nancy.

So Mrs. Blake and I have a long conversation seated out in her garden. Finally, we walk in the house and Nancy and Samantha are in a deep discussion about makeup and clothes. Nancy suggested her and Samantha go upstairs to her room and try on some of Nancy's clothes.

After the two girls headed upstairs Mrs. Blake asked, "Teddy, is that girl Samantha real?"

"I guess so. She's my cousin. She appears so worldly, but I don't know. I'm worried the way she presents herself she will always attract the wrong person, Mrs. Blake."

"Teddy, leave her here. Chet will be home early tonight. I think with Nancy and Chet and I, we may be able to help her make the right choices. Don't worry Honey, she is worth the time. In the end, I'm sure she will be a very proper young woman."

Feeling better, I went into the living room and the two girls are still talking. "Sorry ladies, but I have to feed the horses."

Nancy jumped up and came to me, grabbing me around my neck, giving me a kiss then said, "Leave Samantha here and come back later, Honey. We have a lot to talk over."

Wow. Those two hit it off right now, just like sisters.

"Teddy," said Samantha, "Nancy surely knows the clothes and makeup to look conservative. This is great to have someone give me a hand on what 'I' should wear.

Samantha turned to Nancy. "Let's go upstairs Nancy." Then back to me. "How much time can we spend, Ted?"

"All afternoon. I'll take the folk's car back and comeback later with the Model A."

"Ted, have Mimi call me when you get to the store." Mrs. Blake said.

*   *   *

Mother and Mrs. Blake were on the phone for some time. Mom told me they were discussing Samantha or Flash. "Mrs. Blake could not get over Samantha's nickname 'Flash' and the way the two girls hit it off so soon."

*   *   *

Three hours later I drive my Model A over to the Blake's house. Dr. Blake was home and in a big discussion with Mrs. Blake, Samantha, and Nancy. The talking stopped when I entered the living room.

"Did I interrupt anything?"

"Just not your side of the street, Honey," replied Nancy giving me a wide smile.

"Well, Samantha, time to go because we are having dinner with Gramp and Gram," I said.

Dr. Blake said to me, "Ted, give the Radovichs our best."

Nancy stood up and gave me a squeeze, saying, "Tomorrow, can you take Samantha on a tour of our town or are you working at the store?"

"No, the folks gave me time off to show Samantha around."

"Well, Mr. Radovich, I am going along, if it's all right with you Samantha?"

"Absolutely Nancy. We had a great visit, and I can see why Teddy selected you as a steady. We girls and the Blakes had a wonderful conversation." Samantha gave everyone a benevolent smile. "I could easily live here."

Mrs. Blake looked at me. "You, Samantha, Mimi, and Val are having dinner with us tomorrow night."

I looked at Nancy, "You have a date for tomorrow night?"

"Sure I have, it's you. Mom just forgot I was here."

*   *   *

Samantha and I left the Blake's and headed home.

The redhead, Flash, can't stop talking about Nancy and her folks. "I learned so much talking to Nancy in her room and then down stairs with her folks. No wonder you date Nancy. You know, we will write to each other."

"I have never heard any girl talk about her boyfriend as she does about you. Ted, you must be the best and what you two did at the river, wow. Listening to Nancy, and looking at you two, you guys are like twins. Talk about two people that are alike in studies, thoughts, and appearance, it's unbelievable."

"Dr. Blake is like the father I never had and straighten me out in many things I should have known and didn't. You're so lucky to have the parents you have. They're great just like the Blakes."

"Well, I'm glad you like Nancy. We were born two days apart, were in bassinets in the hospital next to each other and we have gone through all these grades together."

"Ted, Nancy told me she asked you to go steady and then how you saved her life. I never heard that story. We read about it from the clippings your folks sent us, but they didn't even come close to what really happened. She told me you are just like your dad when the danger came from those men you had trouble with. I'm proud of my kissing cousin. Did Uncle Val ever tell you what he did during the war?"

"No, he never talks to me about that side of his life. I do know he had some dangerous and tight events, that's all. Please remember, it wasn't just me down at that river, Samantha. Nancy played a big part in that situation we faced there. We make a strong couple because our minds work together."

"You know, Ted, You have all characteristics I will want in my man."

We were a few miles from home, and I'm driving slow. "If I may, cousin, I would like to offer this suggestion. My feelings only."

"Okay, I would honor your thoughts, Ted."

I take a deep breath and said to Samantha, "You need to change your approach and appearance. Forgive me for saying this, but to all males you appear to be the biggest sex object that walks on two feet. You appear to be a sex machine and you're not. It's too easy for you to be misunderstood just because of your figure, your walk, and the clothes you wear. Every male at the airport was sweating over your appearance as you walked down the airplane stairs. You even had my blood surging through my body."

"Teddy, I just heard nearly the same from Nancy and the Blakes."

"Well, our first impression of you was misunderstood by your friendliness, your great looks that accents a willing and an easy 'put out' body, if you accept my observations. Do you see what I'm saying?"

"Teddy, no one has ever said that to me until today and now twice. I don't date yet, but I would love to find a boy that has every asset you have as a gentleman and concerned person, one I could trust."

"You will find that person, but let that person grow with you and don't overwhelm the boy. Measure him carefully. Do you see where I'm trying to go?"

"Absolutely. Nancy raves about you as person and a gentleman. She trusts you explicitly. Not only the river episode, but you every day, every moment you two are together, and the way you two look at each other, I want a guy like you that keeps his mind and his hands under control. All of my life I have had grouping hands, stupid suggestions, and boys trying for a make on me. I'm going change. Nancy said just about the same to me and Dr. Blake gave me some ideas to follow. Darn, I'm so happy to be here with brand new true friends."

*   *   *

The next day, Nancy, Samantha, and I toured the town. Nancy and Samantha had exchanged some clothes so Samantha looked different, more chaste, and Nancy, well Nancy looked . . . ah, more . . . delightful.

"Nancy, is that one of Samantha's sweaters?" I asked sheepishly.

"Sure, oh, I know what your thinking in your evil mind Honey. I shouldn't wear her sweaters unless I fill them out so I stuffed my bra. Won't have the bounce, though, huh?"

*   *   *

The two girls made me go with them for some quick shopping that lasted all afternoon. Nancy kept telling me, as I traipsed along, "Honey, I'm breaking you in right and proper as we will always be together. I want an understanding husband and never be a groaner. Good time for you to begin to be tolerant, understanding me in particular, and women in general."

"Nancy," Samantha said gripping my hand with her's, "I would take any of your throughway boy friends, anything even close to Teddy here?"

"I've only had one other boy before and he's not your type, believe me. He wasn't my type, that's why I decided Teddy was going to be my man."

So it went all afternoon and early evening. The girls stroking my ego constantly.

Finally it was time to go to the Blake's for dinner.

*   *   *

Inside the Blake's, Mom asked me how it went.

"Mom, I've been walking, standing, listening, and learning; never go shopping with a female, especially two of them."

"You're learning, Honey, but it won't work like you think. To young women shopping is a rite of womanhood."

*   *   *

Next morning, Samantha asked me, "What are we going to do today, leader?" as she got in the Model A. She's wearing one of Nancy's school skirts and sweater. The skirt comes close to her knees, which is something different for this girl once called Flash.

"How about me showing you our town before I take you to Nancy's house? This will give you an insight to tell your friends when you return to Florida."

"Okay leader, lead the way. Are we taking your Model A again?"

"Well, you also have two other choices, a bicycle or walk. I'm sure neither one will interest you as we are four miles from town."

"If Nancy can take the Model A seats so can I, let's go leader."

I'm driving somewhat slow into town and I tell her, "Let me tell you all about this town, Samantha. Just look straight down this street, that's Main, and you can see the Swinjoscie River in the distance? Maybe I should first tell you how our town got started."

"I'd love to get a history lesson from you Ted, but do you really know just what those springs are trying to do to me?"

Giving Samantha a look because I'm not going to bite on that statement I toss her a pillow, then continued my story about Daisy Junction.

"Samantha, we were first settled by a German mercenary soldier who left the British Army during the War of 1812."

"How do you know all this Teddy?"

"I'm kind of know as the assistant town historian and my mentor, Mr. Ivan Stankorvich, is the official expert and the history teacher at the high school. His family has been here from the beginning so his information is accurate."

"Mr. Ivan, we are allowed to call him by his first name, tells us, 'Our town was once a trading post. It was founded by Oleg Petrovich and he came from an area in Europe we now call Poland. Oleg was conscripted into the English Army as a mercenary soldier when the British and German mercenaries were fighting the American Revolutionary Soldiers.'"

"When was that?" Samantha asked, moving to the edge of her seat, getting closer to me. "Those damn springs are doing things to me," she said matter of faculty.

"Way back in 1812, Samantha," I say, kind of leaning away from her.

"According to Mr. Stankorvich, Oleg was not a good soldier and only signed on because it was the only way he could get to America, the promise land. It was during a skirmish with the Americans that Oleg's reputation as a soldier ended. Oleg, trying to act as a soldier, took careful aim on an American. Somehow Oleg mistakenly shot his commanding officer's horse and the officer's right big toe off with the same shot."

Samantha wiggled her butt a little, moving closer to the edge of the offending seat. "Oh Teddy, this seat is doing nasty things to me."

"Since Oleg never could march in step," I gulped nervously, leaning my left arm out the window, "and now with his poor marksmanship he was quickly dismissed from the British Army and was told to get lost.

Samantha makes a sound I'm sure is a moan.

"Then he then tried to join up with the American Army, the revolutionists. This group told poor old Oleg, 'Your reputation as a soldier is well known to us.' I guess word traveled fast even back then. The Americans also suggested Oleg take a hike."

"He wandered away and eventually came to an unnamed river so Oleg named this river, Swinjoscie, for the town he came from in Poland."

"Teddy are you making this story up?" Samantha asked, leaning forward and pulling Nancy's sweater up over her head.

"I would never make up a story, Samantha?" I replied, looking over at her. My god, she doesn't have a bra under her blouse.

I quickly look back to the road. "Because this is documented history," I said seriously, trying not to look at Samantha who is now stretching her upper body, pulling the material tight, with no damn bra on.

"Around the new Swinjoscie River grew a flower, now known as the Dandelion, a native plant in America. However, these flowers reminded Oleg of the daisy's that grew around his native home so he called this place, in English, Daisy Crossing. Eventually, he set up a trading post and traded a husky wine he made from the dandelions he thought were daisies and the wild grapes that also grew profusely in this area. He fortified his wine with alcohol made from the abundant grapes and honey he gathered.

"It is getting hot, Teddy," Samantha said, then threw her arms high over her head, pulling the material of the blouse tight against her chest.

In my peripheral I can see a nipple poking through the tight fabric.

"Oleg's wine kept the Indians in a mellow state of alcohol suspension. Well, actually, these Indians were never war like, like some of the other tribes."

Then Samantha grabbed the inside ridge of the Model A roof, hanging her upper body weight from her outstretched shoulders and arms. "That's better," she said in a soft, seductive voice.

"Finally," I continued like I was oblivious to what she was doing, "he hooked up with an Indian maiden named

Sleeping Moon. They made more wine and traded with Indians far and wide for furs.

"Sleeping Moon," said Samantha. "That's what you need Teddy, a sleeping moon." Samantha let her head fall toward me, like she is going to fall asleep on my shoulder, but luckily she is just a little to far away.

"Then Oleg decided to have the Indians make braided deer hide into something like rope," I continue, thankful because I can't get any tighter to my door and still drive. "This was to aid people crossing the Swinjoscie River and this became his toll crossing. The local Indians and the French fur traders had to pay a toll, in furs, to get back and forth across the river. When they were on Oleg's trading post side of the river his wine was sold or traded for furs, and Oleg became very successful."

"Many more people came to this area because it was very prosperous, but many left because of the weather conditions. You name the day and you might find winter in summer, summer in winter and spring in the fall."

"Like today huh, Teddy?" Samantha purred, "It is supposed to be spring and yet here we are driving around and it's getting hot." Flash spread her legs, sliding down on the seat, the skirt riding up her fabulous legs.

I need to do something, now . . . come on Ted, if you don't stop this it is going to get out of control.

"I do enjoy describing our town," I blunder on with the description of the town. "Look down Main Street, it's right in front of us. This is the only street that is straight in our town. It starts at the bridge that crosses Swinjoscie River and it ends at our park, that big green area with trees we're coming up to. We have a statue right in the middle of

Daisy Junction Park and it's, supposedly a likeness of Oleg Petrovich."

Flash stops me dead in my speech when she pulls her legs up, thrusts them out and slams them on the dashboard. The skirt rides up farther.

Luckily old Oleg's statue is out my window and I can look way from Flash and her creamy, shapely legs. "Notice how proudly he stands pointing, supposedly to the West, but, anyone carrying anything better than a cracker box, ten-cent compass will say he is pointing south."

"Which way is that?" Flash asked me.

"Huh?" I turned to look at the direction she wants to know about and immediately realized I had been suckered because Flash was half laying in the seat, the leg nearest me splayed out in my direction. I saw her flat belly and a little way down between her legs before I whipped my head back to straight in front.

Flash just lets out with a wicked giggle.

"Right behind this statue of Oleg is a World War One cannon," I plodded on with the narrative, but something was not right, "and it seems to point to the rear end of Oleg. Sometime during our school year the senior class students will paint a bulls eye on the rear end of Oleg Petrovich's statue.

I didn't see any hair."

"About every ten years some people in our community will try to have Oleg turned around, facing the old cannon. Two things are wrong with that thought: first, the cannon will point directly to Oleg's crotch," There's no hair in her crotch. "and second, Oleg will be pointing East, and he came west to get here, unless he is pointing to his homeland."

I heard Flash move in the seat, but didn't look her way to see what adjustment she's made. "Our local rug and curtain merchant, Ali Mustafa, wants Oleg pointing east. Local people always asks Mustafa, Why east, Ali?"

"I want him to point to Mecca."

"Why? What's Mecca, Ali?"

Ali Mustafa always replied, "You Christians are all alike."

All the other girls that let me look at them all had hair down there.

"Look down Main Street and you will see a blue sign hanging next to the Bank of Parish. Yes, the bank was named after our county seat. I always wondered where the name Parish came from."

I hazard a glance Flash's way and get what I deserve. She was lying back in the corner of the cab, looking my way intently. Her legs were apart and for the first time in my life I got a look at the real thing, right there, right in front of me and there was nothing hiding the female part of the anatomy. Now I knew where the nasty words that were used to describe a woman came from.

Flash smiled at me and said, "Go on Teddy, I like the way you can describe things."

All of a sudden, Flash had made me comfortable and I was excited to tell her more about Daisy Junction. "Some say it refers to a house, or an a religious area of certain denomination tightly controlled by a church or a civil division within a state and that is used throughout Louisiana. We are a way far from that state, but it appeals to me because they don't have any snow or cold weather. When I go to a college, it has to be where the sun shines most of the time and there is no snow or cold weather."

"That's what it's like where I live," Flash said. "You would like Florida."

Again, it's like she was calming me with the voice of a siren.

"Look over there by that bank and the drug store." This time the direction was over Flash and I looked and pointed right over her, not nervous about the future.

Flash pulled herself up and turned to look out the window and now I got a different look of the female lower half. Again, it was nothing but fascinating.

Flash rested her chin on the door frame, her butt cheeks right up there for my inspection and said, "Oh look, The All American Cafe and Confectionary Store, your family store.

"Belonged, to my Grandpa Egor and Grandma Olena. Dad bought it when he was still in the Army and my mom left nursing and operated the store with my grandparents until dad retired from the army in 1948. Dad worked four years with the OSS in the old Yugoslavian countries during World War Two. Dad did some type of secret work in that part of the world. He never talks to me about it."

I was actually so involve in my history lesson that it was an equal to my fascination with the fully exposed female there with me.

Flash turned back toward me and scratched herself. I know she is relieving an itch and it had everything to do with male, female.

"Our cafe is a hangout for all the kids in high school," I continued. "They come in for lunch and then after school for something sweet like sodas and sundaes. We also make candy right in front of the customers. Gramps still makes the candy and Grandma is the chocolate candy dipper. She makes them V's, and C's, and the other signs showing what kind of centers are in the chocolate creamers.

Right over to your right." Flash again turned to look, exposing her bare rear end. "goes Diego Blanca. Right there by the post office, see him? He is always bent over when he walks.

Usually, he goes by the name 'Mule.' He's one of the elected Aldermen that run the town. Supposedly, Diego's hand is in a couple of our local entertainment businesses that are on the slightly illegal side. Think gambling and six houses of prostitution.

Samantha asked, "How much do the girls get?"

"Huh?" I asked, caught off guard.

"How much do they charge?"

"Who are you talking about?"

"The girls, the business, how much does it take to get a girl?"

"How should I know?" I'm trying to be aloof about this latest twist, but I suddenly get the feeling Flash is asking questions for a reason.

"Teddy, you know what I'm talking about."

"Yeah, I guess I do. Well, it depends on the girl." I look over to Flash who has this grin on her face. She indicates her exposed womanhood with a nod and asked," What would they pay for this?"

"Samantha!" I shouted, trying to look shocked, but she again nodded to the thing between her legs.

"How much would 'you' pay?" she looked at me seriously.

"I, ah, I . . . ah, I," I stammered, completely exposed as a rube.

"Oh Teddy, if we were doing business, you couldn't afford it."

"Now wait a minute, how do you know how much money I have?"

"I don't exactly, but it's not enough for this." Flash spread her legs wide and I got the premium view.

"Holly shit!" I exclaimed.

"Teddy, anytime you want, you can have it for free. Now I want to hear more about this goofy town. Back home in Florida there isn't any real interest in history. The direction of choice is forward, forward. I want to hear more about this Mule guy."

"Yes, Mule. Mule raised mules one time, but now he lives up on the Heights area. That is where the people with money live. No flood waters can reach the Heights. Also, a slight breeze in the summer gives this area a cooling effect, but in the winter a damn cold feeling."

"A rich mule skinner?" Flash seemed amused.

"Dad says; if someone can figure mules out, watch out for them because they are stubborn beyond reason. Mule is rightly named for he's one stubborn money grabber. He surely got his money, but not for raising mules.

"Look to your right, see that woman going into the bank? That is Rose Mary Klatch, known to all as Rosy. Built like a brick, well you know what I mean."

Am I built like a brick?" Samantha giggled, putting both hands down into her crotch and rubbing her inner thighs.

I look at Samantha rubbing away and say, "I 'cannot' imagine where that term came from. Doesn't make any sense now, looking at you."

Samantha started laughing and pulled her hands up.

"She is put together," I continued, "for a forty-something woman, never married. I understand she is a fun person to be with if you know what I mean?"

"I do, I do," Samantha giggled.

"Once I delivered some ice cream to her house and she came to the door with just a towel in front of her, and not very big towel at that. Her towel nearly wrapped around her, but lots of her skin still showed. I was in the eighth grade, and Rosy said to me, 'Honey, I just got out of the shower, come on in and stick it in the fridge.' That's what she said and I was shocked."

Samantha giggled, "If that is true, it sure sounded like an offer, Teddy?"

"Now that I'm older and I think back to her remark and that small towel she had in front of her, yes, it was an invitation."

"Did you take it, Ted?"

"Heaven's no. I was confused for a week.

This caused Flash to burst out laughing.

"Now, see that blue building there?" I pointed ahead as we got close to the bridge over the Swinjoscie. "What's in that Blue Building you ask?"

"Did I?"

"Yes you should have. Card rooms with all types of poker and blackjack. I understand they handle the number's game as well."

"What else do you have in this town that is illegal, Ted?"

"We already covered that, we really have houses of prostitution?"

"Do you really? Tell me about them, how do they work?"

"Again, how would I know?"

"You're right, you wouldn't, but I do!"

I looked over at Flash.

She shrugged her shoulders. "Teddy, come on, you must have figured by now that I'm a working girl."

I again looked at her.

"I sell this for a great deal of money," she said, putting one hand down and spreading herself wide. "More money than anyone in Daisy Junction could ever imagine."

It was my turn to laugh. "Before you leave, I might tell you about my delivery to a house of prostitution."

*   *   *

Finally, the two weeks with Samantha came to an end. I drove the folks's car with Mom, Dad, Samantha, and Nancy to the airport to see Samantha off.

Samantha pulled me aside and said, "Teddy, I have gotten to know you better than any man."

"Samantha, you're still very young, you will meet many more men."

"No Teddy, they will be nothing more than business. I have decided my direction in life and it doesn't involve making friends."

"We're friends," I say with genuine affection.

"Yes, we are. See, you have gotten to know me as well. Do we approve of each other?" Samantha asked, looking up into my eyes with a serious look.

"We do," I affirmed.

An apparently, entirely different young lady waved good bye to us, walked up the steps and disappeared into her airplane. I'm sure she had tears in her eyes as we had. What a two week experience.

On the way home Nancy asked me, "Would you like me to be more like Samantha?"

"Heavens no. You're tough enough as it is without adding any more problems for me. Why did you ask me that?"

"Just to see how long my leash on you is."

Dad pulled off the road, laughing, with Mom joining in.

*   *   *

The next morning as I was sitting in the kitchen when Dad walked in. "Teddy, we want to thank you for befriending Samantha."

"Oh, it was nothing, she turned out to be a nice kid."

"You think of her as a kid?"

I could tell Dad found something amusing about the conversation. "I guess, I don't know how else I would think of her."

"Samantha, aka, Flash, is far from a child as you well found out," Dad said.

"I don't know what you mean?"

"The Flash has been the bread winner of the family for three years now," Dad said calmly.

"I, I didn't know."

"She talked to me as soon as she got here because she wanted to know if it would be okay to hang around with you and Nancy."

"You knew about her?"

"Teddy, her mother is my sister, who I love dearly because she is a hard but fair woman. My sister always had a little different style and until she had that accident, she took good care of her brood. Samantha does what she does because she loves her mother and takes good care of her."

I shook my head and thought, What the hell kind of future does that hard, hard child have?

"I can see you have a concern for her, Teddy. You are a good boy, wish her well."

CHAPTER 14

Summer did not end fast enough for me. Swimming lessons, life guarding, working in the store kept me busy and out of trouble, not that I get into trouble, especially since I survived 'The Flash' with my pants still up.

Nancy and I were enjoying the Rainbow dances and the new steps Dee Dee showed me while we were in the store's kitchen.

At the formal dances Nancy and I put on a show because two weeks before the dance I gave our dance band leader, Freddy, the dances we want him to put in his band's repertoire so we have the heads up.

Then it's football practice and every Saturday afternoon a game. Sometimes I really wanted to go to Miss L'Affaire's place and take a dip in their Jacuzzi, but Nancy always had something planned for us.

In our first game the other team was waiting for me. Man-oh-man, were they waiting for me. We beat them, but those guys really took it out on me. They got penalties for piling on when I had the ball and even when I didn't. I was even blocked when I was out of the play.

Then I remembered what Dad told me. Don't give them an inch. Make them pay when they are going to tackle you. Get those knees up and rattle their box if they have the guts to take you head on. So I finally tried it. It worked.

Oscar kept telling me, You're doing good, Ted. Them guys just don't want to take you head on so our blockers are getting better angles on them. Keep it up, Ted. We've got them on the run."

Toward the end of the third quarter the would be tacklers started to shy away from a straight on tackle because they knew I was going to make them pay the price so I would try to overrun them, then they would try to grab me on a side hit, then I would show them because I had one more gear in my legs to slip past them.

Dad told me, "Ted, you got it down, and that is what college scouts like to see, big power runners."

* * *

After the games, I'm so sore and tired I'm hurting all over. Nancy, by this time, had figured me out and instructed, "You're coming home, and I'll give you something to eat and a rub down, Hon."

After the games I went to the Blake's for food and desert along with that precious rub down. She had a pair of my gym shorts in her house, and Dr. Blake was the one who showed Nancy the proper way to give a rub down.

I kept telling Nancy, "Not to hard, lady. You just wait until spring and you're playing field hockey, then it'll be my turn to give you a rub down, Slovenian style."

"No way, Ted. I'm a girl and I like tender caresses."

Once, I really got stupid and said, "Why don't you call Lisa Roberts and the two of you can give me a rub down, but that's not a good idea because the two of you will probably fight over where you will do the rubbing.

After that stupid remark, I received a hard slap from Nancy. "This is for even thinking about Lisa." Then she slapped me even harder. "And this slap is for being really insensitive."

*　　*　　*

That year we went undefeated for the third year in a row. Our last game would be against our traditional rivals, Seamons Locks Joint Union High School.

No matter what year or what town hosted the final game, everyone from both towns showed up. Most of the businesses in the two towns would close for the traditional home game.

All week, we worked hard to prepare ourselves for the 'biggy.' I know Seamons was doing the same as they are also undefeated.

The game, this year, would be held in Daisy Junction. Our town was in a holiday mood. Coach had us learning new plays. We would use our old plays the first half and then in the second half, if we needed, we would spring our new ones on them. Sounded easy.

*　　*　　*

Saturday at one thirty in the afternoon we ran onto the field, and Seamons Locks came in from the opposite end. Both teams, obviously, had that extra adrenaline pumping into their system.

The crowd erupted. Everyone was yelling and screaming. Our ears rang from the noise of everyone standing and making every type of noise possible.

Oscar and I were the co-captains. We were met in the center of the field by Buss Mitchell, a long time referee and the head official. Since our towns were not too far away, we know the opposing players.

Coming from the opposite direction, walking cocky-smart were the co-captains for Seamons Lock. Buzz greeted us, "Last game of the season and the last game for four great guys. I'm proud to be the official here. He was referring to Oscar and I, and Seamons's, Jimmy Ocho and Eddie Mitchell.

We had met on the field of battle a few times, and Jimmy's folks had a restaurant in Seamons Locks. The Radovichs went there, the Ochos came to our place so the four of us and our parents knew each other very well.

Buzz had us in the middle of the field. "Since you fellows know each other," he checked his watch then said, "do you have you anything you would like to share or tell each other. This is the last high school football game you will ever play. So, is there anything you would like to share with each other."

Oscar asked Jimmy Ocho, a good quarterback for Seamons, "You ready for a good go this afternoon, Jimmy."

He laughed. "Oscar, we have a picture of you and Ted stuck up over the urinal in the locker room. We look at your ugly faces every day. One more day, and I'm gunna throw up, you bet we're ready."

Buzz hadn't tossed the coin yet. He and the other officials were letting us jabber away. I told Jimmy, "How about the losers will soda jerk for one day in the winners store, fair enough?"

"You're on Ted. This is our last game together, but what about these two nobodies standing here that just hand us the ball and stand around on defense watching the game?"

I asked, "Jimmy, you got something for them to wager?"

"How about I have Oscar wait on the customers with a sign around his neck saying, 'I'm the loser?'"

"Sounds good, Jimmy, but I don't think you can afford to feed Oscar or I, Eddie. That's almost a losing bet for us, either way."

"You're right, Teddy. When you bring Oscar over to our store we'll give him a coke or two for his losing effort."

I perked up. "Your store, Jimmy, don't you mean my store? Rest assured, I'll do the same for Eddie because we will win."

Our officials were doing nothing but standing and smiling over our chatter.

I said to Jimmy, "I enjoyed the talk, Jim. Who won the flip?"

"Don't ask me. I wasn't watching. Buster, who won the toss?"

Buster laughed, "We haven't had the toss yet. Are you gentleman ready to play a football game? I want a good fair game because my team has worked many games with you boys over the four years and we know your sportsmanship. This is your last high school game so don't let your team screw it up."

Buster made the proper introductions of his officials and the introductions of the captains. Then came the flip of the coin and Seamons won the toss and elected to receive. We picked a goal to defend.

Today, we four boys, as in every game, will go offense and defense.

*   *   *

This was some game and at half time Seamons was ahead twelve to zip. None of our old plays worked. They had us cold.

In the locker room, at half time, our coach came in, looked as us and turned to leave. At the door he said, "You boys sure can play better than you did in the first half. Try running the new plays if you remember them and still want to play football." And he left us alone.

Being one of the captains, I looked at Oscar and he stood up and walked over to me. I said to our team mates, "Oscar and I are going out to play a real football game this half. Anyone who wants to come along with us, you're invited, but you had better play football."

With a roar the team erupted from the locker room and ran, and I mean we charged out onto the field.

*   *   *

The second half was a complete reverse from the first. I took the kickoff and went ninety-one yards right down the center of the field for our first touchdown, but we missed the extra point. Every time we got on offense we scored a touchdown or it was close.

Oscar, playing defense, spent a good part of the second half in the backfield of the Seamons team. Most times, when they snapped the ball, Oscar was right there among them before they could get anything going. He kept telling Jimmy, "This is some game Jimmy. You and Eddie sure know how to treat us well. I'm really enjoying the second half."

However, Seamons made two more touchdowns. For some reason both team's kickers were off on their tries for the extra points or the kicks were blocked.

Jimmy Ocho never made more than one yard per carry and only completed a couple of passes for any yards. Both their scores came from dumb luck on our side, a fumble, from me, and an interception on an open field. Our team was a complete opposite from our first half. We played with vengeance and executed our plays like we were supposed to the first half, but didn't. I ran in two touchdowns on kickoffs and one on a punt and one from a pass. By the time the game was over I didn't know what the score was. I grabbed Oscar and ask. "Did we really win?"

"Damned if I know, Ted. I'm so tired I can't even lift my head to check the score board." Jimmy and Eddie had to fight their way to the center of the field to hugs us.

Jimmy was gasping, "Hard way to end this football season with a twenty-four, twenty-four tie. Just one good kick and one of us could have won, Ted."

"Jimmy, you mean this game ended in a tie?"

"That's what the scoreboard shows," he said pointing. "I had to ask what the score was. Wow! Some game! Think, Ted, four guys that have playing against each other since grade school, and we end our competing days with a tie."

"Jimmy, that's the only way it should have ended."

"Where you plan to go to college, Ted?"

"Gee Jimmy, I hope it won't be where there is snow. I have been looking at California. Been thinking of San Diego, but we'll see. They have some good schools out on the coast, and you?"

"The same. Maybe we'll meet again. I sure would like to be on the same team with you for a change." Jimmy gave me a soft slap on my head.

"Same here, buddy." I returned the slap. "Bring your date and we'll have dinner together at my place. You can pick a Saturday evening because I'm not playing basketball this year, only track. Got to keep my grades up."

Dad and Mom with Jimmy's parents were walking toward us.

Nancy was fighting her way to the center of the field, hopefully to kiss me.

Hey, Ted, isn't that your steady, Nancy, the tall blond girl running toward you?"

"Sure is Jimmy, and here comes family time and a kiss from my steady."

"I should get a kiss from her because I made you look good this afternoon."

I believe Nancy took off five feet from me and flew into my arms with wet kisses. "I was so worried about you and the way they treated you on the field. I thought you were going to get hurt, Honey. I cried all through the game worrying about you. Those players were mean to you."

I had my hands wrapped around Nancy and I nodded toward Jimmy. "Don't you recognize him, Nancy. It's Jimmy Ocho and he's the one who tried to beat me up. We've been competing since grade school." With Nancy still wrapped around me I looked at Jimmy. "Jimmy, I think, she might just punch your eyes out, the way you treated me."

Nancy turned to look at Jimmy. "Oh Jimmy, I'm sorry? You were almost on every tackle when Teddy had the ball. I was ready to go down and beat you up, damn I was mad at you Jimmy."

"You and Ted will be having dinner next Saturday at my folks restaurant with my date, Monica. Maybe I'll put you at another table if your so fired up," Jimmy laughed. "And you have no idea what Ted did to 'me' tonight. I'm not getting out of bed for three days."

"I was so scared all through the game, the way you guys were pounding on each other, and you two are friends," Nancy said. "How come you've never told me much about Jimmy?"

"Not much to say about Jimmy, Hon."

Jimmy hit me on the shoulder. "Ted, I'll see you next week. I could not run one more play this afternoon. When that gun went off I was very glad. See you buddy."

Nancy looked at Jimmy. "Wait. I don't understand you guys. You beat each other on the field and laugh about it afterwards. When I play field hockey no girl from the other team will even come close to me after our games, and I sure don't want to chat with them at anytime."

Jimmy replied, "Well, next Saturday night you're probably going to have to talk to Monica Weedon, my steady date."

Nancy stomped her foot. "I don't believe this life, sure I know Monica. I still have the bumps on my shins from her wielding that stick of hers. Okay, maybe you guys have the right attitude. I'll try to be decent to Monica. I think I learned something this afternoon.

Monica Weedon was walking toward us. She came over to Nancy who was hanging on to me.

Monica said, "So you two are having dinner with us next Saturday night. Are you going to bring that nasty hockey stick with you? I hope not because my shins have finally healed."

Nancy reached over and touched Monica saying, "Only if you leave yours at home."

Monica replied, "If you don't bring your stick, I'll keep mine at home."

Nancy replied. "Monica, we have learned a lesson from these two men, our steadies."

Dad and Mom stayed back and let us have the stage. Now my folks and the Blakes moved on in along with Jimmy's mom and dad. We all stand in the middle of field talking. Jimmy and I are trying to keep the flavor of our last game together with us forever. Then we slowly walk off the field. Nancy is hanging on to me not paying any attention to my sweaty, dirty football attire.

Mom and Nancy said they were concerned I might get hurt from the tough game we had tonight.

Dad tells everyone, "In sports you fight hard and at the end you appreciate the other person. This is called sportsmanship. We all watched Ted and Jimmy demonstrate sportsmanship this afternoon. Nancy and Monica also realized the concept.

Dad turned to me. "Well, Ted, with four years of football you leave behind four years of hard work and well spent years. The most important contribution you can give to the game is the friends you made."

Nancy was hanging on me, squeezing my arm and giving me kisses. "Ted Honey, please take a good shower and be sure to shave, we're all going out for dinner."

"Where? I didn't bring any special clothes, you should have told me, Nancy."

"My love, you're going to my house and I'm cooking the dinner. Most of it is prepared and waiting. Shower Honey, but don't look at me like that. I can cook and tonight I'm going to prove it. Hurry, you don't want this cook in a bad mood or do you?

CHAPTER 15

It's April, now well into my Senior year. Walking down the corridor of our high school I see Oscar and grab him, pulling him off to the side, whispering in his ear, "I've got a plan I want you to know about. I think we should leave our school something to remember. See you at track practice this afternoon.

"What's up, Ted?" Oscar was excited.

"Tell you later. We'll talk about it at practice."

*   *   *

At practice, carrying our shoes out to the field, I move close to Oscar. "Let's go to the back side of the track."

Oscar is our weight man. He tosses the shot-put, the discus, and the javelin. His events only gather a small crowd, unlike the races, pole vaults, and high jump events.

Oscar is shorter than I, about five eleven and built like a fire plug and weights in around 235 pounds of muscle. He has great upper body strength, but he's slow of foot in running. However, he handles his feet like a classic ballet dancer with the shot put, discus and javelin.

I tried his discus and shot-put once and thankfully only in practice. That was enough for me. I got my feet tangled up and fell on my face trying to spin and throw the discus.

Then I dropped the darn shot-put just missing my toes. Our track coach hollered over to me, "Teddy, stay on your side of the field."

Oscar was also a very smooth dancer, when he had money to take Patty out on a date. He also was a strong center in football and no defensive player ever found it easy to go over, or around him.

* * *

We are now on the back side of our track and he tells me, "You suggested we leave our school with something they will never forget. What's your plan?"

"Oscar. We have to come up with some type of prank or trick we can pull."

"Okay, Ted, but not the Limburger Cheese stunt that the Senior class did two years ago. Shoving a bunch of cheese into the school's heating ducts on a hot day didn't work as well as those guys thought it would."

I laughed, "No one could have foreseen all the mice showing up like they did? I thought I would split a gut when those mice were going everywhere in the hall ways, and the girls all panicking."

"Okay Teddy, what's on your mind for us to do? Better than the cheese and mice?"

"Much better, Oscar, you're working on Saturday at Chester's Dairy?"

"Yeah, I need the money to take Patty out. She sure is expensive just to get one sisterly kiss when I take her home."

"I do feel sorry for you, but we need a bunch of the fly paper they use."

"You bet. Cleaning the milking shed I've got to keep ducking away from them darn strips hanging down from the ceiling, I would be nice to get some fun out of that stuff. What do you have planned?"

"Do they have just plain flat sheets of fly paper?"

"Yeah, they've got a whole bunch of them flat sheets."

"Good, this Saturday, on your way home can you ditch two sheets of fly paper under the culvert where the lane meets the highway just before the road to our house?"

"Easy, what's on your mind, smart one? What are you going to do with the fly paper?"

"I have a prank in mind for us."

"You mean better than the cheese and mice?"

"Much better and easier."

"Easy, what's on your mind?"

"I'll tell you later. Don't mentioned what I've told you now, understand? That includes Patty?"

"Right on, Ted. If I tell Patty anything, she hotfoots it to her church for guidance or whatever prayers she needs to protect herself. That's all they do in her church."

"Okay, plan to spend Sunday night at our house for dinner, and then we have to study Calculus because we have a tough test on Monday. No car, bring your bicycle, got it?"

*   *   *

We did study Calculus at our house on Sunday. Monday morning Oscar and I leave real early from my house and head into town, riding our bicycles. The first stop is at the culvert to pick up the sheets of fly paper and continue biking to town.

"Where are we going with the fly paper?" Oscar is dying to know what the prank is going to be, but I'm tight lipped.

"We'll stop at Rosie Kallich's house, and ditch our bicycles by her hedge where they can't be seen."

"Won't she hear us?"

"No, her bedroom is on the other side of her house."

"How did you know that? I know she has big tits, but she's old. What, around forty?"

"I have no idea."

"Doesn't she go with that police officer you ride and rope with?"

"Yup."

"I still got to ask you, smart one, what's next? Your faithful man servant needs to know."

I slowly answer, "My faithful servant needs to keep quiet and take orders from his smart leader this morning. Dusty and Juan should be in the Old Building because they clean the New Building first as that is where the first morning classes are held."

"You're right about that leader."

We ditched our bicycles under Rosie's living room window, hidden from the street by her thick overgrown bushes.

"She won't wake up, will she, Teddy?"

"Nah, she sleeps till ten in the morning."

"How come you know all that?"

"Cowboy told me that. He knows her well, he knows her very well."

"That well, Ted? I always wondered about Rosie. For an older woman she has some set of jugs and legs."

"Forget it. Come on, lets get across this street quick like and head for the girls bathroom."

"Are you out of your mind," Oscar squeals. "Why are we going in the girl's bathroom? Oh, I get it. What a good one, Ted, if anyone finds out we did it, we will be killed."

I add. "Right. Then we won't tell anyone, correct?"

Oscar and I hurried across the street and entered the New Building. I peeked around the corner and saw Dusty and Juan, our two janitors, just leaving, going toward the Old Building. We are in the clear.

I grabbed Oscar and puledl him into the girl's bathroom. He tells me, in a shaking voice, "I've never been in one of these places Teddy. Sure smells clean, I don't think our toilets smell like this."

"Quit shaking, Oscar, just hold one sheet of the fly paper sticky side down."

"But I've never been in a girl's bathroom, Ted."

"Yes you have, you're in one now. They're just like ours, but instead of urinals and stalls they only have stalls. Quit shaking."

I pulled a stick match out of my pocket and lit it. "Just hold one sheet over this match, Oscar."

I worked the match back and forth and about thirty-seconds later part of this sheet was runny.

"Oscar, put that sheet on the floor sticky side up. Great, now the other sheet."

Another half a minute and we had two warm and slightly runny sheets of fly paper.

"Oscar, take this sheet and come with me and watch. Now Oscar, this requires not much fly paper goo on the seats. Just a slight dab on each side of the seat, slightly back from the middle is enough. Use only one finger. See, three dabs. This is all we need to do. Got it?"

"Exactly, Ted. We don't want the girls to see it on the seats. I'll take this side, and lets go. What a great idea."

We cover twenty stools, quickly leave the building, recover our bicycles, and head off to the store.

"What do I do with the fly sheets, Ted?"

"Dump them in the big garbage can behind A and B Furniture Store and pile some stuff over them so they can't be seen. I'll see you at the store, and come in the back. I'll be waiting for you and looking for a place to stash our bicycles. We'll walk to school."

*   *   *

We pushed our bicycles into the store-room at the rear of the store. Oscar helped me sweep and mop the floor. I fixed breakfast for us and we were eating when Dee Dee walked in at seven, right on the dot.

"Hi Oscar," she said. "Ted has you working this morning?"

"Sort of. I spent the night at his house studying Calculus so I had to do something for my breakfast Dee Dee."

"Anything Oscar and I can do for you before we leave for school, Dee Dee?" I asked.

"No. I can handle it myself. Why are you so polite this morning, Ted?"

"Don't know, maybe because it's Monday?"

*   *   *

Cowboy came in and had his usual coffee and Sunday's left over donuts.

Oscar and I helped Dee Dee fill the fountain with ice and topped off the syrup containers. Then we headed to school, walking, arriving four minutes late, and we had no excuse.

We stopped at the attendance office, and Kathy Small, a secretary in the school office, wrote out our two late attendance cards. We needed them so we could enter our classroom late and we'll collect four demerits.

As we left the office, I tell Oscar, "Remember, no smiles and no telling anyone including Patty. We'll split up and I'll see you at track practice. We don't want to be seen together, even in Calculus this morning, or in any class today. Understand? Remember, Oscar, no smiling or laughing unless everyone else laughs. You have your story down, and we were together helping Dee Dee in the store. That is why we were late to school."

Oscar had a history class, and I had an English class first thing in the morning. We agreed not to talk to each other until school was over and we are at track practice.

As I moved to my second class, Calculus, I noticed a couple of girls walking down the hallway pulling on their dresses. Oscar and I were able to sit away from each other.

By the third class change, more girls were tugging on their dresses, and there was now a group of mothers, with stern faces, standing with their daughters outside Miss Orr's office. She was the Dean of Girls This was certainly not a happy bunch of people.

When I walked to my forth period English Class, I passed Oscar in the hallway.

He whispered to me, "Patty had to go home this morning. She got the flypaper."

"How do you know?"

"In Chemistry, I looked out the window and saw Patty and her mother leaving school. Patty was tugging on her dress. If she finds out it was you and me, we are worse than dead."

Eleven in the morning the school public address system scratched out an announcement going to all the classes. "Attention all students and instructors. In ten minutes all students will assemble in the auditorium. No excuses or tardiness will be tolerated. Absolutely no excuses allowed. All instructors will lock their classrooms and meet in Mr. White's conference room in fifteen minutes."

I left my class and slowly walked down the hallway passing Miss Orr's office. Outside her office was now a large gathering of mothers, some with their daughters. No one looked happy as they stood talking in groups.

Walking ahead of me was Nancy. I touched her shoulder and asked her, "What is going on, my dear?"

"Don't know, love. I heard something about the girl's bathroom. I had PE first period, and my classes have been in the Old Building. Don't know anything more. How about you, Hon?"

"Not a smell. However, many mothers and daughters are outside Miss Orr's office and they don't look too happy."

"Maybe that's why there is a school meeting, love."

"Yeah, I guess so."

We walked together into the auditorium and took our seats in the front row.

In our school the seniors have the front seats in the auditorium, and the freshmen sit in the back. Juniors sit behind the seniors and the sophomores in front of the freshmen.

As student body president I have two front row seats always reserved. My seats have this sign painted, "Reserved for the Student Body President and guest." Along side is the Senior Class president with two seats reserved. Nancy and I sat talking in a low voice until Oscar arrived. He didn't look at me.

"Where's Patty, Oscar?" asked Nancy.

Oscar looked straight ahead and answered, "Don't know. Saw her in English and thought I saw her walking out with her mother while I was in Chem class."

Nancy was looking at Oscar, but he wouldn't return the gaze. Nancy looked at me and whispered in my ear, "Is there something I don't know that you two did?"

I looked into her blue eyes and said, "Probably a whole lot, depends on what you're thinking. Why?"

"Just wondering. Shuu, here comes Miss Orr."

All our teachers were now lining up along on both sides of the aisles and down the center with their back's to the stage.

Every one of them was staring at the students. I know they are posted to see whether they can find the guilty student or students. Fortunately, they have their backs to the first two senior front rows.

*   *   *

Miss Orr was our Dean of Women and was once a Commander of the Waves in the Navy during World War

Two. She was nearly six feet tall and always walked with a military stride.

This morning, she and Mr. White, our principal, walk together to the center of the stage where a microphone was placed.

Mr. White was rather round and short, and walked with short fast steps as he tried to keep up with Miss Orr.

Mr. White approached the microphone to test it. He blew into it. That caught our attention because the volume was on full, and almost every student, including Oscar and me yelled out, "Ow, my ears!"

Dusty, the lead custodian, arrived on the double to turn the volume down, and the students clapped. Mr. White, once again, approached the microphone and announced, "We have a problem with the girl's bathroom in the New Building this morning. The boy's bathroom in the New Building will be used by the girls until this matter is taken care of." A long groan came from the boys.

Mr. White continued, "Miss Orr will proceed with her announcements."

Miss Oar approached the microphone. Then her eyes slowly searched the seated student body before she said, "We had to send many girls home today because one or perhaps two boys, we believe, put something on the girls toilet seats like glue or something sticky in the New Building.

The student body, boys mostly, let out yells and laughed. I smiled and shook my head, as Miss Orr was now looking down at Oscar and I. It was all I could do not to look over to Oscar. Talk about being under the evil eye because we definitely were.

Miss Orr mentioned the loss of state funds when many of our girls had to leave early this morning. "Now, today's attendance cannot include these girls in the class rolls of morning. We just lost state money." And then she dropped the bomb. "As of today, until further notice, all outside school activities will be halted until we find the person or persons that pulled this dastardly deed on our girls."

A loud moan raced through the student body. She continued, "I shall read out some names of class and student body officers and I want to see these people in my office as soon as this meeting is over. The names I call out are not under any suspicion, but I will need their help and advice to get to the bottom of this."

Guess whose name was first, mine, followed by Oscar's. Nancy leaned over to me as Miss Orr was reading more names and she whispered, "What ever you do look her in the eyes and tell Oscar the same. Keep your story short." She gives me a quick lick of her tongue on my ear and a squeeze of her hand on my arm.

The meeting was mercifully over, and we all stood up to leave. Nancy said as she left, "Hon, be careful and do what I told you."

I look at her with surprise. Does she know?

Then Nancy mouthed two words to me, "Castor Oil."

Our auditorium was now clearing out after Miss Orr's ax on outside activities. This ultimatum caused a mass of quiet conversations regarding the outside school activities penalty, and the students appeared to be murmuring on their way back to classes.

Oscar and I left to meet with Miss Orr. I tell him what Nancy said about looking Miss Orr in the eye and keeping our story short.

"Does Nancy know?" Oscar asked.

"No, but she thinks she knows something. Damn woman."

We walked down the wide school hallway to Miss Orr's office. Many mothers were still gathered outside Miss Orr's office looking as though they were ready for a lynch party. Not a smile in the bunch.

Ever wanted to see pissed off mothers? These mothers were ready to toss the rope over a tree limb. The only thing they needed was a place to hang the rope and a victim, and from the look in their eyes any boy would do. These mothers certainly glare at Oscar and I with hungry eyes.

Katy Small, Miss Orr's secretary, was waiting for us and ushered Oscar and I into Miss Orr's office. Katy sat in the corner to take notes. This was like a courtroom atmosphere with Miss Orr looking very severe.

She told Oscar and I, "You boys are the leaders of the student body and the senior class and you both are looked up to as role models. I need the name of the person or persons that did this deed to our girls. Where were you this morning Teddy?"

"May I start with Sunday night, Miss Orr?" I asked.

"If it helps your story, go ahead, Ted."

I sure didn't like that remark. I told Miss Orr, "Oscar and I had a Calculus test, second period this morning and Oscar came to our house, Sunday night, to study with me. We rode our bicycles into town and Oscar helped me sweep and mop the store. We had breakfast and then we helped

Dee Dee ice the fountain. Also, Cowboy Pat McGrath joined us for breakfast with his coffee and donuts. Oscar and I arrived a little late to school and we picked up four demerits for being late to class, just only a few minutes or so. Kathy wrote out the demerits, right Kathy?"

She nodded her head.

"Oscar, is their anything you may add to Teddy's story?" Miss Orr asked.

"Well, the only thing that bothers me about Teddy's story is he didn't tell you how hard I had to work to get breakfast."

Miss Orr smiled over that remark, then told us, "You boys may know who did this terrible stunt this morning, or will find out later. I want names, but I promise any help will not be in the file or mentioned, trust me. Oh, your late demerits will be erased, You got that Kathy?"

We both smiled and said, "Thank you Miss Orr."

She continued, "I shall contact Dee Dee, and would that be Pat McGrath, the police officer you call Cowboy, Ted?"

"Yes, Mam, the same."

"I will check out your stories. You two are excused. Remember, if you hear anything let me know."

We said we would and left her office and went to our classes without speaking with each other.

*   *   *

Our 'lock down' of outside activities lasted just three days. When the after school academic programs were stopped, Daisy Junction's parents objected to the stern methods used by the school administrators in their attempt to find the party or parties that pulled the 'heinous' stunt.

Our local morning newspaper, on Tuesday, noted this same stunt was done over twenty years ago and that time in the Old Building because they didn't have a New Building then.

Walking out to track I'm talking to Oscar for the first time since the incident. "Oscar, there is no way they can find us out. Don't worry, we did a clean job. Remember don't ever say a word."

"Don't worry about that Ted. We are both too young to die and if I'm caught my chances of one of the academies may suddenly disappear. I'll keep my mouth closed, and I know you will so let's warm up."

*   *   *

One week after the crime, Dee Dee at seven in the morning, bounced into the store from the back door and announced, "Well Ted, you owe me one."

I haven't the slightest idea what she was talking about.

"Owe you what Dee Dee?"

"I saved your sweet ass, I surely did."

"I have no idea what you are talking about, Dee Dee."

"You thought I didn't know something was going on when you and Oscar stayed so long in the store to be late to school. You two were trying to reinforce your alibi using me as your witness in your sticky toilet seat incident at the high school. When I heard about it, I just knew you two had done it. So you just owe me one."

"Owe you what, Dee Dee?"

"Let's just say, you owe me, and I'll collect when I'm ready. Have a good day at school."

*   *   *

I grabbed Oscar between classes. "What did you say to Dee Dee the morning we put the fly paper on the girls toilet seats?"

"Nothing, why?"

"Well, she says she knows, and I'm sure she will try to blackmail me."

"I wish Dee Dee would try to blackmail me. I'd help her. She sure has some tits. Tell her I'm willing to pay the price because I can't get to first base with Patty."

"Listen, Oscar, get off that subject right now. Someone besides Dee Dee knows because Nancy thinks she knows, and if one knows, then two may know, and then everyone will know, and then we are flat ass dead in the water. Do you understand what I'm saying?"

"Ted, I haven't told anyone, trust me. I got an application to the Naval Academy and I want to go. I've got an uncle with pull, I hope. What can we do?"

"Well, let's leave it as it is and not say one word. That includes Patty and Nancy, but I'm pretty sure Nancy has the idea we were involved."

"How would she know, Ted?"

"Just after Miss Orr let us go from the auditorium. She gripped my arm and told me to look Miss Orr in the eyes and keep my story simple. I don't know how she figured it out, but she hasn't said one word about that subject since then. Damn women."

CHAPTER 16

Two weeks later on a Tuesday in the late afternoon after track practice, Dee Dee and I were in back of the store talking to Cookie and I hear, "Ted, your mother and I will be gone this weekend to Chicago for a meeting, and you and Dee Dee will have to run the store until Monday when we'll be back. We'll leave the car at the airport. Will that mess up your weekend with Nancy?"

"No problem Dad. Nancy is going to check out a couple of colleges in the New England area with her mother and father this weekend. So I'm free so I think Dee Dee and I can handle the chores, right, Dee Dee?"

"No problem Mr. R. I thought Ted and Nancy were going to the same college?"

"No, I don't think so, Dee Dee," replied Dad.

Dad left and Dee Dee asked, "You and Nancy aren't going to the same college. I thought it was all settled, except where?"

I told Dee Dee, "Well, it was a yes and no. Going to school on the East coast with the Eastern winter weather is not for me. I really want to see sun and an ocean together. I received a few good offers, but living and playing in the ice and snow is not exactly what I want to do for four years. Nancy has an academic and athletic scholarship for a college back east. A school out west offered an athletic scholarship as well, but I don't know which school it was because she never told me. Nancy is more interested in the academics. Anyway, we'll be able to see each other on vacation time and Christmas holidays."

Dad walked in and asked me, "You have a college picked out Ted?"

"Well, one of the best, honest offers came from San Diego State. Sounds good to me. Rather small school, but close to the ocean. Other college offers in the Los Angeles area came slightly on the sweet side, like money in the pocket without a job, all easy classes, and even a car. Didn't like that at all.

I think I'll take San Diego's offer on a full academic and athletic scholarship. One thing they require is to take ROTC. I don't know why, but they said for me to plan on a four year ROTC program. Oh, by the way Dad they want the three of us to fly to San Diego, late this spring, and tour the campus. They even have a place for me to live off campus."

"Say silent one, now you tell me this. When is this to take place?"

"Sorry, I forgot to tell you. The end of Easter Week. Coach Barrows, an assistant coach, called last night, and you and Mom were out. I just forgot. He told me the tickets for the flight are in the mail."

Dad looked at Dee Dee. "Yes, Sir, Dee Dee, nothing like being informed. Well, don't plan anything for Easter Week, Dee Dee. You may have the store all to yourself."

Dad left, and whenI heard the back door slam, I looked at Dee Dee. She was smiling. "Ted. Why don't you come over for dinner Saturday night at my house? Mom and Sis will be gone this weekend, and we can have dinner alone. How does that sound to you?"

"Anything is better than restaurant cooking. What time Dee Dee?"

"Make it seven thirty. I know you have a suit, so wear it. This will be your lesson on what to wear, how to eat correctly, and how to be a gentleman with a lady. I'll teach you everything."

"You say, to teach me? Well, okay. What can I bring?"

"Yourself, I have everything else." She arose from the stool she was sitting on and walked past me giving me a pat on my rear end. See you in the morning, bye."

*   *   *

The week went by slow, too slow for me, but finally on Saturday my folks had gone and left the store to Dee Dee and me to run and we had the dinner date for that night.

During the week, Dee Dee stayed away from me until Saturday afternoon. "I'mgoing home early to make sure everything is correct for your lessons, Ted. Remember, it is seven-thirty and come with a clean shirt and tie, and shave. See you later." Flashing her smile, Dee Dee wiggled off and left me with growing excitement.

I stayed at the store until five and then went home to shower and shave. I didn't have much of a beard yet, but I know women are sure particular because Nancy kept telling me, "I don't want any type of red whisker burn on my face, like some of the girls I know who show up at school with."

Before my shower, I shined my shoes, although they didn't need it. After my shower, I prowled around my bathroom cabinet and found an underarm deodorant, I had never used. I got it for a Christmas present from someone, Don't know who, but it smelled great.

I made four attempts to get my tie tied correctly, then finally stuffed it in my white shirt pocket, checked my shoes, slapped some Vitalis on my hair, and combed it carefully making a good looking part.

I was ready for my lessons, whatever that meant. Would this be the night? At least if it was, it wouldn't be in my Model A Ford rusty panel truck because any woman or girl that got in there always complained about the springs.

I stopped at Magic's Grocery Store. Mary Magic was behind the counter so I asked, "Do you have red roses for sale, Mary." She was a junior in high school and worked in her dad's store.

"Sure have, Teddy. I'll bring some out for you to see from the cold room."

"Just one red rose is all I need Mary."

"I'll bring more out, Teddy. I think you need more than one."

"Mary, let me say this slow so you can understand what I am saying." I'm being a wise-ass because Mary was one of the smartest girls in school. "I want just one rose, period."

"You need more than one rose, Teddy. I know Nancy is out of town and one rose won't work for you."

I looked around and see Mr. Magic sweeping the floor. "One more time, Mary, or I'll go and talk to your father and tell him that his little girl is trying to sell me something I don't need. Can you understand what I'm now telling you."

"Loud and clear, Teddy. How about two roses at the price of one. You must understand one rose means something that you did, and I know you didn't."

"What I did do and what didn't I do, and you know it? What kind of talk is that, Mary?"

Mary spun around and left to go into the cold room.

I'm thinking. Why more that one, I don't know. She returned smiling as if she is the smartest person around.

She handed me my two roses wrapped with a red ribbon. "Sometime, Teddy, when you have time, check out a book on etiquette from the library. I'm not going to tell you why now, but I'm giving you two roses for the price of one and that is that. I'll wrap them so you won't crush them in the Ford panel truck. Don't they look nice and neat with a red bow, Mr. Teddy Radovich?"

Mary handed me the red roses and said with a smile on her face, "Next time, let's hope it will be one rose, and have a great evening."

I almost shoved the two roses into Mary's face.

*   *   *

It was still light outside as I drove slowly to Dee Dee's house, still wondering what the difference between one red rose and two roses meant. Dumb girl, She was just trying to kid me. I'll ask Dee Dee.

Dee Dee lived in an old neighborhood that once had barns for their horses and wagons. Many of these barns still stand and were used for storage and garages. I turned off Van Ness to Second Street and then into the driveway that ran along side Dee Dee's house. In front of the barn was a big turnaround.

Dee Dee must have been waiting for me. As I slowly drove down the gravel driveway along side of her house, I see her standing on the porch. Huumm, she is not exactly dressed. She just has on a flimsy housecoat.

Dee Dee hurried down, bouncing all the way and flagged me to a stop. What she was wearing was a thin pink house coat with lace and flowers on it. Her housecoat was buttoned, but not all the way up or all they way down.

She was barefoot and everything was giggling. "Ted," she gave me a big smile, "park behind the house, away from the driveway in the turnaround area and your Ford can't be seen from the street."

Hum, could this be an all night lesson? I wonder if that's the reason she doesn't want the old Ford to be seen from the street. Ah, neighbors, of course.

I parked where directed so the Ford can't be seen from the street. Dee Dee was waiting for me still standing on the gravel driveway. She gave me a big hug as I handed her the two roses.

I told her, "Mary Magic would not sell me one rose, why?"

Dee Dee flashed her wide smile. "That will come later. Let's get inside because I'm not dressed to be running around outside. My you smell nice. What's the name of your deodorant, it smells dangerous?"

"Something called Musk. Got it a Christmas ago and never used it until tonight."

"You surely picked the right time to use it. Let's get inside before the neighbors smell it and want to come over and, well, perhaps, smell you."

Dee Dee's house had a front door, a back door, and this side door, similar to the two story yellow house on 52 Virgin Street where I delivered the candies and ice cream a few years ago, except her house is one story. Inside there appeared to be an old fashioned parlor with family pictures everywhere. Off to one side was the dining room. I saw dishes on a large round oak table, set for two places only.

Dee Dee asked. "May I pour you a glass of wine while I finish dressing, Teddy? Just sip it easy like, not down the hatch, please. It is Uncle Gorya's private wine. You'll like it?"

I nodded my head, and she handed me a glass of red wine. "I'll be right back. Remember, just a sip, no gulping."

Man-oh-man everything moves under her housecoat. The top of her breasts were very apparent. The same ones I had in my hands a couple of years ago. Their bounce appears unchanged from what I can see. Is it possible they'll feel the same after all this time?

Sipping Uncle Gorya's private stock, I guess one might say this wine is smooth. I wandered around the parlor looking at the family pictures of stern looking women, and men with bushy mustaches like Dad's.

The men stand, and the women sit for their pictures. I wonder why no one smiles except the little children. Some of the older kids try to make that stern look, but it doesn't work well. I know Dee Dee comes from a large family scattered all over the state.

Finally, Dee Dee entered the parlor and she was dressed in a long rose colored gown of some type that doesn't appear to have anything under it. She now took the roses and placed them in a narrow vase and smiled at me. "Two roses is just right for this room"

I asked her. "What is the difference of giving one or two to a girl, Dee Dee?"

Smiling she answered, "As I said earlier that will come later, Teddy. Let's sit and talk. Dinner will be ready in fifteen minutes. I'll get some more wine for us."

My glass was still nearly full.

She wiggled and bounced out to the kitchen and returned with a bottle of wine with no label on it. "Remember, Teddy, you must slowly sip Uncle Gorya's wine as it is very strong, so take it easy. If not you'll be on the floor and ruin our evening. Trust me as I have done it a time or two myself."

We talked about the college where I hope to go to and my subject choice, international politics. She did not bring up the subject of girls. Nancy was never mentioned and neither was the fly paper episode at school.

Dinner was ready, and she lifted her hand to me to help her up. Now I could see down her gown. She had nothing on, at least on the upper half. We walked together to the dining room. Two places were set. Trying to remember my manners, I helped her into the chair. Another look down, and her breasts were nearly visible. Wow!

I went to my chair and sat. If the dinner will be anything as I think I see it, then this is my night.

On my plate was a half chicken. This would r equire some decorous knife and fork maneuvers. Red potatoes and asparagus rounded out our meal.

She told me. "Teddy we will have our salad later."

*   *   *

I thought I got through dinner quite well; no big mistakes in using the knife, fork, and no need to use the spoon or my fingers.

Salad was with another fork, and this one was chilled. The crisp asparagus and tomatoes were over a bed of chilled butter lettuce, and the dressing was some creamy type with no garlic in it. Huuummm?

Dee Dee poured me another glass of wine, my second. She told me, "This bottle is Uncle Gorya's favorite wine. He calls it, 'My special defrocking help mate.'"

"What does that mean, Dee Dee?"

"I guess it means, let's see, 'Too much of this wine and any resistance is lost.'"

"Well, I'd better drink up," I joked.

"No, no, Teddy. Lets go into the parlor. I have some new records and I want you to hear them. Maybe we can do some slow dancing. We'll have dessert later."

"What about my wine, Dee Dee?"

"Of course, bring your wine with you."

I helped her out of her chair. I grabbed another look; they sure look nice and they haven't changed from what I remember.

She put on a stack of records, slow dreamy music. Dee Dee held out her hands, and I went to her and we began to dance very slow. She was right up against me; I mean she is moving against me hard like.

Finally, she unlatched her hand from mine and her hands went around my neck. My hands dropped down to her hips, and now we were dancing very slow in a body rubbing configuration. Her gown began to slip off her shoulders. She stopped and asked me to take off my jacket.

"How come you didn't wear the tie like I asked?"

"I couldn't get it knotted right."

"Now it doesn't really matter, you were right, it makes it simpler," she said going back to dancing, but now she began to unbutton my shirt, one button every ten or so seconds.

Too damn slow.

I didn't know how she did it, but the buttons on her gown became unbuttoned. I could feel her breasts against my, now, bare chest. Well, tonight must be the night. She looked up to me and mummers, "Would you feel more relaxed if we went to my bedroom for a while?"

"Well, of course, sure, yes, I think that is a great idea."

"Leave your coat and tie here. You can pick them up in the morning."

Tonight is the night. She is ready and so am I.

"Teddy, is this your first?"

"If you mean sex, yes Mam it is."

"Good. I will be your teacher tonight. Let's go."

We entered her bedroom and she sat on her bed to remove her slippers. I could now see right down her dressing gown which was hanging on her plump stomach. Not the same stomach as Flash because Dee Dee's was rounded and Flash's was flat, and I can see hair. I really conduct a detailed inspection of her nipples, breasts and stomach. Dee Dee looked up to me and smiled. You have to get undressed Teddy."

Then that damnable telephone began to ring. "Shit, who can that be?" Dee Dee snarled as she grabbed the telephone with no attempt to button up her gown. I followed her and as she bent over to pick up the phone, from behind her my hands find her breasts.

"Hello. Oh Auntie Duscha how nice for you to call. Yes, yes, I'm alone. You are where? Yes, I'll have the light on. I'll wait for you."

She hung up the phone and said, "Oh damnit, it's my maiden aunt and she wants to stay the weekend before going to the city. She called from Sonny's Chevron Station and will be here in ten minuets so you'll have to hurry out of here. Damn, we were going to have a hell of a weekend together. Grab your clothes quick because you have to beat Auntie Duscha, she's a fast driver."

Dee Dee gave me a quick kiss and hands me my jacket and tie and almost pushed me out the side door. "Hurry Teddy, she's got a heavy foot. I've got to clean up the kitchen."

I left and climbed into the Ford and drove out the driveway and onto Second Street. At the corner of Second and Van Ness a black car squealed around the corner and headed down Second Street."

"Goddamn relatives!" I holler out as the car passed me and turned into Dee Dee's driveway. Well, this was another night that failed, and I was so close.

*   *   *

My evening was still young so I drove back to the store, parked in the alley, combed my hair. Using my key I opened the back door.

I made my way past the kitchen to the swinging doors and looked through the curtains to see who might be in the store tonight. In the back booth I can see a blond haired girl sitting alone. It's Nancy Oliva Blake.

*　　*　　*

From what Nancy had told me; she would be spending all weekend touring colleges in the Northeast.

I straightened out my jacket and walked briskly past her as she sat alone in the back booth.

"Hey, stuck up. Can't you say hello to your steady?"

I turned around and tried to look surprised. "My word, it is you Nancy. I thought you would be gone all weekend. What happened?"

"Can you sit with me? Why are you so dressed up, Hon?"

I bent over to give her a kiss. She latched on to me as though I would leave her. We have real mouth to mouth kisses before I can unlatch myself from her arms.

Finally, I'm able to answer her. "Had dinner with friends of Dad and Mom. My folks are gone until Monday night so I dressed for this dinner."

"It's so early, what happened? Did they kick you out of the house? Wow, you smell dangerous. No wonder you were kicked out, what in the world do you have on?"

"Something I haven't used for a year or so, why do you ask?"

"I don't know, but it but it smells like sex in grand style so keep it away from me."

"If a chicken dinner with two older people is sex? Tell me about your Eastern trip with your mom and dad?"

The first college we visited, U of Mass, they're the ones that offered me a full academic and athletic scholarship. Good program, chance to join a sorority, good diggings everywhere I looked so I signed up. Came right home as Dad had a patient he was concerned about, so no sightseeing for us."

"You decided on a major?" I asked trying to keep the attention off myself.

"International Relations," Nancy answered. "I may want to work in the State Department so I'll probably need a Masters for that and they have one, with good hiring possibilities. Going to go east, Hon. Have you decided yet?" Nancy continued. "With all those offers I'm sure some were hard to turn down."

"No, I haven't quite signed up or sent in my acceptance. The folks and I will fly to San Diego at Easter. They have a good program and I'll also take International Relations. How about that? Dad wants me to take ROTC, and I may receive a full ride on an athletic and academic scholarship. They even have a place for me to live off campus, if I decide to go there."

"That school of mine and yours will have a field hockey game during the season and the finals are there three years from now. Ted, we can get together?"

"You mean not before college?"

"Try now."

"Say Nancy, how did you get here, walk, car, or bicycle?"

"Roberto picked me up and we drove because he wanted to park and talk. We needed to talk, or rather I needed to talk to him. I told him, "You're history Roberto, take me to Radovich's, and he did, but you were gone and that's why I'm here. Either I call Mom, or you take me home the long way. Why haven't you really kissed me yet?"

I just did, but I'll gladly kiss my steady again." I leaned over and gave her a tongue searching kiss.

"Where did you get that wine taste?"

"I had one glass of wine with dinner, nosey one. Let's go out the back door."

"To your Model A with that rude seat that tries to violate me?"

"Correct. It wouldn't be a 'good old Model A' if it didn't, my dear, just like me."

"Well, as long as it's the seat and not you, end of subject."

We left the store and we walked hand in hand in the dark to the Ford. I let her in the passenger side and walked around and entered the driver's side.

Nancy moved over to my side and put her arms around me saying, "More kisses. I missed you so much. How can I function in college with a million miles between us?"

"You'll make friends. Sororities are great for that, I'm told. I should be the jealous one."

"Hon, we'll have Christmas vacation, also this summer together, and don't forget the hockey game. We can get together then."

"Nancy we can park or go to the house as the folks are gone. Which is for you?"

"Your house or park, hummm. I guess your house. These seats are not to sit on, and the smell of horse blankets is not very romantic."

"What's with you woman? It was my tennis shoes you said smelled, and now it is the horse blankets. They were just washed, and I'm returning them to the barn."

"I like your smell better, Hon."

We drove home with Nancy rubbing my back and kissing me in the ear, making it hard to concentrate for the six miles. The house was dark with no lights on outside as we walked around to the front door. She was shaking. "No problem Nancy, nothing will happen to you, I promise."

"It's not you that bothers me, it's me I'm worried about. I have to be home at one, can you remember that in case I forget, Hon?"

Once inside I asked her whether she would like a soft drink.

"Water will be just fine. What are you having since you had wine with your dinner?"

"Water for me."

We sat side by side on the couch and sipped our water not saying anything. Nancy carefully placed her water glass down on our coffee table and took mine out of my hand and placed it next to her glass. She turned and put her head in my lap and brought her hands up and around my neck and pulled my head to hers. We kissed.

"Please dim the light, it bothers my eyes, Hon," she said.

Our kissing became fast and moving with ears, nose, eyes, and neck, all covered. We moaned and groaned as we continued kissing. My hands reached underneath her blouse. It's a tight fit and it's hard to slip my hands under there. I can just touch, I think, Her brassiere catches, how can I unsnap them through her tight blouse? Her body was moving around me and on the couch. Every time I moved my hands down to her hips she took my hands and replaced them somewhere else, saying, "Not there."

I still tried to get under her blouse then she sat up. "This is Mom's blouse, and I better take it off before it rips."

Off came the blouse and then her hands went behind her back and the brassiere slipped off her shoulders. In the low light I can see the small mounds with her nipples erect.

Nancy returned to my lap and again pulled my head to her face. Then more kissing and my hands found those small breasts and hard nipples, smaller than Miss L'Affaire's and lot smaller than Dee Dee's.

Nancy was twisting and turning as I rubbed my hands over her breasts. Her kissing became almost a frantic attack on my eyes, nose, my lips, and mouth. She was aggressive. I tried to unlatch her mouth from mine because I want to go to her breasts, but she refused my efforts.

Suddenly, she sat up and switched on the table lamp. She was breathing fast, almost panting, her face glowing with perspiration. Looking at her watch, she swallowed and checked her watch again. Nancy quietly told me, "Nearly one Honey. I've got to get home before I climb all over you, and our college plans include one other person we don't need now."

"Ten more minutes," I begged.

"No way, not now!" Nancy said forcibly. "We have got to find a place we can be alone. I want a nice hotel room away from our town, where no one knows us. You must bring the protection, understand what I'm trying to say to you, Honey?"

"Yeah, but in this town if I go to a drug store and ask for those things everyone will know about it."

"Sweetheart, druggists don't talk, just like doctors. They just don't talk. Listen to me, I have more to loose than you. You are a man and you must lead me through the act. You have read the books, haven't you?"

As she was talking to me she snapped on her brassiere, and then put the blouse back on and buttoned up.

"Only the dog and cat books," I tell her. "That is all I've seen, oh, chickens and roosters, and the horses I've watched."

"Well, I have a book Mom gave me to read," Nancy said. "I've only looked at the pictures and drawings so far."

"This is great, Nancy," I complained. "We can go away, and you can bring the book and who leads who through the sex act? Do I hold the book or do you, and who reads what to do? I understand there are many positions."

"Huh? All I know, Hon, is what I have heard in the gym from girls that have done it. It hurts the first time, and some boys are real animals not thinking about the girl. They jump on and just pump and pump away not thinking about anyone other than themselves. Then they jump off and leave. That's the scary part."

"I won't do that to you, anytime. I'll take my lovely lady home now, untouched."

*　　*　　*

We drove slowly with Nancy, somehow, lying with her head on my lap. We talked about when and where we could go. Each suggestion didn't see to work out for the other person. She mentioned that she could feel me. "I'm so sorry for you tonight," she said sincerely.

Arriving at her house we had many kisses then I walked her to the front door for another very long kiss.

"See you in church, happy dreams my dearest Nancy."

"Same to you, Hon. Sorry, but the time will come for us. See you in church. Love you. Take a cold shower when you go home, you'll sleep better."

Walking slowly down the walkway, I wondered when, if ever, I would reach that goal of finding what sex is. Oh sure, there was always Dee Dee, or even that hot Lisa, but that wasn't what I really wanted. I couldn't figure out why, but I was confused, thinking about the opportunities lost. I had had the perfect chance with Flash, but didn't take it. I still think of Flash, but the raw womanhood she showed me isn't what I see in my mind, I see Flash, the friend. I've always realized how powerful that little girl is.

Wait a minute, smart man, maybe Miss L'Affaire. No one is home so why not. I'll go and see her and maybe she wouldn't be occupied, after all, it was only onefifteen in the morning, and I was awake and ready because, well, it was some night already. Two times at bat and no hits.

A few cars were on Virgin Street, and I didn't think there were any in front of 52 Virgin. I walked up to the side door and knocked three times. The door was opened by Mrs. Angel.

"Well, welcome Teddy. I bet I know who you wish to see. I'll get Miss L'Affaire so wait here in the parlor. Would you care for a coke or something stronger?"

"No Mam, I'll stand and wait." If I held anything in my hand, I'd shake it all over the rug.

Not longer than one minute, and Miss L'Affaire walked through the door from the stairs. "Teddy dear, you finally came. I'm free for the night. Let's go up to my room." She grabbed my hand and pulled me upstairs, pulled me into her room, sat me on the bed, closed her door and locked it, then stood in front of me with her hands on her hips.

I looked at her and could see almost everything. The pink whatever she had on appeared to be nearly transparent. With her white skin, her sparkling blue eyes, and her bright red lipstick, she looked like a movie actress. Not a flaw, but I wasn't really looking for flaws.

She sniffed the air. "You smell great. What have you been doing tonight so well dressed up?"

I told her about Dee Dee and the aunt who came and messed up my night. Then I told her about Nancy and how we would try to get together before summer. "I need help Miss L'Affaire. I've been reading some books, but they don't tell me what I think I should do correctly. I need your help. I have no one else I can ask."

Miss L'Affaire turned around and sat next to me and then hugged me. She gave me a big kiss. It was a kiss all right. Wow! Some kiss. "So, I will be your first? I'm thrilled you finally picked me. You are such a dear boy, I would be thrilled even if I was third."

Okay Ted, we'll go through it carefully as you surely don't want to hurt your girlfriend who I assume is very special to you."

"That's right Miss L'Affaire. I want to do it right and have Nancy enjoy it with me."

"Teddy, you do plan to use protection, don't you?"

"I guess so. I'll buy them at the Harvey's Drug store if he won't tell?"

"He won't, pharmacists are like doctors. Do you know how to use them correctly?"

"No Mam, I surely don't, and I don't even know how to ask for them?"

Miss L'Affaire laughed, "First, you ask for a box of condoms. That is easy to remember." Slowly she said again, "C o n d o m s." They slip over your penis. Don't you dare have any sex, anytime, without condoms. I don't care who may say you don't need them, you do. I'm the expert.

She stood up and walked to her bathroom and returned with a sweeping broom. "You might as well get undressed, Teddy. I will do the same."

"Right here?"

"Of course, silly, right here? Put your clothes over on that green stuffed chair."

I did as asked with my back to her. My erection was growing. I walked over to her with both hands trying to hid the erection.

Miss L'Affaire had taken off her blue smock and was sitting on the middle edge of her airframe tube of her waterbed. "Sit next to me, Honey."

I tried not to look at her totally naked body, but even with my peripheral vision, I got a real sense of woman, just like when Flash was messing with me, but this time was for sure. I hope?

She took the broom and said, "Pretend this is your penis. I shall show you how to put on a condom correctly and not tear it. If it tears use another. Don't ever use the torn one. It's too easy to get an infection or cause the girl to become pregnant. Neither one is an option you need to have."

I've got a total erection, and Miss L'Affaire appears not to notice it.

"Now in the heat of the battle, this is where the inexperienced may ruin the mood," Miss L'Affaire said, holding a condom package in front of my face. "It may seem unnecessary to worry about something as simple as getting the condom out of the package, but believe me if you don't learn this part, you may turn a moment of passion into a joke." She took the package and showed me how to tear it open with my teeth.

She took another condom package and said, "Now, you do it."

I'm thinking, How hard can this be, as I go to tear open the package with my teeth? It took me three tries before I got it right.

"Good, good Teddy, see where you can run into trouble right away?"

"Yes, I do, thank you."

Next, she told me, "Let me show you how to put one on. Many women will do it for you, but if they aren't sure how to do it, it might not go on properly and this is where it could get torn and then trouble is just over the hill. Watch how I do it." She placed the condom over the top of her broomstick and rolled it down.

"See how it is rolled. If you get it upside down, it won't roll down."

She rolled the condom backup, and then turned it over. "Watch me now. You see it won't go down and may tear." She rolled the condom back up, "Okay you do it on the broomstick.

As I rolled out the condom, she continued, "I think, right now, for you and your special lady friend a lubricated condom would be the best. Forget the other tacky ones they may try to sell you and stay with the lubricated ones with a reserve end. It would best for you, for the first few times, to put the condom on yourself. Then you'll know it's done correctly.

Another thing to remember, Teddy, and it is very important. Do not use the same condom for a second go-around. These are easy to tear, and when you ejaculate the sperm is in the end."

Miss L'Affaire stood up and asked, "Any questions so far?"

"No Mam." I kept my head down. I'm not sure why, but it's like I respected Miss L'Affaire for helping me with this and want to show it by not ogling her body.

"Maybe you're in a hurry and may want to continue without changing your condom. Two things may occur: one, it is easy for the condom to loosen and come off inside the lady after you have ejaculated, and that kinda spoils the fun as she must fish inside for it, while you wait, two, the condom may tear and your protection is gone. Then she might become pregnant if just one, you can't see them without a microscope, sperm escapes from the torn condom, or if she has a disease then you may catch it."

Miss L'Affaire standing there in front of me asked, "Any questions?"

I shook my head. Wow this will be my first, and she explained things I surely didn't know.

Now Miss L'Affaire turned half around, bent over, I snuck a peek, pulled back the covers of her waterbed and climbed on the bed and situated herself on her back. She told me, "Take an another condom and lie next to me on your stomach. I'll show you how to prepare the lady for your entry without the fumbling and hurting like most first timers end up doing. Many men still do it wrong because think they are macho. Some jerks think they are the only ones that should enjoy sex so they are no better than animals."

I climbed onto the moving waterbed and I could feel the silk sheets under my knees and hands. It's was kinda slippery and the bed was moving under me with a wave action. I was now next to Miss L'Affaire. I looked up to the big mirrors above me, and I could see us both.

"Teddy, pretend I am either Dee Dee or your girl friend. You can kiss me and my breasts like you tried to do a few years back, remember?"

"You were too strong for me."

"Not this time Teddy, not this time. I'll turn the lights down low." She reached up and played with some type of switch and the lights dimmed. Somewhat on my right side, I placed my left hand over her one pointed, full breast and I began kissing her.

Did she ever respond! Wow! I had never kissed anyone like that. She rolled over on top of me, and we continued to kiss. Her legs were on each side of me. Miss L'Affaire raised up. "Oh Teddy how proud of you I am. I've watched you grow from a curious little boy to now a man and ready to go out in the world.

"Well," I replied, "Dad says I am almost a man, just a few more weeks to go."

"What does your dad define as a man?"

"Oh he says that I act like a man already, but the law won't recognize me until I turn eighteen in three months."

"God dammit! Shit!" She rolled off of me and moved quickly off the water bed. She stood up with her hands on her hips. "I can't do it with you. I just can't."

"What's wrong? Did I do something or say something?"

"No, it's not you honey. I assumed you were eighteen because you were a Senior, but I can't have any real sex with anyone under eighteen years of age, or I'll go to prison for a few years. I just can't let that happen."

"Who will know?" I whined.

"There is a house full of girls that can talk, and Mrs. Maude Angel will know, and that is bad because she has connections. Terrible things have happened to girls working under the association protection breaking the rules, and I can't chance it. Wait till you are eighteen, and it's my treat. But, at least now you know about condoms. I'm sorry. Get dressed honey, and I'll see you to the door."

It was now two thirty in the morning. When would I learn? It was a long drive back to the dark house, and I was alone, again, and frustrated, really frustrated. My only thought was, I've got to find a place to do it with Nancy.

CHAPTER 17

MONDAY MORNING, I WAS in the kitchen having breakfast when Dee Dee entered from the back door, and I asked, "Has your aunt gone?"

"No dammit. She has parked her fat ass in the parlor and will be here for a week. I hope I didn't scare you Saturday night. What did you do after leaving the house?"

"I came down here to the store and found Nancy alone so we went driving."

"You did it with her?" Dee Dee sounded disappointed. "Were you careful with her? I hope you used protection? I know you sure were ready before my aunt showed up."

"No, we talked and tried to think of a place we could go so we could be unseen and anywhere in this town seemed too risky."

"Ted, I'll be out of town this weekend. Your dad promised me a long one off. You two can have my house. Just clean it up before you leave and do the sheets. Bring some food and enjoy your stay. Nancy is a very nice girl and be careful with her. She is too good to put her through some dumb sex act in the back seat of a car, especially that Model A you drive.

"Are you serious Dee Dee?"

"Absolutely. If you two aren't sure how to go about it properly, I have a book that explains everything in detail

Even if you two know what you're doing, this book can help. I'll leave the book on the bed. Now, I've got to get to work and you to school, bye."

*   *   *

Sixth period was my Chemistry class. I walked in and slid into my seat at my regular work station. Nancy was taking to another girl. I touched my steady on the arm. "Hi lovely one, how are you today?"

She gave me her blue eyed look and a wide, red lipstick smile. I could just grab her and kiss her right there, except that was a good way to be suspended from our school. Graduation was close, and I think I was still under the microscope of Miss Orr.

"Hon, enjoy your weekend?" Nancy gave me an appraising look and was waiting for my answer.

"Cleaned out the barn and stalls and mowed the lawn, and you?"

"Just thought about you and me. We've just got to get together."

"Well, sweet one, I have a place for the whole weekend, how's that?"

"Once you get started on a project, Ted, there is no stopping you. What a fast worker. Where?" She had a very serious look on her face.

"Dee Dee told me this morning we can have her house this weekend. She will be out of town. How's that sound?"

"Dee Dee? She has been trying to get into your pants since you were a freshman so how did this come about, you and me and not her?"

"Don't know, and for your information it will always be you. She told me about her house this morning."

"Last Saturday evening you had a scent on I have never smelled on you before and Blossom said she saw your Ford down by Dee Dee's. Didn't you have, as they say in the gym, a roll in the hay with Dee Dee?"

"No, she just takes an interest in me, that's all. Does that offer sound right for you?"

"I'll consider it, but let's read the book first. What's the deal on her house?"

"Dee Dee says she has a good book to guide us through and she will leave it on the bed. All we have to do is clean up when we leave and be sure to wash the sheets if we leave a mess behind."

"A mess? What mess?" questioned Nancy.

"Food, I guess?" I got to thinking about that. It sounded serious. Well, maybe there will be something in the book about that, but back to chemistry because here comes Dr. James, the chemistry teacher.

*   *   *

Three days later, Nancy told me, "Let's take Dee Dee up on her offer, but maybe only late Saturday afternoon and part of the evening. My folks aren't going out of town like I thought. You have to get the protection. You're the man, and you should know how, or I don't go. What about that book, does one of us hold it for the other one. How does that work and what would you call that?

"I think the word is kinky, Nancy. Great news, my folks are going out of town with another couple, and Dad tells me I can have the new family car to drive while they're gone, but no scratches or messing around in the car."

"Good, anything would be better than your old Ford with those seats."

*   *   *

Now, all I had to do was buy the protection. Jimmy Johnson's Drug Store was next to our store and there is an archway between the two businesses in the back by the counter.

I know Jimmy because he comes into our place for coffee breaks and once or twice a week for lunch. I waited, peeking around the arch way until there was no one in the drug store. Then I quickly approached the drug counter.

Jimmy met me. "Hey Ted, that was some track meet last Saturday. You had a full day, winning the hundred and two twenty and then the relay. You sure smoked them guys. What college are you going to?"

"I've looked at a number of schools, Jimmy, and finally decided on a small school in San Diego. They have a good program and no snow. Had some other offers, but either there was snow, cold weather, or the offers were on the fuzzy side of the recruitment rules, and that is not for me."

"Good for you, Lad. I went to a university that had a nearly professional football and basketball program. Them guys never studied and how a few of them graduated, I don't know? Those that didn't graduate got tossed into jail sooner or later. They had some dumb classes for the jocks, but they couldn't run anything unless they hired someone who could count and make change. What an animal college it was, and still is. What can I do for you, Son?"

"I'd like a box of them protection things; I think they are called condoms."

"Sure, no problem Son. You want the reservoir end, the ribbed ones, the lubricated ones, or I have a brand-new type in colors, and they say some of them glow in the dark. Which is your selection."

"Jimmy, are you pulling my leg. I came in here for condoms, and you give me a line I care not to hear."

"Sorry Ted, but I have to ask. Some people are very picky about these items.

"If your lady friend is new to this, I would suggest the lubricated ones with a reservoir. A box you say, hmmm. A box coming up in a brown paper wrap, and just because you are a friend and I've known you since you wore diapers, I'm giving these to you as a gift. Here, let me put them in a bag."

Jimmy handed me the bag. I took the bag and then squeezed his thin upper arm. "Jimmy, this is between you and me and no one else, Do you understand me?" I gave him a hard stare.

"Absolutely Ted. I'm the same as a doctor and always keep my mouth shut on anything bought in my store, professionalism is the word. Mum is my code. Have good day and I envy you youngsters."

That Saturday night, Nancy and I planned to use Dee Dee's house, but Friday, Nancy was jumpy at school. I asked her. "Why don't we go out to dinner to Elk Grove and be away from people we know before we go to Dee Dee's?"

"Teddy, this is why I love you so. You're are so understanding and such a gentle person."

*   *   *

The drive, in my folks's new car, to her house was long as I had some thinking to do. One question kept popping up; How do we start?

She was alone in her house because her folks went out to dinner. I received a kiss from Nancy as we walked to the new car.

"Sure is lovely honey," Nancy said. "I can sit right next to you without some mechanical thing trying to do something to me."

We drove to Elk Grove for a nice, quiet dinner with limited talking. Our conversation was rather sedated at dinner because we were both nervous. Nancy kept her eyes down and when she drank some water she had to use both hands on the glass? I really worked hard to keep a light conversation going.

*   *   *

After dinner we drove the long way back to Dee Dee's. Just as we entered Daisy Junction, Nancy asked me, "Do you have the protection I asked you to get?"

"Sure, the box is in the back seat."

"Can I look at it?"

"Go ahead, no problem with me."

She bent over the front seat showing me a slim rear end view, then came back with the paper sack. "They are in this box?" How many are there?" she asked me in a hushed voice.

"Don't know, just what Jimmy gave me."

"You didn't tell him about me did you?"

"Of course not. It's no one's business but ours, honey. Why don't you open the box and let's take a look at them?"

Nancy took the box out the brown paper bag and tore off the lid like she had to get into the box in a hurry, causing the damn box to nearly explode with condoms going everywhere in my folks's new car.

"How many are in the box Ted?"

"Don't know, check the box, they should have the amount on the label, I'd think."

She fished around under the front seat and on the floor and found the lid. Using the car's dash lights she read and then exclaimed in a loud voice, "Holy cats, this box has a dozen of them things in there You really planned to use a dozen on me. I won't be able to walk for a week. Are you nuts? This is our first time. If you don't kill 'me' first, you'll certainly die from the exhaustion."

"Come on Nancy, be serious. Only one, or maybe two for starters."

"For starters you say? You meant for 'enders'. My book doesn't say anything about this. Maybe when we get there, I'll read one of them pages again and with you this time."

I'm laughing at her statements because I know she is nervous and just trying to keep busy. "Slow down honey."

Nancy, in a high voice asked, "Ted, have you decided who will hold the book and who will do the work?"

"In the dark, Hon?" I chuckled. "We will both read the book first. We have to be serious my sweet."

"All right, Ted, we will read it together with our clothes on."

"Honey, now gather up our little toys and stick them back in the box."

"They aren't our toys Mr. Radovich, they're yours. All I did was open the box."

"Well, gather them all up. I sure don't want the folks finding anything like this in their new car."

"You don't!" Nancy shrieked, "I see your mother every Wednesday night at Rainbow and this is not a subject I would care to discuss with her. Also, my Dad treats you like a son and he certainly won't if he finds out about this!

Nancy started picking up the separately wrapped condoms, counting as she put each into the drug store bag. "Eight, nine, ten . . . that's all I can find."

"Nancy there are twelve in the box, you even said so. Somewhere there are two more. We have to find them."

"Maybe the company made a mistake and only put in ten instead of twelve?" Nancy said, diving around under the seat.

"No way Nancy, I'll stop and let's look together."

With all four doors open and the dome light on we looked and felt around the seats and floor for the other two. We hadn't found even one, when suddenly we were bathed in bright white light with a flashing red light backdrop. Surprised, I looked up. It was a police car. I hear a familiar voice. "You two in trouble?"

"Stick everything in the glove compartment, Nancy," I instructed under my breath, then stepped out into the light and see Pat McGrath and his deputy Chino headed my way.

"High Pat, high Chino, what's up?"

"Thought we saw some people in trouble and came to help. Val's new car?" Pat asked.

"High Pat, hi Chino, haven't seen you for some time," Nancy added as she stood up and appeared to brush her hair back, then she straightened out her dress. I noticed Nancy had just palmed her right earring into the pocket of her dress.

"Just lost an earring and Ted and I were looking for it. Not expensive, dime store thing."

"Chino," Pat ordered, "get the flashlight and we'll help two young people in distress."

"No need Pat," I hurriedly countered, "I have to get Nancy home early tonight, and I'll look for it tomorrow in the daylight."

"No problem, Son, tame night, nothing is happening. Chino will take the front, and I'll take the back. Won't take long."

The two police officers were bending over to start their search of Val's new car.

Nancy and I looked at each other. She has a shocked look on her face, and I'm sure my face is red.

Thankfully a call comes over their new police radio. They are needed somewhere about a fender bender.

Whew.

Both officers left and roared off with their red light on.

I placed my arm around her shoulders. "They didn't find them, talk about lucky."

We got back in the car, and Nancy told me, "I'm sorry, I'm not in the mood, and it is late. We'll do it when we have time lots of time. I'm sorry Honey, but it's a girl's prerogative and I've lost the mood now, and I don't want to disappoint you Honey."

"I think you are right. I don't want a hurry up affair with you so we'll wait. I'll check out the car very carefully when I get home and find them."

She leaned over to me and gave me a kiss, then a number of kisses. I drove her home with her head in my lap, and the seat pushed back. I had my hand on her breast as I drove one handed. She held my hand tight against her small breast.

*   *   *

I got a long kiss at the door and I thought I felt and tasted salty tears from her eyes when I kissed her cheeks, her eyes, and her lips.

I had the longest, ever, drive home for me.

*   *   *

Early Sunday morning, I spent a half hour looking and checking under the seats with no luck. Maybe the two condoms fell out of the car. I'll accept that and will tell Nancy Monday morning at school, and she'll be relieved and so will I.

CHAPTER 18

Monday morning I was having breakfast in our restaurant and just before I left for school, Cowboy Pat McGrath came in from the back door.

"Is the coffee and them old stale donuts for a tired, overworked and underpaid police officer ready, Son?"

"Always waiting for you Pat."

"Did you find that earring Nancy lost Saturday night?"

"No, might have fallen out of the car while we were looking for it inside. It's a cheap earring so Nancy's not real upset."

We talked school and games and just when Pat was getting ready to leave, Dee Dee came in. A few words were exchanged between Dee Dee and Pat.

I walked to the back the store with Pat. He stopped and motioned to me, "You know that problem in school, a month or so ago with the stuff on the girls toilet seats?"

"There was talk all over school about it," I tried to sound nonchalant, "but I think it blew over because the schools quiet about it now, that's all."

"Well, Ted, I can tell you this. Them school people, and that Miss Orr called and wanted a police investigation. So did I. Then I remembered when I was in school many years ago, twenty or so years I believe, we did the same thing then and used fly paper. Now how do you suppose anyone would know about fly paper these days. Don't we have chemicals for flies, Ted?"

"We do at the store, Pat." I was trying to look calm and collected.

"So I got to thinking, now who uses fly paper? Probably someone got it from the same source I did, right from Chester's Dairy. Now, who do I know that is a smart thinking lad? Some guy who might just be the Student Body President and his loyal friend who is the Senior Class President and works weekends in a dairy? If I know two guys that can keep their mouths shut, it's them guys. What do you think of that, Ted?"

"Well, I would think you are one smart policeman, Cowboy."

He slapped me on the shoulder. "Some great prank. Miss Orr has no idea who did it. I swear she would give up her virginity to find out who it was. I know the two guys that pulled the latest version of this stunt wouldn't want to be taking original credit because they weren't the first to pull it, or even the second. When I was in school, I was a person who could keep his mouth closed and I did the same thing. See you later Ted."

"Wait a minute Pat, who was that person who did it with you?"

"Huumm. I really shouldn't say because it was his idea, and I only I got them fly papers from Chester's Dairy just like Oscar did for you."

"Who was the other person?"

"Oh, just our local pharmacy druggist."

"You mean, Jimmy Johnson?"

"You said it, not me, see you later son."

I watched Pat leaving and he was whistling. I got to front of the store to tell Dee Dee I was leaving for school.

Dee Dee was cleaning off the counter where Pat sat.

"Are these yours?" She held up two sealed condoms.

"Not that I know of," I gulped. "Where did you get those, Dee Dee?"

"Right under Pats saucer, anything you wish to tell me? You didn't use my house like you wanted, why?"

"Shit! Well, okay. Nancy wanted to look at the box of condoms I got from Jimmy's Pharmacy, and she tore the box open and we lost two. Pat helped us look with no luck. I guess he found them and played a trick on me."

"You bought two only? They come three to an envelope."

"No, I got a box of twelve."

"Jesus, God and all the Saints. You bought twelve condoms for your first sex episode. Good Heavens, you could have killed that girl or yourself if you two tried to use all of them?"

"Well, I don't know about those things, Dee Dee."

"Listen, Ted, let me tell you something. Way back, when I was a very young girl, there was some trouble and the soldiers came. I hooked up with one of them soldiers, and I'm somewhat brand new in the world of sexual knowledge. In fact, I was just beyond looking for babies under rocks or behind flowers in the garden.

"That soldier and I spent one long episode in a one room shack. We had plenty of food and water and we didn't surface until four days later and when we did we looked like starved and beaten prisoners of war. He left because the trouble fizzled out and that was the last I saw or heard of him.

"Maybe he died of exhaustion, Dee Dee."

"He easily could of. You know Ted, I have since read that there are over one hundred sexual positions. I think we did about fifty. In the classic book Karma Sutra sexual positions there is a quotation I still remember; 'Once the wheel of Love has been set in motion, there is no absolute rule there after.' You may want to checkout one of these books, 'Selected Positions' or 'The Perfumed Garden' or Modern Lovers or 'Ancient Lovers'."

"But, you two may have to become acrobats, contortionists, or be double jointed to do anything close to even fifty positions if you're going to try to run through the various positions of sex in the book."

"You mean the Missionary Position isn't the only way?"

"As I told you, it is only one of a hundred positions. There are plenty of books printed on the sex habits and positions so read up on it before the next time."

"I guess, I'll have to wait, but I don't have much time left before graduation. I have an appointment in San Diego. I'm going alone; Mom and Dad are going to Mom's Nurses class reunion, so I'll fly to San Diego by myself. Nancy wants to go, but I don't think either of our parents will allow that to happen."

"You're right on that statement, Ted. There was a Federal Law called the Mann Act that prohibits a man and woman, not married to each other, from crossing state borders for sexual pleasure. It may still be in force."

Dee Dee was standing behind the counter wiping her hands and she continued, "Well, you have most of the summer with Nancy. Just find a quiet place like somewhere up state, not out of state, mind you, like in the woods with a lake. You need to get to know each other before you go separate ways because I understand the coast of California is full of girls that are all blonds and they all surf and have great tans. You may forget Nancy in a few months or, she will forget you with all those rich eastern playboy from New York after her."

"That is something I do worry about," I mentioned to Dee Dee. "Those Eastern boys and Nancy, that and the distance we will have to travel to get together."

"Ted, sometimes the distance is better. This gives each of you a chance to size up other people and see the good and the bad compared with what each of you have in common. How does your schedule look for dates coming up?"

"It's going to be tough. I'll be traveling to meet the coaches and see where I will stay in San Diego. Have to work on my graduation speech and go to many meetings. Then our conference track finals and if I'm lucky, the state finals.

Then Nancy will be busy as well, banging away with her field hockey team. They are good and looking toward their state finals, so I don't know?"

"One good thing, Ted, you do have a good supply of protection to last you a while?"

"Yeah, if I ever get the chance to see her alone, otherwise, they will rot in my bedroom."

"I doubt that, Ted, remember I always have a bedroom for you to consider with or without Nancy. Think about it, the bedroom I mean, not you and I. Now you're off to school, so see you later, and I'm not kidding. I'd love to have you for a night or two.

"We'll see," I said, hurrying off.

CHAPTER 19

I TELEGRAPHED COACH HECKY, OF San Diego State, and let him know I'd be traveling alone, April 1, and would bring the two unused tickets with me.

*   *   *

My first airplane ride. Wow, it was exciting. I though I could see forever. I didn't know how high we were, but it was some view. The flight had a few bumpy spots along the way and a change of airplanes.

My seat companion on the final leg was a salesman and he told me he traveled on commercial planes all over the United States.

He must have noticed my scared look as I gripped the hand rests when we hit those bumps. He assured me, "Don't worry now, Son, the time to worry is just before we hit the ground.

Then there was one especially big bump, and I grabbed the arm rests with all my might.

My seat mate told me, "Those guys in the cockpit know what they're doing. Some of them flew in the war with me. I'll tell you this, we had all the thrills needed for three life times. Sit back and relax."

Relax he says? Then he mentioned to me, "Have you noticed the tight asses on those two stewardesses? To bad you have a coach waiting for you in San Diego. I could fix you up with one of them. I make this run every two to three weeks. Those gals rent a two bedroom apartment next to Mission Beach in San Diego."

He was right. They were nice looking and very polite to me and everyone else on the airplane. They looked like movie stars.

Coming in over San Diego the town seemed to go on forever. My seat companion pointed Mexico in the distance just before we landed. "Maybe you should make a trip into Mexico and experience the nightlife," he suggested.

"Well, I'm meeting a man to show me a college in San Diego and I don't think I'll have the time."

"Well, Son, if you can make the time, you should at lease take a day drip to Tijuana because you can get anything you want there, but listen, taking up with one of them Mexican girls can give you a possible disease, so be careful and always use rubbers."

After gathering my one bag from the pile of luggage dumped in the San Diego Airport, I walked outside. The sun was out and it was warm and it's only April. This is my country, I decide right then and there.

My instructions from Coach Hecky were; 'look for a station wagon with an Indian painted on the front doors'. I see a man holding up a hand lettered sign with Radovich in large letters. This must be Coach Hecky. He walked up to me and gave me a big hug. "So you are Ted Radovich. I'm Coach Hecky, and welcome to San Diego. I'll shove your bags in the back and hop in front, next to me."

He's driving a Ford Woody station wagon with a large Indian head painted in red on both front doors. He tells me, slapping the Indian head on the drivers door, "Ted, this head is an Aztec Indian head and we go by the name Aztec's.

First, Ted, I'll show where you will be living, then we will go visit the college. You know you are already programed for four years of ROTC here. You'll meet our coaches at the gym and have a look around. We'll have dinner with a friend of mine. I was at Notre Dam, and he was at West Point. We played against each other for four years, and he knows your father, mother, along with your grandparents."

I have no idea whom he is talking about.

*   *   *

Dad, Mom and Nancy met me at the Parish County Airport when I arrived back home four days later. It was a smooth flight with different stewardesses, but still good looking women. Made me wish I was older.

It's a cold windy evening on my return, and I missed San Diego already. I got a hug from Dad, a kiss from Mom, and a couple of real wet kisses from Nancy.

She had a tight grip on me as if I was going to run away, as we walked to the car. Everyone was talking, but me and Dad. The women keep firing questions at me and before I could answer one, I had two or three more heaped on top of me.

I was sitting in the back seat with Nancy, and she was as close as she could get without sitting on my lap. Her hands kept going up and down my shirt sleeve.

Mom turned to look at me and finally asked, "Now, Teddy, tell us about San Diego and where will you live on campus?"

"Not quite, Mom, I'm not living on campus." Nancy and Mother said in unison. "You're not living on campus and not in a dorm? Are you going to be living in a frat house?"

"No, I have a room above a garage on an estate in La Jolla."

"Where's La Jolla?" asked Mom.

I could see Dad through the rear view mirror. He's smiling, looking at me. He knew, damnit, how did he know?

Nancy was staring at me, and Dad finally replied, "It's a wealthy area on the beach with lots of young, blond, suntan girls hanging around the sidewalks, the beach, or surfing, right Ted?"

"Well, there were a few as we drove along the beach," I confessed.

In reality, I had two warm days with lots of young women bicycling or walking along the sidewalks in La Jolla and at the campus. I figured, kind of a laid back school with most of the kids in shorts, tee shirts and sandals.

Nancy jumped in with, "Mr. Radovich, I have a surfing cousin and she lives close to La Jolla." Nancy looked at Mom. "I haven't met her, but we exchange pictures and letters. Nancy looked at me and withdrew her hand. "I'm not going to tell you her name or give you her address. I just don't like the idea of you living in an estate?"

"It is an estate owned by a very wealthy widow," I added, "and she supports the college athletic program and I 'am' required to keep my grades up to be able to stay there."

Mother added, "It is amazing. Ted, you're always able to get the best out of any situation."

I went on, "I also have a job, waiting tables for her, the wealthy lady when she is entertaining. I also have a car to use for my transportation to school and back. Part of my job will be to pick up her bridge, swimming, and tennis lady friends, then drive them to their homes after whatever they were doing. For that job I will be driving a new Rolls-Royce. Part of my job is to keep Mrs. Andrew's cars polished.

"You said a Rolls Royce and there are other cars, Ted?" Mom asked me.

"Yes, she has three cars for herself, and—"

Before I can go on about the cars, Nancy erupted with, "Four cars? You said she has four cars?

My God what's next?" Mom exclaimed.

"Well, she doesn't really have only four cars, She has six cars in a big garage Three for her use, one for Jose her man in charge of the grounds, one for me, and one for the woman that lives in the other apartment next to me. Her name is Coach Van Tunstall."

Nancy jumped in with, "You said Coach Van Tunstall, is that Janice van Tunstall?"

"I don't know, I didn't meet her, but she has the apartment next to me. I was told she—"

"I got a letter from Coach van Tunstall," Nancy interrupted. "She said she might be interested in me playing field hockey for her team. She said she heard, I could possibly be the one defensive player she's always wanted and when she found out you and I were dating I guess she thought the two of us would come together to San Diego. Did the coaches tell you about me and the hockey offer?"

"Not a word. I *never* met my neighbor and nothing was said to me, and you never *told* me anything."

"I wanted to surprise you, Hon, *but* Mom and Dad had other ideas."

*   *   *

Dad wanted to know more about the school and what my plans were for this summer and when I'd have to report for practice.

I paused, I really did not want to tell them this, but I guessed I must. I didn't know if they would be excited, or not. "Well, let's see, how shall I explain this? Well, all right. I'm reporting to Fort Benning two days after our high school graduation. The airplane ticket will arrive next week. I, uh, I was selected for a special basic training this summer.

Somebody called Gunner Skiloski set it up. Is he the same man that used to stop by and visit us? I guess he's really something in the Army. I met him. He told me he knows you Dad."

Now the car erupted with two women asking questions. Finally, Dad is able to silence them.

"Now start from the beginning and tell us just what really happened in San Diego," he said to me. "Wait, lets stop at the restaurant up ahead and have dinner and you can tell us eye ball to eye ball. You will start from the beginning, won't you Son?"

It was very quiet in the car. Nancy had scooted over to the right rear window away from me and she refused to hold my hand. All she's doing was looking out the side window. Not a word was said when we stopped. I guess everyone was waiting for my story about San Diego and why I was going to Fort Benning, so quick.

Walking to the restaurant, Nancy was ahead with Mom and Dad, and I'm walking behind, alone. We took a table and placed our orders, the whole time I had two pairs of women's blue eyes looking at me. Dad had a smile on his face. Damn it, again, he knew something.

I took a deep breath and looking at Dad, announced, "I joined the Army."

Mom and Nancy sat up and almost in one voice exclaimed, "You what?

Nancy exclaimed angrily, "You gave up two college scholarships to join the Army without notifying anyone. But you're living in La Jolla? How can you do all that?'

I looked at Dad. His smile had not left his face and I knew, he knew the whole story. I tried to explain to the women.

"Well, it's not exactly like you think. You see, I am taking ROTC and I met a man, a General Skiloski. I had dinner with him and Coach Hickey."

This General said if I signed up now, they will pay me Army pay for four years, while I go to school, and I will be required to take four summer training courses at Fort Benning.

He told me; I will graduate from college as a First Lieutenant instead of a Second Lieutenant. Also, if I do well, I may be able to pick a better slot in what I want to do in the Army when I'm out of college, and Oscar will have to salute me because I will out rank him when he graduates from Annapolis."

Mom looked at Dad. "I'm not interested in Oscar right now. Skiloski, that's the same Army buddy called Gunner that used to stay with us when Ted was little?"

"That's the man, Marie. His name is General Gunner Skiloski. Ted, you had better learn that from now on you to refer to him as General Skiloski because he carries three stars. He will be watching you during your four years of college and summer training."

"What about you and me, Ted?" Nancy had tears in her eyes and her lips were quivering. "I thought we would have the whole summer to, well, you know, do some things together, and now you will be gone all summer, then football at that school probably starts for you in August. You aren't being fair to me. I'll end up as an old maid, or maybe I'll up and become a nun!" She slapped my thigh hard.

Nancy was ready to cry.

Mom looked at Nancy. "Lets make a quick trip to the ladies room Nancy and freshen up."

Dad and I both stood and helped the women leave the booth. We watched Mom and Nancy leave with Mom's arm around Nancy's shoulders that appear to be shaking.

"Ted, I can't tell your mother right now, but you made an excellent choice. General Skiloski will have you on the fast track in the Army."

"I guess so. He does not want me to take any language except Spanish in college. He mentioned to me he likes my idea of taking all the courses in International World Relations. He said that I will be able go to a school in Monterey for my languages after I graduate from college. He emphasized languages. What's in Fort Benning that is so important for me to attend, Dad?"

"First: Monterey is the finest language school anywhere. You'll learn right from the start not only a foreign language, but the food they eat, the clothes they wear, the newspapers and the magazines they read, and even the movies they see. It is a nine-month course of full immersion in the culture and language of the country you will be sent to. Second, Fort Benning is an elite Army post for the Special Forces, Paratroopers, Rangers, and the Delta bunch. Even the Navy Seals do some training there, and the FBI has a training area there as well. I don't know how General Skiloski did it, but you'll train with the best troopers in the world. You'll also meet some soldiers from our friendly foreign countries.

Ted, you'll be with the absolute best soldiers anywhere. Also, you'll be in top shape when your football practice begins. What a great way to get in shape for football and still improve yourself in catching hold of the Army life."

"Dad, how long have you known this, uh, General Skiloski?"

"Ted, I don't think you really remember him. He used to come over to the house when you were a little tike. Gunner never came over to the house when you were older because he stayed with Grandpa and Grandma. You might remember his singing Russian songs with Grandpa.

He was often in the stands watching you play football. He also used to watch Nancy play field hockey. Gunner was always across the field from us. He's a quiet man."

He played ball at West Point as a guard, as I recall. Tough guy, squatty, but with moves like a ballet dancer. Quick with his feet and hands, kinda like Oscar, and Oscar's foot work is similar to Gunner's."

"Then you knew this General when you were in the Army?" I asked Dad."

"Yes, I had him in my regiment when I was Command Sergeant Major, and he was fresh out of the academy.

This is funny; he's a brand new second lieutenant. He marched into my office wearing some misfit sloppy uniform, kind of like a South American jungle soldier. Get this, he tosses his papers on my desk knocking over my coffee cup.

I told him, 'Mr. Whatever you are, you are in my house and you just made a mess, Sir. You'll clean it up, right now, or you will spend the rest of your time here in my Army, Sir, being the Officer of the KP's, and I'll dump all the latrine inspections in your direction, Sir. I promise you, Sir, you'll never leave this regiment until I retire and you'll be catching every shit detail I can find for your pleasure, Sir, and I'll even invent a couple just for you, Sonny, oh excuse me, Sir!'"

"What did he do?" I asked.

"He gave me a mean look then bent over and picked up his papers and wiped my desk clean, using his handkerchief. I never moved out of my chair.

Then he asked me, 'I'm an officer, aren't you going to stand up and salute me?'

Certainly 'Sir', but only when you become an officer. Right now, I can't tell what rag tag army you're with the way you're dressed, but it's certainly not in 'my' army, and you'll not dress like that on my post starting right now.

He said, 'I'm sorry Sergeant. I had bad flights and lost all my luggage, had multiple transfers and storm delays between New York and here. Those airlines pushed me all over the United States dodging storms.'

I stood up, saluted him and said, 'You are now in my country. I'll get you fitted correctly because you can't have my colonel see you like this. Come with me and we'll get you squared away. Fortunately, your commanding officer, Colonel Jefferson, is out and won't be back until later because right now, you couldn't pass for an officer of some back water country we never heard of.'

I stuck him in my jeep and drove to the commissary and arranged for him to be outfitted with new uniforms, then showed him his quarters and waited until he changed into a decent uniform. I checked him over to see if he was dressed correctly. I made a few changes and we returned to my office.

My boss was in, and I took the new Second Lieutenant Skiloski, now dressed correctly, into meet his commanding officer. This is always an unwelcome thrill for a new Second Lieutenant or any officer under a Colonel.

My boss told me, 'Sergeant, grab that chair and stay seated.' Only two chairs were in his office, and he had one and now I had the other, and for five minuets this Full-bird Colonel Jefferson chewed on Second Lieutenant Gunner Skiloski standing at attention. I think the office people must have told my boss what happened with the coffee cup.

When he was through he ended by saying. 'When you were at the Point, you obviously didn't pay any attention to the Code of Conduct regarding enlisted men and especially those sergeants that wear a star in the middle of their chevrons like Sergeant Major Radovich. Listen to me, you dragging ass Second Lieutenant. Only two people in this man's army wear stars: one are Generals, and the others are Command Sergeant Majors, and you never shove your rank on them for any reason, or your tour in this man's army will be a longest and most painful experience you'll ever have. Your name will go on a list that will follow you clear to the Old Soldiers Home.

My Sergeant Major is my right hand and when I'm out on business he is in charge of this office and everything else that goes with it under my eagle. Get this straight now or you'll discover how much crap can be stacked on top of you. So much you'll never find your way out of the jobs these people can give you because every Command Sergeant Major in this army will follow you to your grave giving you more cow crap than you can swallow.

Second Lieutenant Skiloski, one more rank pulling on this man and your life will be one solid shit detail that will never end. Got it, 'Second Lieutenant' Skiloski?

Lieutenant Skiloski, still standing at attention, demonstrating a perfect West Point brace and not blinking an eye, replied, 'I completely understand and will comply, Sir!'

The colonial continued, 'My advice is; read and know, thoroughly, the book on Code of Conduct. I'm sure I made myself clear? My Sergeant will treat you fair as he holds no grudges, but he is one hundred and ten percent military and when you accept that maybe you'll become a soldier, and not just another drag ass second lieutenant. You're dismissed and get out of my sight until you learn to be a professional soldier.'"

I asked Dad, "Then what happened? How did you two become friends?"

"Afterwards, it was a while before we became friends. First, Gunner and I met in the gym as we worked out, then slowly we began to work out together. Finally we began to spar with gloves. For a while, in the beginning, he would try to catch me off guard and I was always waiting for him. I'd pop him a good right cross and buckle his knees.

He never held it against me. He'd laugh and say; 'You rotten Slav, you got this Russian again. Okay, I'll buy the beer again. I'm getting damn tired buying all the beer for some stupid Slav's lucky hit. When do you buy the beer?'

When some stupid Russian learns not to drop his right glove when he telegraphs his left jab."

'You rotten bastard, you have known that all this time, and I've been buying beer for your despicable, sneaky ass every night for a year?'"

Dad continued, "I watched his rapid rise up in the ranks and we became better friends from then on? He and your Coach Hecky are friends going back to their football days, Gunner at the Point and Hecky at Notre Dame."

Dad looked at me seriously and continued, "We, your mother and I, had a meeting with the Blakes. We all decided a separation would be the best for you and Nancy."

I didn't know what to say because the thought of no Nancy made my stomach hurt. I was about to complain bitterly and lash out, but decided it was probably for the best. "I guess that's for the best," I said unconvincingly. "I'll accept it, but Nancy probably won't so don't tell her you and the Blakes discussed it."

"We agreed on that too," Dad said.

"I still can't get over it, Oscar will have to salute me when he graduates from Annapolis. He'll be only an Ensign and I'll be a First Lieutenant."

"You're right about that and perhaps throughout both of your military careers you can stay ahead. Here come the ladies, don't mention what I told you. Just tell the ladies how proud you are be selected for special attention in the Army and will have the chance to go to college. I'll run the interference for you at home with your mother."

I pulled out the chair for Nancy, when her and Mom returned, and she gave me a smile. Her blue eyes appeared to be red from crying.

Dad told the women how lucky I was to have this early training and be under the eyes of a man he had known for years, and how fortunate I would be to advance one grade when I graduated from college.

Nancy was trying to accept it. During dinner she had her hand on my thigh and was constantly squeezing, but she still wanted to know if I would be home for a while after Fort Benning and before I reported to football practice in August.

I told her I didn't really know, but I was sure I would be.

Nancy asked me, "Ted, Hon, what will your major be, besides, the Army?"

"Government and Foreign Affairs, similar to yours, Nancy."

"Maybe we can study together when you are home for the holidays, if I'm not too booked up with the Eastern boys." She gave me a kiss on my cheek.

Dinner was quiet. Nancy kept her hand on my thigh, rubbing and squeezing. Finally, she turned to me and asked, "Are we still going to the prom, Hon?"

"Of course, there is no reason not to. I always knew my Senior Prom would be with you, or do you have another date?" I joked.

"Absolutely not. You are my date and we're going to the prom, and graduation night we'll be at my folks house with lots of our schoolmates. Understand? You are still my steady and that's an order Mister Radovich."

CHAPTER 20

Every May, my folks held a barbecue at our home on Mallard Lake for the Senior Class of Daisy Junction High School. Before I was a Senior I was shipped off to Oscar's house for the day.

My family offered boating, swimming, and eating as the fare of the day at the Radovich's Senior Bash. That year I could finally go.

Gramp Egor and Gram Olena, old then, still helped cook and barbecue the food. Gramp always cooked with his old leather shirt, short pants, jaunty leather hat covered with medals, and his scuffed and patched hiking boots."

He made a fine figure because he would dance the Slovenian dances with any girl he picked out. Many of the Slav girls knew some of the dances and they stomped and whirled around the patio.

He was always on his good behavior and never swore, not even once. During the parties, held each June, Grandma Olena, Mom, and Dad always held their breath for fear Gramp Egor would let out with one of his favorite bleeps.

The kids loved his stories of the old country and his leather shorts and alpine hat. Even his bad legs don't seem to bother him as he jauntily struts around the garden teasing the boys and dancing with the girls.

During the afternoon, the kids would beg Gramp Egor to play his concertina and sing some of his family songs. Gram would watch carefully and would try to stop Gramp when he started on one of his questionable barroom songs. Heck, many kids knew those songs from their folks and would ignore Gram's request to halt the singing. Gram then would throw up her hands and hurry back into the kitchen.

*   *   *

Toward the evening, even with all the fun, I realized; I have to make plans for college. Nancy and I thought, once, we might find a college or university that we could both attend or at least be close to each other for the next four years. Nancy had suggested that maybe we could be roommates if we share a place with any other students. We were certainly wrong.

CHAPTER 21

ONE SUNDAY, JUST BEFORE graduation, I came home from church and slammed the front door. Mom and Dad were in the living room reading the Sunday paper.

Both looked up, surprised, and Mom asked, "What's all that for, Teddy? Did you have a fight with Nancy?"

"No."

"Well, something certainly has got you upset," Mom added. "Ah, let me guess. It's Pastor Roberts. This was his day for his sermon about the evil doings of teenagers, am I right."

"No Mom, it's not the fourth Sunday, that's next week, but this Sunday he started in on us early. What in the devil is wrong with that man? He picks on us continually, and that brother of his, 'Georgie Boy,' is just as bad. What do they think we do all day, just go out and have sex, drink and smoke? I'm telling you, the next time he preaches on the evils of us kids I'm walking out of his church right in the middle of his righteous sermon. He should spend more time with his oldest daughter Lisa and find out how she entertains the boys."

Dad asked, "What are Nancy's thoughts regarding Pastor Robert's sermons?"

Same as mine. She was wiggling around in the choir bench during his sermon and kept mumbling to herself.

When she starts mumbling, watch out. The minute we marched out of the church and went to the choir room she threw her choir robe off into a corner. Georgie Boy' went up to Nancy to say something and she got into his face, saying, "Don't you even start on me if you want to see me at another choir practice. You two, you and your brother, are so old fashioned it's a wonder you two don't travel around in horse and carriage. Let's get of this place, Ted."

Taking Nancy home was some project. She was so steamed up she was sitting right next to the door of your car with her arms crossed and still muttering. I tried to calm her down and she blew up at me. I told her, "Whoa, easy, Nancy, remember, I'm on your side. Let me tell you what we can do?"

"I don't want to listen,' Nancy yelled at me. What does he know about the youth today or even yesterday, and what gets me, the darn church members all nod their heads in agreement. I guess they were never young. I'm so mad and embarrassed by his attacks on all of us kids, including you and."

"Okay, okay, Nancy, I want you to hear me out. I agree with you," I explained.

She wanted to know, "What are you going to do about it, Ted? You're so smart, what is your plan since you always have a closet full of ideas?"

I returned, "Only if you calm down and listen to me, Nancy."

She snapped, "I'm calmed down!"

So I explained my plan; "Next Sunday, if he begins on us, like we know he will, we will just get up and walk out of his church right in front of everyone. I'll bet some of the other kids will do the same and follow us. I'm sure some of them will join us."

"Ted. We have to make an impact on everyone, not just our high school friends," Nancy added."

"You're right," I advised, "so next Sunday you'll wear something flashy with high heels, and I will wear my new brown suit and my shoes with the leather soles and heels."

"Your dancing shoes?"

"Absolutely. We need the clicking noise when as we leave the church."

"I don't understand."

"When we get up and leave, and walk down the center aisle, everyone in the church not only will see us, but hear us leave because it's a wooden floor on centeraisle. We won't look at the people sitting in the aisles. You and I will just focus our eyes on the two big doors at the church entrance. Can you do that with me?"

"I'm sorry I was such a bitch," Nancy apologized, "Okay Ted, I'm with you. Of course you knew I would be the whole time. I feel better, but we have to understand that we 'will' receive some criticism from various people after our grand exit. Are you ready for that, love?"

"As long as I'm with you, my dear. So that's what we will do next Sunday.

We agreed not tell anyone our plans. We are just going to do it.

Dad was sitting in his chair and had a smile on his face. He asked, "You two talked this over with the Blakes?"

"Yes, we did, and they agreed."

* * *

All week, Nancy and I did not mention, to anyone, our plans for this coming Sunday.

I picked up Nancy on Sunday morning for church, driving my folks new car. Nancy showed up in high heels and a dress that was made just for a spring morning. I told her, "Damn you look great."

"Well, you certainly don't look like a country boy yourself," Nancy returned.

As we were ready to leave the Blake's, Dr. Blake told us, "Good Luck kids and remember no smiles. We'll see you after church, over at Mimi and Val's. I think you two might strike a cord that will hopefully be remembered for a long time, and maybe change Pastor Roberts for the best."

I was in my new, light brown, soon to be graduation suit. I had on a starched white shirt and tie.

Nancy told me, "You'll be the best dressed and the most handsome man in church today."

"You mean only today?" I joked.

"I don't care if you are in your filthy manure boots and jeans, you are always good looking, and I'm the envy of almost every girl in school."

"Who are the ones that don't envy you?"

"I'll never tell. Why did you ask, Ted?"

"Well, when you dump me for someone else, I would like to know whose shoulder I can't cry on."

"Honey, if that time comes you'll be so old nobody will want you, so, 1 guess it will be little old me forever. There will never be another other woman in your life like me. Keep that in mind. We are going to stay together no matter how many miles apart we will be. Let's get into the church."

I gave Nancy a hug, and she wanted a kiss, so I kissed her lightly.

"Come on, you have done better than that," she purred up at me.

"I didn't want to walk into church with lipstick all over me."

"Since when?"

"Remember Nancy, we have to get seats up close to Pastor Roberts."

We held hands as we walked into our church. Nancy's high heels, and my brown shoes with the hard heels seem to reverberated off the church floor and sound like we are pounding our way forward purposefully.

We walked toward the front of the church and entered the front pews right under the pulpit used by Pastor Roberts. No one joined us as most of the church goers, seemed to me, occupied the middle to the back of the church pews. Why? I haven't the slightest idea.

At ten o clock the choir enters from the two huge wooden doors in the front of the church and they slowly walk up the center aisle, singing, led by 'Georgie Boy'.

He almost tripped over his long choir robe looking at Nancy and I. We both smile to him, but he didn't smile back at us. I really think the choir could have used our voices this Sunday.

Then came the various prayers and songs with George Boy giving us long questioning looks all morning. Now our time was getting close when Pastor Roberts walked slowly to his pulpit and Nancy and I are right under him.

Pastor Roberts placed his notes on the lectern, then he gave us a long stare before he began his sermon. We gave him our best, most benevolent smiles.

Nancy had a tight grip on my hand. I thought I could feel a slight tremble in her grip.

Now came the sermon and about five minutes into it, Pastor Roberts slid into his favorite subject; the younger generation. We gave him about ten minutes to get up to speed and just when he was about to totally slander Nancy, myself, and the rest of the younger generation, I felt a clench and unclench signal from Nancy's hand.

I returned the signal. Then we stood up and headed for the center aisle. Hand in hand, with our eyes glued to the two big, now closed, entry doors, and with clicks of our heels on the wooden floor, we walked, standing tall, toward those impressive doors.

As we passed, everyone watched with interest."

Pastor Roberts just continued lecturing.

Dad Lerfervre, the custodian of the doors and lot of other things, quickly left his seat at the last pew and stood in front of those high, thick, and carved wooden doors.

I pointed to the doors showing we wanted to leave. He nodded and opened the doors.

He followed us outside, closing the doors behind himself.

Outside he inquired; "There's something wrong?"

Nancy was ready and in a firm voice explained, "Yes, there certainly is. Pastor Roberts gave one too many unacceptable sermons on our evil intents, and he is dead wrong, again. We have heard the last of his patented, 'lets bash the kids 'again' sermons."

Almost in one voice Nancy and I say, "Good day, Dad Lerfervre."

She and I turned to leave, but Dad Lerfervre said to us, "Just one minute please. You two are exactly on target. I've been telling Pastor Roberts he has been making a big mistake by his continual attacks on you and your friends. I've told him, it must be over hundred times, 'Our kids today are no different from when I was a kid and you young. Ease up on them.'

I've told him so many times, 'Don't tear the young generation down.' He feels your generation is the worst of the worst. He just doesn't pay any attention to me."

The big doors to the church opened and out walked Oscar, the Benton sisters, George Photopolis, the butchers son, and Carey Roberts, Pastor Roberts's nephew. They joined up with Nancy and I.

"Boy, am I going to hear about this," Carey Roberts said.

"You might want to go back," advised Dad Lerfervre.

"Hell no, I hear that crap more than you do, even at home, and I'm fed up."

"I figured you'd need some support," Oscar threw in.

"The whole choir is ready to bolt, but 'George Boy' and his assistant have the getaway routes blocked," said Jenny Benton.

"How's Pastor Roberts doing?" I asked.

"Still blowing his horn, but the congregation is restless," Oscar answered.

Dad Lerfervre turned to the new pilgrims and continued, "Like I was telling Nancy and Teddy, I told Pastor Roberts; 'I was once an archeologist and I remember, in my early career, when I finally was able to decipher all the symbols on the Egyptian tombs and walls. Pastor, you won't believe this. The people in those times were as concerned about their young ones as we are now. They just knew their children were on the road to ruin.'

He told me, 'Dad, these are modern times, and new vices are here. Much different now than them olden times.'

I told him, 'Come on Pastor Roberts. Don't you hear what I've been trying to telling you? Older people always think the youth are headed downhill, but they aren't. It's been the same for over 2000 years, probably much longer. The youths have been considered, going to the dogs, or where ever people want to place them as being bad, according to their standards, and it's only our thinking. Young folks have been the same for hundreds of centuries.'

I know he won't pay any attention to me, now or ever. I'll tell you all, I used to give this talk to all my first-year students at the university, concerning how kids have always been.'

Last week I told him again, 'Ease up, please Pastor Roberts, or you will lose them for good.'

Maybe he will pay attention now. Nancy, Teddy, and you others. Thank you for your effort today. Let's hope we came to a turn in that road this Sunday. Thanks for your bravery and conviction. Have a good day kids." Dad Lerfervre headed back for the large doors, opened one and went back inside the church.

When we got to the parking lot, there were an additional six rebellious youths coming from around the back of the church, followed by at least fifteen adults.

Nancy and I left and drove to my folks home, feeling great after listening to Dad Lerfervre.

As we were walking up to the door Nancy said to me, "I feel wonderful, and I'm sure we did the right thing, Honey." Nancy then gave me an 'oh so good kiss', and then we went inside.

"Time for breakfast, kids," Dad hollered out, "and how was your morning." Dr. and Mrs. Blake were there.

Nancy and I began telling them that we followed through on our plan, and got some support because quite a few people joined our protest, and we mentioned what Dad Lerfervre told us."

There was much talking during our breakfast, and then a telephone call for me, then seven more in quick succession, kids calling to tell me after we left the church they did the same."

Dr. Blake certainly didn't let me bask in my so called glory. "Ted, since you are the Student Body President it will be you that will select the civic leader to give the blessings at graduation? You know it's been a tradition to use one of church leaders to give the graduation prayers and a short talk. The four churches in town are on a four year rotation, and I'm pretty sure this year is Pastor Roberts's turn. Do you have a decision on that situation? Remember, Ted, you will give the introduction to the official and you will be sitting right next to him while you're on the stage."

"I did forget that gem? Wow! Well, Oscar is the class president, but on the other hand Nancy and I did the walking out, and the others followed us later. I have no intentions of changing the routine so I'll have to talk to Pastor Roberts.

"Ted," Dr. Blake remarked, "I'm sure you'll handle the situation correctly because I know you very well. You take sticky problems and handle them correctly. Remember Ted, I've seen you under stress, make us all proud of you."

"Thank you for those kind words Doctor Blake. I'll call this week and make an appointment to see Pastor Roberts. I'm really not looking forward to it, but I led the movement out of his church."

Nancy chirped in with, "Well, I'm going with you when you talk to Pastor Roberts because I have a few things to tell him."

"Nancy, I think it would be best if I handled this alone because we've made our point and now need to compromise."

"Okay, just make sure his daughter, Lisa the sex pot, doesn't waylay you before you see her father."

"I can hardly wait for that to happen."

I received a quick tongue showing from Nancy.

With all the projects I have in front of me, besides school work, I have to see Pastor Roberts, and the only time I have is this week.

*   *   *

The Daily Register's article the next morning read, "Pastor Roberts claims, 'The Devil Made Them Do It.'"

CHAPTER 22

Another problem was the lack of a decent hall in Daisy Junction for the prom. It was suggested that maybe we can use our gym.

Coach Able, our basketball coach, was somewhat upset with the thought of having street shoes on his carefully protected gym floor, and wearing just socks instead of shoes in a suit or a formal dress just did not set right with me or my committee.

Past years, the proms were held in the Masonic Hall, the same place the Rainbow dances were, but because our class is the largest to ever graduate it's just too small. Dancing in the Masonic Hall would be a bump and shove event so our committee decided we needed a change. Going out of town was not acceptable by the school and the our parents. Among all my projects surrounding the prom and graduation I have to find a place for our prom.

I made arrangements to meet Pastor Roberts Saturday evening at seven.

I drove to the church and entered his study.

"Good evening Pastor Roberts, I want to thank you for giving me the time out of your busy schedule to talk to you."

"Before you begin, Ted, let me start. I have been a preacher for thirty years right here in Daisy Junction. I don't think you know it, but being the leader of our church community has its problems. Even to come up with a sermon every Sunday is demanding. I struggle every week to find something interesting for my flock.

When you and Nancy walked out of my sermon, the only time in thirty years anyone has done that, it hurt me. It hurt me very deeply. I'm so glad that my daughter Lisa was not a part of that. She is such a sweet and innocent girl. I know people say different, but that is just the devil trying to distract me from my appointed mission."

I had to hold my tongue and just let him go.

Pastor Roberts was leaning over his desk, looking at me. "Dad Lerfervre got hold of me after everyone had left. I was sitting right here at my desk trying to figure out what happened. Eight or twelve young kids also left after you and Nancy Blake. I'll tell you the truth, I was not feeling chipper.

Then Dad came into this office and sat down right there where you are now. He gave me a talking to as a father would give his wayward son. Finally, after all his suggestions to me, I heard what he has been telling me for some time. He was right, I have to bend a little.

Let me tell you a little about my youth. I came from a struggling family life. My father was a bartender and my mother took in children during the day, babysitting so to speak, and I had no childhood supervision and ran wild. I thought all kids did the same as me. My doing 'God's Work' is what save me, and I know that salvation is what can save you and your friends.

This week I realized that the Devil is stronger than I thought. You, Nancy, Dad Lerfervre and the other kids convinced me of that. I'm going to tone the sermons down because the Devil threw me a curve. I mustn't continue to berate his attempts so openly because then he will win out. I must make my mission more attractive because I realize that's what he does.

Don't say anything yet." Pastor Roberts held his hands up. "You have prom coming up. Where will it be held?"

"I have no idea yet Pastor Roberts. I would like to have a different place and yet stay in town. We just don't have anything. I even thought the fire house would work, but it's too small."

"Ted, may I offer you a suggestion?"

"Well, yes, certainly," I quickly replied.

"Now this is between you and I only. No one knows this, but I have a brother who ran away from home and joined the circus. Many of my sermons are featured around our escapades. Anyway, he has worked himself up to a part owner of that circus. I'm going to give you his phone number, and you call him tonight at eight, he's expecting to hear from you. Don't tell anyone I had anything to do with it, just take the credit. You can figure out some plausible story, I'm sure of that."

Pastor Robbers stood up and that was my clue, 'times up'. He walked me to the door and asked. "Am I on for graduation?"

"You'd better be, I have your name on the graduation program, Pastor."

He laughed. "I'll have a surprise for you at graduation. Thank you for allowing me to share a peek of my early life with you. Now, all his is still between you and I, right?"

"Always." I walked away seeing another side of Pastor Robbers.

*   *   *

After my phone call to Pastor Roberts's brother, Arnold, Dad, Dr. Blake, Mr. Torres, Mr. Roosevelt, Mr. Otsuki, and Mr. Lee came to the rescue because this project came with a series of complicated moves. Everyone wanted to know how I found a circus tent, and I told them I just took a chance and phoned a circus for help.

Now, I had obtained this huge circus tent for free, but it had to be shipped by two flat cars to a siding in Daisy Junction. With a couple of big farm tractors and two huge implement trailers the rolled up tent with poles and stakes and miles of rope had to be taken to our football field.

With the tent came an unassembled floor. Also, the tent came with Arnold to guide us through the complicated erection process. He used a different name while in town, again to keep our secret.

With fathers, students, and Arnold, hollering and sometimes cussing, the tent was raised successfully.

Our local electrical company brought in the electricity and donated the cost of the lighting. I asked Freddy if his band could have some new music. Maybe a native dance, along with a tango, maybe a samba or rumba, and of course a couple waltzes for us on this special night.

Freddy called me and said, "I can assure you, Ted, the band will come prepared and South American and European dances will be played. We have never played under a circus tent and are looking forward to our big night as well. We'll have that music ready."

*   *   *

My parents were chaperones along with The Blakes, The Torres, The Otskis, The Roosevelts, the Lees, along with Cowboy Pat McGrath and his guest Rosie Kallich, Captain and Mrs. Shumaker, Miss Orr and Mr. White.

The chaperones, school administration, and the senior student committee made a couple of rules, also requested by the secret circus man: leave the tent once and don't bother to return, any alcohol before or during the prom, and the police will handle that part. The parents will be notified, and if they are not home, the perpetrator will stay in jail until an adult member of the family arrives for their release. Another couple of rules from the senior committee: girls must be in formals and dates in suits, no tuxes. The reason? The cost. Every girl must have a dance bid and her date will bring a corsage for her. I know my mother had her hand in those rules.

Mr. Otsuki was sold out of carnations at his two florists shops."

Portable restrooms were at one end of this gigantic tent. The restrooms for the women were in an enclosed area because gowns would be difficult to handle in a portable restroom. This was Nancy's idea and was well received.

Freddy's band was on the other side of the tent, the large wooden dance floor in the center, and tables and chairs on the other side along with the midnight buffet. Finger food and soft drinks were available all night long.

* * *

I drove the folks' car to pick up Nancy at eight in the evening.

Nancy opened the front door without my ringing the door bell and I almost didn't recognize her.

She was wearing a new, off the shoulder light purple gown. Nancy's long blond hair was cut short. I guess I stood in the door way just staring at her. Damn she was just beautiful.

Finally she said, "Won't you please close your mouth and come in Mr. Radovich."

Inside, Dr. and Mrs. Blake were dressed very formal, Dr. Blake in a Tux and Mrs. Blake in a blue formal gown. Mom and Dad were dressed down a little compared to the Blakes.

Mom and Dad and the Blakes were grinning at me, waiting for me to say something intelligent.

I'm trying to remember the poem I spend all day memorizing for this moment.

"My lovely date," I started with a frog in my throat. I took a deep, deep breath and launched.

*　　*　　*

She Walks in Beauty. May I say this to you
If it doesn't take all night
She he walks in beauty, like the night.
Of cloudless climes and starry skies
and all that is best and bright
Meet in her aspect and her eyes.

*　　*　　*

I took another deep breath when I was done, and there was an applause from the Blakes and my folks.

"Well done, Ted, well done," said Dr. Blake.

Nancy was smiling. "My handsome poet, allow me to quote from the Mirada by W.S. Gilbert.

*   *   *

I have a left shoulder-blade that is a miracle of loveliness. People come miles to see it.

My right elbow has a fascination that few can resist.

*   *   *

Mom, Dad and the Blakes erupted in laughter.

Mrs. Blake, laughing so hard she has tears in her eyes, says, "Those two are going to their prom and they quote from the masters trying to get one up on the other,"

Nancy gave me a long look and then a kiss. Then she held out a box, but did not give it to me.

"What's this, my lovely date that is much older than I?"

"This is for a very young boy, if he opens the box, maybe he will know." Nancy was smiling and handed me the box.

I opened the box and inside was a lovely carnation boutonniere. All the times I took Nancy to the formal Rainbow dances she never once gave me a boutonniere.

I asked her, "May I give this beautiful blond flower giver a kiss?"

"You had better if you want that boutonniere."

After a very wet kiss I asked to be excused, then I brought in three wrapped gift boxes.

I gave one to Dr. Blake, another to Mrs. Blake, and the third I held in my hand. Of course Dr. and Mrs. Blake were surprised, or appeared to be surprised. I knew Mother might have said something to them days before. I wouldn't doubt it because I'm sure Dr. Blake would certainly have had a corsage for his wife.

Nancy was looking at me as I still held the third box while Dr. and Mrs. Blake were thanking me.

Not looking at Nancy, I said, "My gosh, somehow the florist must have made a mistake and I didn't catch the error until now. She gave me three boxes instead of two. Well, I guess I can drop this box off tonight when we go to the prom. Maybe some lonely girl could use this? Ready Nancy?"

She tossed her coat over her shoulder and walked to the front door, not once looking at me. "You plan on opening this door, or do I have to do it myself?"

The Blakes and Mom and Dad have smiles as they wait to see what will happen.

"Sure," I told her, "go ahead and maybe I can give this box to either Lisa Roberts or to Blossom Ann. I'll bet they'll know what to do with a special corsage that a very beautiful blond lass in an outstanding formal dress will not be wearing. A corsage that I had made special for her."

Nancy turned around and came back to me. "You'll have to pin it on my dress, and if you can't, I'll get Roberto to do the honors. Your move Mr. Radovich."

I handed her the white box with silver bow.

That corsage I bought for Nancy cost me a fortune. Mrs. Blake told me the color of Nancy's dress, and I let the florists do the rest of the job.

The florist guaranteed me; "Nancy's corsage will be the prettiest and most unusual that I have made up in years, and you two will be the most handsome couple at your prom.

Nancy opened the box and picked up the card on top and opened it. It read, "May this night join us for the years ahead and return us back to our first and only true love we will ever have. Ted."

Nancy was crying as she reached in the box again and pulled out the orchid corsage with small ferns that matched her dress. "Darn you Ted," Nancy sniffled, "I'll have to redo my make up." She hurried toward the stairs with Mrs. Blake and Mom close behind. They were all wiping their eyes

"Well, Son," Dr. Blake placed his arm around me. "You are leaving a young lady that is very much in love with you. Both of you will be miles apart in, what, two days after graduation, six days from now?"

"Exactly. Maybe I shouldn't have put that note in the corsage box. I didn't plan on that happening. I didn't think I would make them cry."

"No, no. I would guess they are shedding tears for your good manners. Now you have two more ladies to dance with tonight. Your poetry, the note, the corsage, and the timing will make this night one to remember."

Dad added, "Silent and surprising Ted, you planned this event perfect. Well, well, here comes our ladies down the stairs and for heaven sakes, Ted, please don't make them cry again."

*　　*　　*

A full moon was starting to rise that night as Nancy and I drove slowly to 'The Prom in a Tent'. If she had been sitting on my lap, Nancy couldn't have gotten much closer to me.

"Ted, honey, how many days do we have together before you leave for that fort or what ever you call it?"

"Six days my dear."

"It's just not going to work out, darn it."

Without her saying it, I know. "Okay, then I'll be home for a short time before I head for San Diego, maybe then?"

"Honey," I said to her, "I just don't want to hurry up my affair with you, for you I'll wait."

She placed her head on my shoulder. "I'm going to love you forever."

"And I'm proud to say the same my dear Nancy. You've had me since I first saw you in the crib next to me at the hospital. I promise you we'll be together even if we're miles apart."

*   *   *

As Nancy and I came to the gate to enter the tent we were held up by Oscar.

"Slight problem, wait," he said.

I ask, "What's the problem, Oscar?"

"Just wait."

I noticed Oscar trying to hide a wire and some type of speaking device. I heard him say, "Okay, ready to roll."

Then all the lights went out. Oscar took Nancy by the arm and told me, "Follow."

Inside the tent it was dark. A spotlight hit us, and Freddy and his band gave out a long musical cord.

Standing on the stage was Lincoln and Washington dressed in suits and each holding a microphone.

Together they announced in perfect unison, "Here is 'the' man, with his beautiful lady, that got us this fabulous circus tent. Hit it Freddy!"

The band played that great circus march 'Entrance of the Gladiators'. Nancy and I, with misty eyes, slowly walked toward Freddy's band stand. When we got there, Nancy handed me the box I gave her earlier.

Oscar went to the microphone and announced, "Lets all watch Teddy pin Nancy."

After the cheers, Oscar continued looking at Nancy. "Now, I'll read Ted's inscription, 'May the day come, years from now, when we will be together forever.'"

Nancy turned and grabbed me. "Damn, there goes my makeup again. I'll need your handkerchief, I'll love you for ever. Pin me."

*   *   *

Just before the party was about over, Dad went over to Miss Orr and asked her for a dance. No one knew Dad had made arrangements with Freddy to play a couple of Schottisches, Slovene folk dancing. Dad whipped out of his jacket, and put on Grandpa's old leather hat with all of Gramp's medals pinned on it.

With that weather beaten and well used hat on the side of his head he and Miss Orr put on a display that cleared the dance floor amid continuous and enthusiastic clapping of us Seniors.

Later, Nancy and I did a Tango to the applause of our classmates. Freddy then repeated another Tango, and again, Nancy and I performed a near perfect dance step of love.

Miss Orr, laughing, came up to us at the end of that Tango and said, "You two are lucky you're graduating because your dance movements to the Tangos, especially the last one, could get you suspended from school for a couple of weeks." She was both laughing and crying.

While she was using my damp handkerchief, she asked "Where did you two learn that dance?

Nancy replied. "Dee Dee showed us the steps, and we did our practicing at her house."

Miss Orr shook her head. "Can you believe it, a Rainbow girl dancing like that."

I tell Miss Orr, "Well, Nancy and I did some improvising tonight. By the way, Miss Orr, how did you learn a dance the Slovenian Schottische style?"

"I shortened my name when I graduated from college. I was a first born generation of our family in America. My full name is Orrmaranovich. Your father knew about my name someway or other. He wouldn't tell me how he found out, but I know he was in the old country, where my folks came from, during the war, He had to assume with a name like that I could dance the various Schottische's steps, and my minor in collage was folk dancing.

We didn't end dancing until daylight. Freddy told as he was packing up, "My band's never had a night like this. The kids, the setting, the food, no complaints. Your suggestions to add other dances worked out fantastic. I think you set a very high standard, Ted. Other proms may try to follow, but there will never be one like this."

It was some night to remember. I danced with Mrs. Blake and of course Mother and even with Miss Orr, and she never asked me a thing about the girls bathroom incident.

While dancing with Mom, she told me, "The Blakes are really pleased with you. The card you gave to Nancy was wonderful, but of course the topper of the night was the pin you gave her. It was a surprise to everyone. You two are not ready, or even close, for marriage, but another woman like Nancy will be hard to find, Ted. Honey, steer a careful course in your young life and where you are going, and I'm sure Nancy will be there waiting for you."

Our 'Prom in the Tent' was an outstanding success. Absolutely no problems and no mistakes of any type. Give it to the Senior class, the parents, and the setting.

*   *   *

The two families along with friends ended up at the Blake's after dawn for tea and toast. Nancy turned her record player on and we danced together outside on the patio.

She kept telling me how much she wanted to get together during vacations. She hopped we would meet in San Diego for the home hockey games.

She grabbed me tight just before we went into the house for something to eat. "Honey. I'm going to count those things you have every time I see you, and they had better count up to twelve and all in the same brand Mr. Radovich."

"You mean, I'm not to use them when we meet again?"

"Of course, they are just for you and I. I don't care if they have moss on them. All twelve belong to you and I."

"My lovely lady, that promise I will keep."

CHAPTER 23

It was a mad house up to graduation. I gave my Student Body President speech, and Nancy was the Valedictorian. I never told Nancy I beat her by one decimal point, but I let her take my place. Miss Orr and I are the only ones that know.

Oscar give his Senior Class President remarks.

Pastor Roberts handled the religious part of our graduation and he added an interesting, yet short talk about young people today. He said, "We all should try to be tolerant of our youth as we might have been the same when we were young."

When he made that comment to the graduation class, they all stood up and cheered.

After graduation I thanked Pastor Roberts, and he said to me with his arm around me. "Ted. I do believe, we, the two of us, just graduated."

Surprise, surprise.

Then we all left for a late dinner at the Blake's house and Nancy claimed she, the cook, prepared everything just for us. A happy, but sad day for me.

Nancy kept asking me, "How will we will stay together with so many miles separating us?"

"Because it is us, you and me we are talking about. Of course we'll stay together. For our college graduation I'll have a wedding ring for you, unless you are involved with some rich boy."

"No, I found my rich man with manners right here. I have plans for you, Ted, Honey."

"Like what? We can't spend every day in bed."

"My time will be devoted in making mad and very passionate love to you, with some housebreaking thrown in. I'll be busy training you to wash dishes, do the ironing, keep the floors clean with a vacuum and a mop. Of course the windows will need to be shining. Remember, I've been on the East coast and you've been spending too much time with the laid back Californians. You'll be from another kennel and will have to be retrained."

"For your information, Miss Blake, in four years it will be Mrs. Radovich, and I, the master of the house will be First Lieutenant Radovich, I'll have done floors, windows, and every thing else that didn't move, plus a lot that did. It's you that will need to be retrained."

"Hmm. Well, I'll have four years to settle that problem. Do you think you'll have time from the Army to visit me occasionally? We'll get a motel for a weekend."

"Certainly, my love. A motel huh?"

Nancy kept dabbing her eyes. "I need one more kisses from you to seal this arrangement between you and I and I am so happy because Lisa Roberts told me I was the luckiest girl in town."

Nancy was holding on to me like she thought I was going to escape her.

Never.

However, tomorrow, I was leaving from our local airport with no family or friends allowed to see me off. I was told;

I'm on a fast eight to ten week training program. Only Dad will drive me to the airport.

Toothbrush, comb, and the civilian clothes I'll be wearing was all I was allowed to carry aboard the plane.

General Skiloski will not be on the US Army plane, just me, two pilots and a crew chief. Besides being a physical program, I was told by Dad, it will be a mental test as well. Well, I'll be ready for football practice in August.

I did not tell anyone but Dad what I'll be doing this summer in the Army. This came as an order from General Skiloski. "Do not tell anyone, but your dad, what you think you will be doing, or afterwards what your training was. The moment you step on that plane, you will be one of us."

Nancy would leave in six weeks to go out East to her college, Oscar in one week to attend an indoctrinating training at the Navel Academy. Oscar's girl friend, Patty, would take a three week backpack trip through Italy with her church group, especially to visit Rome. Now I know why Patty seldom kissed Oscar, like Nancy kissed me. She will be training to be a Nun.

PROLOGUE

THIS STORY ENDS AS I'm sitting reading the Daisy Junction news paper my folks sent me. The only story of interest to me is the wedding of Nancy Olivia Blake. We were so sure we would be together forever and it's been nearly three years since the last letter, seven since the last face to face. I wish her well because she was an integral part of Teddy, but now I've moved on to Lieutenant Colonel Theodore Radovich.

Oscar went on to Annapolis, did well in football, then to sea for couple of years, and finally, as a military attaché. Now he is assigned to various back water consuls throughout the world where they need him most.

Oh, Oscar's Patty? She did become a nun in the Dominican Order and is teaching in Africa.

Lisa Roberts followed in her fathers footsteps and now preaches about the failings of the new younger generation.

Dee Dee still looks good and still works at the All American Confectionary Store and Restaurant, part time.

Flash is now on the campaign trail, vying to be the first woman Senator and the poles say she has a substantial lead.

Oh, and, Miss L'Affaire, she is now mayor of Daisy Junction and is doing a bang-up job of cleaning out the gambling and prostitution.